Get a Clue

THE NOVELS OF JILL SHALVIS

Aussie Rules
Get a Clue
Out of This World
Smart and Sexy
Strong and Sexy
Superb and Sexy
Instant Attraction
Instant Gratification
Instant Temptation

ANTHOLOGIES FEATURING JILL

Bad Boys Southern Style
He's the One
Merry and Bright

Get a Clue

JILL SHALVIS

KENSINGTON BOOKS
www.kensingtonbooks.com

KENSINGTON BOOKS are published by

Kensington Publishing Corp.
119 W. 40th Street
New York, NY 10018

ISBN-13: 978-0-7582-5344-6 (ebook)
ISBN-10: 0-7582-5344-3 (ebook)

ISBN-13: 978-1-4967-2530-1
ISBN-10: 1-4967-2530-1
First Brava Trade Paperback Printing: September 2005
First Kensington Trade Paperback Printing: April 2019

10 9 8 7 6 5 4

Printed in the United States of America

Dear Reader,

Thank you SO MUCH for buying a Shalvis classic romance! These books might predate the digital age, but they're still super fun and sexy! We hope you enjoy this peek at my earlier work!

When I first came up with the idea for *Get a Clue* (over a decade ago now—where did the time go??), it was my first time putting a mystery in with my romances. As a family, we'd been playing the game Clue and I just kept wondering . . . what if this were a romance! So I started with a dead body and worked backwards. I added in a bunch of wacky suspects, a huge old creaky place for a setting, and mixed it all together. I added in a jilted-at-the-altar heroine and a sexy hero who isn't sure what just hit him. ☺ It added up to a fun madcap mystery and a whole lot of heated romance!

Best wishes and happy reading!

Jill Shalvis
www.jillshalvis.com

One

It took her a while, but eventually Breanne Mooreland realized she had a naked man in her shower. Normally that would be the icing on a double-fudge chocolate cake, but in today's case, where she'd already had more failures than she could face, it felt like the last straw.

Consider her the camel, back broken.

In the interest of sanity—hers—she pretended to be fine as she dropped her small carry-on bag to the chair by the bed and stepped to the closed bathroom door. "Um . . . hello?"

Nothing but the sound of water hitting tiles. She glanced around the bedroom, exquisitely decorated in rustic wooden-log furniture and soft, fluffy, equally exquisite bedding with pillows piled higher than Mt. Everest. Just what she and Dean had ordered for their honeymoon.

That she was on said honeymoon alone caused her throat to tighten, but she'd cried bucketfuls on the plane and had promised herself no more pity parties.

But, of course, that had been when she'd merely been stood up at the altar in front of two hundred of her closest friends and family members. Before she'd gotten on the plane from hell all by her lonesome, where the turbulence had been so bad she'd had to stay seated between a three-hundred-pound

Louisiana woman crying, "Oh, Lordy, Lordy, have mercy—save us, Jesus!" and an Alaskan fisherman who smelled as if he'd kept some of his daily catch in his pockets.

Thinking she'd hit rock bottom—oh, how wrong she'd been—she'd gotten off the plane to discover that the rest of her luggage had never made it from San Francisco. That landing in the rugged, unpredictable Sierras in the middle of a snowstorm was equal to being shaken *and* stirred. The storm had only increased in severity since, so that the Jeep that had driven her to her "secluded, exclusive, fully staffed manse on the lake" honeymoon house could barely even get down the narrow, windy roads.

Breanne had distracted herself on the terrifying drive by pulling out her Palm Pilot and opening her journal. There she had her life—her hopes, her dreams, her failures, everything. Her last entry, made on the plane: *No more failures.*

Ha! That was going to be tricky, as she tended to make bad decisions. Maybe she wasn't enough of a giver. Maybe she just took, took, took. Maybe concentrating on others more would somehow turn the tide for her. Yeah, that's what she'd do, she'd give back. Do favors. Perform public service. Try harder at work, where, granted, she slaved over the books for a large accounting firm, but with an attitude.

She knew being the baby of a large family allowed her to fly beneath the radar. Even with her older brothers looking over her shoulder, she'd sought out trouble like a moth to the proverbial flame, beginning back in elementary school, where her sharp tongue and naughty pranks had regularly gotten her into hot water. By middle school she'd switched from pranks to boys, having developed an early fascination.

Of course, her mother always put it more simply: Breanne was drawn to the wrong type—jobs, friends, it didn't matter. Even men. Especially men. Hence, being stood up at the altar—for the third time.

On second thought, chances were she needed more direction than "no failures," so she added: *And especially, no more men.*

That's when her driver had begun four-wheeling up a narrow private road lined by tall pines covered in so much snow they looked like two-hundred-foot ghosts, swaying in the wind. On either side of them was a dramatic drop as they rose in altitude with every mile. Hues of peach, pink, blue, and purple colored the sheer granite escarpment of the Sierras through the falling snow in the deepening dusk.

Finally they'd maneuvered down a long, steep driveway, stopping in front of a beautiful log-cabin mansion. The backdrop should have been a private alpine lake, but the ascending dark and thick precipitation kept it from view.

"Here you go." The driver had reached over and opened her door instead of getting out and coming around for her.

She supposed she couldn't blame him; night was nearly upon them, and there was at least three feet of white, fluffy snow all around. She ruined her new suede boots just by hoofing it to the front door, clutching her only possession, her carry-on bag. She felt a little awed at how fast it was getting dark, and at the utter lack of city lights—or any lights, for that matter.

As she'd raised her hand to knock, a blast of wind pummeled her, plastering the snow from face to toe, going in her mouth, stinging her eyes, snaking like chilled fingers down her cashmere, open-necked sweater. Gasping for breath at the shocking cold, she staggered around to face her driver, intending to ask him for help.

He was gone.

As she contemplated the aloneness of that, a small streak rushed out from the corner of the house and practically across her feet, ripping a startled scream from her.

Then the streak *howled*. A coyote.

The sound had the hair on the back of her neck rising as

she stumbled back against the door. *Don't panic, coyotes don't eat humans. Probably.* Hugging herself, she felt very alone.

Alone, alone, alone . . . the word echoed in her head in the voice of her mother, who was certain her troubled youngest child would never marry, would never bring forth grandchildren into the world to spoil, and therefore would never amount to anything.

Shrugging that off—no more pity parties!—Breanne eyed the house. It certainly looked impressive with mounds and mounds of white snow pressed against the base, more white stuff ·falling, and the sky ominously dark and foreboding. Inside, there was supposedly a huge stone fireplace, a Jacuzzi tub, a sauna, a mini movie theater with an entire library of DVDs to pick from, and much, much more, including her own discreet staff for the week.

A honeymooner's delight, right? Dean had claimed to be excited. A shame he'd not been as excited about showing up for the wedding.

No one answered her second, desperately desperate knock, which for an instant perpetuated the hope that maybe she'd been cast in some sort of new reality show called *Torture the Bride.* Any second now, the director would yell *Cut!* and then, in a *This Is Your Life* moment, Dean would pop out and laugh at her for falling for it.

Only there was no camera, no Dean, laughing or otherwise, nothing but snow in her face, making her eyes water, her lips cold, raising goose bumps over every inch of her flesh.

Oh, and let's not forget the coyote, still howling in the distance with his friends, discussing eating her for dinner.

Forget *polite.* She opened the unlocked front door and gaped in awe at the interior of a most impressive house. She stepped inside the foyer that stretched up to the second story—and came face-to-face with a moose.

Just a head, she told herself, *mounted on the wall.* Slowly, purposely, she let out the air that she'd nearly used to scream.

"Definitely not in Kansas anymore," she whispered. There was also a wood mirror with shelves, each holding glass lamps that sent soft light across shiny, hardwood floors. In complete opposition to the "warm" feel of the room, the air itself danced over her, icy cold.

"Hello?" she called out, trying to stomp the snow off her clothes. Not much of it budged, happier to stick to her every inch, making her wet and miserable.

There was a reception area with a small pine desk, and a sticky note there that read:

Newlyweds get the honeymoon suite, complete with accessory package. Room is open and cleaned.

Well, damn it, she might not be a newlywed, but she was still getting that honeymoon suite, charged as it was to the rat bastard Dean's credit card. She just hoped the suite was warmer than the foyer, because she could make ice cubes in here.

Clutching her small carry-on, which held only her makeup and two extremely naughty negligees that had been meant for her wedding night, she walked to the base of the huge, wooden staircase that slowly curved and vanished up into the second floor, with several big potted plants lining the way. More glass sconces along the wall lit the area so that she could see into the fading daylight. It was an Old West, cabin-style interior, beautifully and tastefully done.

But no one appeared, and she hadn't heard a sound. Along with the daylight, much of her bravado deserted her. She didn't relish the idea of being here alone tonight. *"Hello?"*

She didn't know what the check-in procedure was, but she wondered if the huge storm had sent the staff members running for their homes in town, a one-horse place called Sunshine, of all things, a good ten miles back down the curvy, surely now snowed-in road.

They'd probably left the door unlocked for their guests, never even considering she'd be alone.

But alone she was. *Thanks, Dean.*

Knowing from the brochure that the honeymoon suite was on the second floor, she reached for the banister and began to climb the stairs.

"Anyone here?" she called out again at the top, stopping to pant for air. Damn altitude. The landing looked down to an open, large room below, rustic and cozy, with two forest green and maroon sofas shaped in an L, a large leather recliner, and throw rugs dotting the floor. It looked far more inviting than the cold, silent hallway where she stood, shivering like crazy from her wet clothes, and maybe nerves.

Then she realized she *did* hear something—running water. Proof of life! Hugging herself, she followed the noise, past three doors on the right and left, all of which appeared to be bedrooms.

The hallway walls had old photographs of the Wild West on them: cowboys, wagons, old mining towns. At the end of the hallway, she stopped in front of a set of double wooden doors.

The honeymoon suite?

Hoping so, she stepped inside. That's where she found the log bed, so high she'd need a stool to climb up on it. The bedding was white down, with bear-and-moose pillows, and looked so scrumptiously warm she nearly sank into it. There was a matching armoire and dresser as well, also done in pine logs. The ceiling was open-beamed, and a work of art all by itself. The stone fireplace—not lit, darn it—and floor-to-ceiling windows finished off the room, the windows revealing that the day had fled completely now.

There was a goodie basket on a chair for the honeymooners: body paints in every flavor, a package of edible underwear, and several books on the pleasures of massage and touch therapy, including *How to Make a Woman Come Every Single Time*.

Too bad Dean wasn't here. He could use that one.

There were other fillers, too: body lotion, bath oils, a brand new vibrator in neon-pink and shaped just like a penis she'd once seen that had a terrible curve to the right. She picked it up and took a good look at it, trying to picture the designers of such an item sitting around a table and deciding on the angle of the curve. She considered herself adventurous and fun in bed, but she couldn't imagine Dean figuring out a way to make good use of this. Gee, guess it was a good thing he wasn't here . . .

It penetrated her addled brain that the shower was still running.

Odd. Surely the housekeeper wouldn't be in there . . . Curious, a little unnerved—and if she let herself think about all that had happened to her since she got out of bed that morning, she could add *crazed* to the list—she stepped over a pile of wet clothes on the floor.

Huh?

Turning back, she crouched down to look at them, trying to get a clue as to who was in her shower. Levi's, original fit, size 34x36. Hmm. Tall and lean. There was also a white Hanes Beefy T-shirt, size large, and a soft blue chambray overshirt, both smelling good enough that if she hadn't given up men, she might have pressed her face against the material and inhaled.

But she *had* given up men. She'd written it in her journal and therefore it had become law.

He didn't wear underwear.

Why the hell *that* intrigued her, she had no idea. Rising, shivering because her clothes had become iced to her skin, she knocked on the bathroom door.

Whoever he was, he had the radio on; she could hear the broadcaster talking about the storm of the century—

Storm of the century. That couldn't be good. Pressing her ear to the door, she heard other disturbing words, such as "No one is going anywhere, folks" and "I hope you're all stocked up on whatever you need, because this one's a doozy." At that, she twisted the handle on the door and pushed it open.

The bathroom was as amazingly detailed as the rest of the house. Even through all the thick steam, she could see the stunning granite countertops, the raw wood-framed mirrors, the small overstuffed day couch, the old-fashioned brass fixtures—

And yet another gift basket, filled with more goodies. She looked at the vibrator she still had in her hand. What else could she possibly need? Well, besides a new groom, that is. A shame they didn't come a dime a dozen in a gift basket such as this, selection ready.

The shower took up one full corner, all in clear glass, etched with the outline of the Sierras, which in fact did nothing at all to hide the tall, leanly muscled man standing in it.

Naked.

Gloriously so, she might add. The water sprayed out of four different rain heads, massaging over him. He had his back to her, and what a fine back it was: broad, ropey shoulders, sleek, strong spine, smooth and tanned until, low on his narrow hips, his tan line abruptly ended.

He had a fabulous, mouthwatering butt, and Breanne took a moment to wonder at the man who wore a bathing suit in the sun but not underwear beneath his jeans.

Water sluiced off him, and soap, too, and then, as if God had decided to bestow one tiny little favor on her shitty, rotten day, the guy dropped the soap.

Breanne held her breath. Would he—

Yes. Yes, he would.

Bending for it, blissfully unaware that there were a pair of very curious female eyes on him, he clearly didn't even consider his modesty. Every muscle in his body flexed as he doubled over, legs slightly spread, offering her an eye-popping view of his—

Oh, my.

Lifting her hand, she furiously fanned air to her face, because the front of him lived up to the back, and how. She wondered how old he was, thinking that body couldn't be more than thirty, which was only two years older than herself. In any case, she stood there, rooted to the ground, her own wet misery forgotten, mouth hanging open, drool pooling, eyes locked on the backs of his well-defined thighs.

And what was between them.

But then suddenly he whipped around, staring at her through the glass for one beat before shoving open the shower door, allowing steam and water to pour into the room as he glared at her with an ominous, thunderstruck expression on his face.

More than thirty, she thought inanely. Probably, given those laugh lines bracketing his unsmiling mouth, and startling sky-blue eyes, at least thirty-five.

Not that age mattered, with a majorly heart-stopping body like his.

"What the hell are you doing?" he demanded, looking tough and clearly ready to prove it.

And that's when her brain kicked back into gear and reminded her of her situation. She was in a strange house. In a strange *bathroom*, out in the middle of nowhere, surrounded by rugged mountain peaks and more snow than she'd ever seen.

And she was staring at a furious, naked guy. "Um—"

"Who the hell are you?"

"I—" She glanced at the neon-pink vibrator in her hand and felt every single brain cell desert her.

"Get out."

Yeah. On that, they were perfectly in sync, thank you very much. She might have a secret weak spot for an edgy, difficult bad boy, but she absolutely did not have a weak spot for being stupid.

Whirling, she dropped the vibrator and ran. She ran like

hell through the open bathroom door, slamming it behind her to give her an extra second on him.

He'd told her to get out, so chances were that he wasn't planning on chasing her, but she'd rather be safe than sorry. She hightailed it through the bedroom, leaping over his clothes, moving more quickly in her ruined boots than she'd moved in . . . well, a very long time.

Behind her the bathroom door whipped open.

Oh, God.

He was in pursuit and he was quick.

With a startled squeak, she sped up, thinking no one back home would believe she could ever move this fast, not even to save her life.

"Wait!" that low, almost gravelly voice called out. "*Who are you?*"

Stopping to chat seemed like a bad idea, so she kept moving.

Her only problem was, she really had nowhere to go.

Two

Remember: the better-looking the guy, the less he can be trusted.
It's a direct ratio thing.

       —Breanne Mooreland's Journal Entry

Cooper Scott stood butt-ass-naked, freezing cold and dripping wet in the bathroom doorway, holding the vibrator his mystery guest had just dropped. Bad enough that he'd quit his job, shocking everyone he knew. Bad enough that he wasn't getting laid, now that he'd sent a pretty woman screaming like a banshee into the night.

A woman carrying a vibrator.

He could still hear her, pounding down the stairs in those ridiculous, towering high-heeled boots that were all for show and had absolutely no practicality.

Who would wear such things to the Sierras at the onset of winter, in the middle of an insane storm like the one they were facing?

He had no idea, but he supposed, as she was in his house, he needed to find out. Well, not *his* house, exactly, but his rented vacation house.

And a stunning one at that.

His brother James had sent him here with strict orders to "get his shit together," not mentioning that the place was at least ten thousand square feet of pure luxury. Log-cabin style, it had gorgeous mahogany flooring, pine trim, soft, buttery interior walls filled with rustic prints and old-time equipment such as hare-bone snowshoes and antique wooden skis.

But if the decorating was glorious, old western style, the actual appliances were state of the art, with everything placed and designed for ultimate comfort. He had a week to live in style here, a week in which he'd intended to do nothing but ski his brains out and maybe find a pretty ski bunny to keep him warm at night.

And, as James had ordered, "get his shit together."

As long as he avoided thinking, he was good. All he wanted to do was recover from the job that had nearly sent him to the loony bin, and figure out what the hell to do with the rest of his life.

No sweat.

He'd gotten here from San Francisco via his truck, which was probably buried in the driveway by now. The drive had been treacherous at the least, and given how the snow was still coming down, he doubted he could get off the mountain if he'd wanted to. But the staff that was supposed to greet him had been nonexistent, the house cold as an iceberg. He'd found the heating control and cranked it, but as yet, nothing had happened.

He'd taken a hot shower anyway, intending to start a sizzling fire in all the fireplaces he could find, but instead had been interrupted by a woman watching him soap up. Hoping she was one of the promised staff members, maybe someone who could cook—God, he was starving—he grabbed a thick, plush white towel from its neat pile on the granite counter.

There had been all sorts of toiletries laid out for him on the countertop, including a basket filled with condoms in varying sizes and colors, which had amused him earlier.

How long had it been since he'd needed a condom?

Too damn long, he knew that much.

Towel around his hips, he stepped into the bedroom just as the lights flickered. Perfect.

The electricity was going to go. Then he could be cold, wet, starving . . . *and* in the dark.

Another power surge, making the lights dim with an odd hum, and from somewhere below came the sound of a thud and low cry. Dropping the towel, Cooper grabbed his jeans, jamming first one leg and then the other in, hopping as he made his way out into the hallway, still shirtless and barefoot.

Up here at an altitude of sixty-five-hundred feet, daylight didn't slowly fade, but vanished in the blink of an eye, and today had been no exception. Full darkness had fallen. Any starlight was muted by the heavy snowfall, so the three overhead skylights and the wide range of huge windows in the rooms below were useless.

The lights were flickering nonstop now, offering only a sporadic glow from the wall sconces lined up in the empty hallway. "Hello?"

No answer. Of course not. What had seemed like a beautiful, welcoming house in the daytime suddenly didn't seem so welcoming. Still, he wasn't alone, he knew that much. He might be close to a nervous breakdown, but he wasn't seeing things.

He reached for the banister, just as the lights stopped flickering and went out completely.

"Don't panic, don't panic," Breanne whispered to herself. She'd flown down the stairs and across the hardwood floor at the base of the curved staircase, thankful for the lighting, stingy as it was, because she wasn't happy in the dark. That went back to the days of too many brothers, and too many times they'd happily tortured her. Once she'd even been locked in a closet and left there by accident.

But she was a grown-up now. "You're tough," she said out loud. "You're impenetrable." She wondered where Scary But Gorgeous Naked Guy was.

Coming after her.

At the thought, she tripped over her own two feet and went sprawling face-first across the shiny floor.

That's when the lights went out.

Then, from up above somewhere, she heard footsteps.

For years her brother Danny had been telling her she needed an exercise regime, some sort of weight training to give some tone to her body, and she'd always shuddered at the thought because she and exercise mixed like oil and water.

Now she wished she'd paid attention. Kickboxing, taebo, karate . . . Hell, *anything* aggressive would have been nice.

In the complete dark, she pushed herself up off the floor, breathing like a lunatic, probably looking like a deer caught in the headlights. Only there were no headlights, nothing but an inky blackness that had her stomach falling to her toes.

No groom.

No electricity.

Stuck in a house with a naked guy.

Screwed.

She was a self-proclaimed city girl, she reminded himself. Feisty and independent, not easily cowed or intimidated. Give her a scary downtown alley with a drunk leaning against the wall, or an obnoxious construction worker blocking her path any day. Anything but the big, open, scary, dark space where the unknown waited just out of sight. Bears, spiders, coyotes . . .

Oh, and a gorgeous naked guy with a low, sexy voice in her shower.

Maybe people found gorgeous naked men in their showers all the time out here. Maybe it was a way to greet the new-comers. Maybe . . . maybe she was delusional because her day had gone so badly.

She slipped her hand in her pocket and gripped the com-forting weight of her cell phone. Normally she'd have mace there as well, but who'd have thought she'd be needing any on her faux honeymoon?

Pulling out the phone, the digital display lit up, providing a tiny, welcome bit of light. No bars, though, which meant no reception. She actually shook the thing, as if that would help. She'd heard about this, of course, and she'd seen the "Can you hear me now?" commercials, but having grown up in a city where people walked around with their cell phones permanently attached to their ears, where there were no mysterious pockets of low reception, she'd never had this problem.

Hell of a day to experience it now.

She should never have gotten out of bed, should never have donned that lacy white wedding dress she'd loved, never gone to the church to marry a man simply because it had seemed like a fun, exciting thing to do, and because her mother had suggested this was her last chance to get it right.

And she sure as hell wished she would stop falling for "I love you" when what a guy really meant was "Do me, and also my laundry, while you're at it."

She shivered again. Or maybe that was *still*. Her clothes, still wet and extremely cold against her skin, had stuck to her, probably steaming because despite her bone-deep chill, she'd also begun to sweat in sheer terror.

And then she heard it, a sound from behind her in the dark.

Just a slight scrape on the floor, which could have been a rat, a mere creak in the wood, or . . .

A footstep.

Oh, God.

Ballsy or not, this experience was quickly growing beyond her. She stumbled forward and fell into the front door. Grasping the handle, she wrenched it open.

Icy wind and snow greeted her, blasting her in the face, sliding down her collar. To add insult to injury, the horizon was pure black—no city lights, no stars, nothing but a velvety darkness. Still, propelled by fear, she took a step forward.

And sank up to her thigh.

Once when she'd been little, her grandma had given her one of those snow globes of San Francisco. Shake it up and it snowed down over the city.

In fact, it did snow in the city. Once in a blue moon. During those times the wind would slip in from the shore, chopping and dicing at any exposed skin. But in those rare events she simply stayed indoors. There was lots to do inside: hang out with friends, seduce a boyfriend, drink something warm . . .

But today was a whole new kind of cold. And this fluffy, powdered-sugar kind of snow, thick and currently up to her crotch . . . she'd never seen anything like it. Too bad she'd dressed for a chilly day looking at the snow from the *inside*.

Torn between sinking into the snow, never to be heard from again, or facing the dark, terrifying house, Breanne stood there in rare indecision for exactly one second, during which time another gust of wind hit her, sending her backwards a step, onto her butt in the doorway. More wet cold seeped through her denim.

Quickly scrambling to her feet, she fought the wind and slammed the door shut, then whirled around and flattened herself to it, blinking furiously, trying to adapt to the dark.

But there was no adapting, especially when out of that inky blackness came a low, almost rough masculine voice. "Hello?"

Oh, God. That didn't sound like Gorgeous Naked Guy. Biting her lip to keep quiet, hands out in front of her, she tip-toed toward the reception desk where she'd first seen the note about the honeymoon suite. There'd been a phone there . . . Her fingers closed over it.

Teeth chattering in earnest now, she lifted the receiver to her ear, ready to call . . . she had no idea. It didn't matter; she'd take the Abominable Snowman, for God's sake.

No dial tone.

Okay, this wasn't happening. This couldn't really be happening. She'd stepped into some alternate universe—

She heard a click, and then a small flare of light appeared, and a face, floating in the air.

Breanne clapped her hands over her mouth to hold in her startled scream and pressed back against the wall as if she could vanish into it.

Once for Halloween she'd gone into a haunted house with a group of friends, smug and secure in the fact that having grown up with brothers, she couldn't be frightened. And indeed, her friends had all screamed their lungs out while she calmly walked through, her mind rationally dismissing each scare. Oh, that was just a CD of scary sounds. And there . . . just a skeleton—fake, of course. And that dead body swinging overhead? With all the blood? Just ketchup.

But this was real. Her hollow stomach and slipping grip on her sanity told her that. And while she really wanted to remain cool, calm, and collected, her heart threatened to burst right out of her chest, even as she registered the truth.

The floating face wasn't really a floating face at all, but a man holding a flashlight beneath his chin.

Not Gorgeous Naked Guy.

No, this man was the same height but stockier, and in his twenties. He wore a hoodie sweatshirt over a baseball cap low on his forehead so she could only see a little of his face, but what she could see was overexaggerated by the beam of the flashlight, giving him a dark, almost Frankenstein-like glow that had her breath backing up in her throat.

"It's okay," Frankenstein said to her. "The phones go out all the time."

Oh, okay then. She'd just forget about the panic barreling through her at the speed of light. Her plan was to at least look calm. Get what info she could. "What about the electricity?" she managed, as if asking the time that tea would be served.

After that, she hadn't a clue.

"Yeah, that's new," he admitted, and shrugged as if to say he had no idea.

"Are you . . . the manager?" she asked, hoping the answer was "Yes" and not "No, I'm your murderer."

"No. The manager is . . . temporarily indisposed."

He didn't look so much like Frankenstein at all, she saw when he lowered the flashlight and his hood slipped back, revealing straight black hair to his shoulders, dark skin suggesting a Cuban descent, black eyes, and a long scar down one side of his jaw. "So who are you?" she asked.

But he'd already turned his back on her and was shining his light into the vast cavern that had been the great room before the lights had gone out. "I'll start a fire," he said, moving in that direction. "You should change your wet clothes."

She'd happily strip out of the sweater and jeans that had turned to sheets of ice on her body, but the two sexy nighties in her carry-on didn't have enough material combined to warm a gnat. "Are you going to tell me who you are?"

There was a snap, then a quick flare of light as he held the match to some kindling inside the huge stone fireplace. The resulting glow highlighted him from head to toe. He was built like a linebacker, wearing baggy jeans at least three sizes too big and low enough to reveal equally baggy boxer shorts. His sweatshirt strained across his shoulders as he glanced back at her, those dark, dark eyes of his landing on hers. "I'm Dante. The butler." He shoved up his sleeves, revealing heavy tattooing on both forearms, making him look more like a rapper than a butler, but what did she know about being either?

"Where were you when I first arrived?" she asked, trying to control her shivering but having no luck. Instead she continued to tremble, mixing up her innards like a shake.

"Yeah, sorry about that," Dante said.

"There's someone in my suite."

He gave a palms-up gesture. "A mixup with reservations. Don't worry."

Oh, okay. She wouldn't worry, then. *Not.* Unsatisfied with

the vague answers, she stayed where she was in the doorway, still freezing, wondering what the hell to do.

"You going to get any closer to the heat?" her thug butler asked.

Heat. Her entire body craved it more than her next breath, but there was still the matter of the Naked Guy and his status, and much as she didn't want to be *alone* in this house of horrors, she really, *really* didn't like the idea of being here with these guys, either.

"Suit yourself." With a shrug, Dante faced the burgeoning fire, holding his hands out as if he was cold, too.

On the other hand, Breanne thought, if these guys were going to hurt her, it was probably best that she be warm so she could fight back, right? But before she could move, from above came the unmistakable sound of footsteps coming down the stairs. Breanne tipped her head back, but in the dark couldn't see. "Um, Dante?"

"Relax," he said from his perch by the fire.

Sure. She'd just relax. *After* she died of nerves. From the stairs, a pair of bare feet emerged, then denim-covered legs, long and tough with strength.

Her heart jolted unexpectedly into her throat. She knew those legs; she'd seen them with water and soap raining down the length of them. They'd been tanned and well defined, as if he used his body for more than sitting behind a desk balancing other people's checkbooks for a living as she did.

And he didn't wear underwear.

The unbidden thought caused an inane hot flash. All those male . . . parts, nestled against the denim.

Naked.

She began to sweat some more but didn't bother to say a word to Dante, because if he told her to relax again, she was going to come unglued.

Then a bare chest materialized, still gleaming from the shower, but no less jaw-dropping for it. She already knew the guy had a nice body, muscular without being beefy, lean without being scrawny.

His belly was ridged, carved into a six-pack she envied, since sit-ups were something she occasionally thought about but never actually did. He had a very light smattering of hair between his pecs that narrowed into a line down his belly that vanished into the loose waistband of his jeans, like an arrow toward the hidden prize—

He held up his hand, and in it was . . .

Oh, God.

The neon-pink vibrator, glowing in the dark now.

It was following her, stalking her, all the way down the yellow brick road to hell.

Naked Guy—not quite naked now—came the rest of the way into view, and unerringly turned his head in her direction, and though it was dark in the shadows where she stood, she knew his eyes landed right on her.

He had an odd awareness to him, as if he could see in the dark. As if he knew exactly what was going on around him at all times, a skill she'd never mastered in the best of times, to which today absolutely did not belong.

He also had the look of a man thinking things—things that, even with fear coursing through her, made her face heat and other parts tingle.

He smiled grimly, a lopsided smile that did nothing to dull the fact that he was amazing to look at—and terrifying, all at the same time.

With a pathetic little whimper, Breanne pressed back closer to the wall, swallowing hard, trying to decide if that had been an anticipatory "all the better to eat you with" smile . . .

Or simply a trick of the flickering firelight.

Three

Note to self—give serious thought to becoming an alcoholic.
—Breanne Mooreland's Journal Entry

Cooper took the last step and came face-to-face with his voyeur for one brief flash before she backed up into the darkness. All around them it closed in, except for the low glow of light from the fireplace—and, of course, from the vibrator.

Then he caught a movement and tensed as a shadow to his left materialized into a man.

"Welcome," the man said in utter contradiction to his urban street clothes. He eyed the vibrator in Cooper's hand but whatever his thoughts were on a guy wielding a vibrator, he kept them to himself. "I'll get some candles."

"Who are you?"

"Dante, your butler," he said, without a hint of laughter, indicating he was serious.

A butler? Cooper watched Dante vanish into the darkness. He'd been dressed more like any of the punks he'd encountered over the years on the job, but if the punk had candles to share—

"Unbelievable."

This from the woman somewhere in the dark, beyond him in the foyer.

Turning, Cooper located her faint outline against the foyer windows. She had sunk to the floor, her back to the glass.

There was a low-light digital display in front of her face, and she appeared to be entering something into a handheld digital device.

"No groom," she muttered as she entered. "Flight from hell. More snow than the Arctic Circle. A serious lack of electricity. Oh, and a gorgeous naked guy."

Cooper blinked. Gorgeous naked guy? *Him?* As bad as things had been lately, he'd take it.

"Next up," she said, thumbs furiously hitting the keys. "Is getting knocked off on your honeymoon."

Cooper held up the glowing vibrator to see her better, filling in some of the details he'd only caught glimpses of before. She had long, wavy hair, most of it in her face, and huge, wide eyes. Hard to tell if she was pretty, but something about her grabbed him. Her sweater was pink, snug to her full breasts, and she was damn cold if the hardness of her nipples meant anything. As he moved closer, she gasped.

"No one's getting knocked off," he said softly.

"Easy for you to say." She was shivering out of control. "You're not the one facing death."

"Neither are you."

She lowered her digital unit. "I really, really wish I hadn't come."

She was scared, shaking with it, and probably chilled to the bone. Knowing how she felt, he crouched in front of her. Because he'd come running when he'd heard her cry out he was still wearing only his jeans, so he raised his hands to show that while he might be half-naked, he was harmless, forgetting for a moment that he held the glowing vibrator. "You dropped this."

This got him a vehement head-shake. "Not mine," she said firmly.

"But I saw you—" He broke off at the look of horror on her face. "No? Hmm . . ." Knowing damn well she'd dropped it, he pretended to ponder the ownership as he turned the thing over in his hands. It turned on, humming loudly into the silent foyer.

This drew another gasp from her, so he tried to turn it off, but only succeeded in cranking it into high gear, and it nearly vibrated right out of his hands.

"Oh, for—*here*." Snatching it out of his hand, she turned it off and then stood up, jamming the thing into her back pocket. "Who are you? Not the butler—there's already one of those."

"Cooper Scott." He left out the unemployed loser part as he straightened. "You're right, I'm not another butler. I'm a guest. And you're . . . ?"

"In the twilight zone," she said, peering uneasily into the dark around them.

"So in your twilight zone, you watch people shower?"

Without the glow of the vibrator, he couldn't see her expression clearly, but could feel the heat of her embarrassment. "I didn't intend to intrude on your privacy," she said primly. "I just didn't realize what you were doing."

"You didn't realize that when someone's standing bare-ass naked in the shower, rubbing soap all over their body, it means they're taking a shower?"

Her glare practically lit up the dark.

"Let me give you a helpful hint," he said. "Knocking on a closed door is a good thing."

"And let me give *you* a hint." She punctuated this with a poke to his chest. The contact of her finger with his bare flesh shocked him, and given the funny hitch to her breath, it startled her, too. "Stay out of other people's honeymoon suites."

"*What?*"

Jerking to her feet, she jammed her Palm Pilot in the bag strung over her shoulder. "You were showering in *my* honeymoon suite."

"No. *I* rented this house. Well, my brother did, but it's mine for the week."

She crossed her arms over her chest, plumping her full breasts up and out. She wasn't tall, maybe up to his shoulder, but her jeans and sweater clung to her body, revealing she was quite the package. "Wrong again," she said indignantly. "The place is mine, bucko."

"*Bucko?*"

"I forgot your name."

He stared at her, wondering how it was he felt both annoyed and . . . alive, extremely alive, a feeling he hadn't experienced in too long. He had no idea what she'd look like in the light of day. He had no idea what she really looked like in the dark, either, other than a nice set of curves with sparks of temper coming from her general direction, but it didn't matter. She was as annoying as hell, even if she did think he looked good naked.

She was also shaking like a drowning poodle. Fact was, he was damned cold himself, with no shirt and no socks. "Cooper," he said with a sigh. "My name is Cooper. And you're . . ."

"B-Breanne," she said through her chattering teeth.

"Look, Breanne, the fire is crackling now. Move closer to it."

"Why?"

He sighed again at her wariness. Had he done that, or was she just defensive and cranky all on her own? "Because you're turning into a popsicle." He put his hand on her arm, shocked at how chilled she really was. Her sweater was thin, wet, and nearly iced over, her skin beneath just as bad. "Didn't anyone ever tell you that you need to wear a coat in a snowstorm?"

"It wasn't snowing in San Francisco. Or on the plane. Or in the airport."

Another violent shiver wracked her and he ran his hand up and down her arm, trying to give her some of his body heat. "What about when you left the airport?"

She stared at his bare chest, though he figured that was just her way of avoiding eye contact. "Lost my luggage."

"You've lost your groom *and* your luggage?"

"Yes." Behind her temper was a sadness that got to him. "And I hate the dark, too."

He looked at her for a moment, wondering at the urge to touch her, to open his hand, spread his fingers and stroke her skin. "You're having a hell of a bad day all around, aren't you?" he murmured.

"You have no idea."

"Come here."

She went absolutely still, only her eyes cutting once again to his bare chest. "Why?"

Besides being wary and cold, she was a suspicious thing. And looking as she did, all disheveled and shockingly sexy for it, he could understand she had a good reason to feel that way. He could practically see her heart pounding at her ribs, and her belly rose and fell too quickly. *She was afraid of him.* That cut deep, as he'd spent most of his life helping people not to be afraid. "I'm not going to hurt you. I promise."

"Like I'd take your word," she said bravely, but then let him tug her out of the foyer and into the great room. The flames were roaring now, lighting the place with a soft glow, showing off the inviting leather couches.

But the woman just stood there stiffly, arms still wrapped around herself, shuddering with her chill. Her long, wavy hair was the same color as her eyes—expensive whiskey. She had a light smattering of freckles across her nose and cheeks, and lips that were soft and full. *Made for kissing* came the inane thought.

"You're staring," she said.

And for smart-mouthing. "You're cold. Come warm up."

She just shivered again, continuing to hug herself. He knew those clothes had to be damned uncomfortable against her skin, molding her figure, which happened to be a nice one. Not chunky, but not thin, either.

Just right for holding onto. Not that he'd ever been choosy

when it came to women. Hell, he hadn't had the opportunity to be choosy, not with his job that had taken up every second of his last few years.

Yet another full-body shudder wracked her and he nearly reached for her. The stupid hero in him.

Ignoring him completely, she moved closer to the flames, leaning in, revealing her backside, and the vibrator glowing from the pocket.

"That butler guy . . ." She glanced over her shoulder and caught him grinning. "What?"

"Nothing." To swipe off the grin, he had to look away from the vibrator peeking out of her pants. "Go ahead. The butler guy . . . ?"

She narrowed her eyes. "He said the manager was temporarily unavailable. "But as soon as he shows up, he'll tell you. This place is mine for the week."

"Look, I hate to argue with a lady who's already had a pretty fucked-up day—"

"—then don't."

"—but you're wrong."

"Not about this."

He might have said more, but instead frowned as it occurred to him that her teeth were in danger of rattling right out of her head. "Hey." He put his hand on her arm, which was even icier now than it had been. Beneath his fingers he felt her tense enough to shatter, and he lifted his other hand as well, holding both her arms. She was shaking so hard she nearly shuddered free, so he tightened his grip slightly, trying to hold her steady. "You really need to change your clothes."

She tried to twist away, but newly concerned, he held onto her, sucking in a breath when her hair brushed his own chilled skin.

"Trust me," she said through her rattling teeth. "Given what I have in my carry-on, I can't change."

"You have nothing?"

"Not exactly nothing." She stopped trying to break away from him and looked at her fancy boots, the kind that were made for muddying up a man's brain, not for real use. Her hair fell forward, again against his chest. Normally he loved a woman's hair teasing him there, but these strands were frozen. He sucked in another breath and waited for her to speak.

"Just . . . honeymoon stuff," she said softly.

Everything she'd said finally clicked in. "Are you really on your honeymoon? Alone?"

"Well, the tickets were paid for, weren't they?"

"What happened to your husband?"

"No husband. He never . . . we didn't—" Taking a step back, she lifted her head, eyes proud. "He didn't show up, all right? And there was no use sticking around to face the sympathy and barely masked glee that being dumped at the altar brings." Another violent shiver followed this statement, along with a very disparaging sigh.

Cooper swore softly, softening in spite of himself, and he pushed her into a large leather recliner. It was entirely possible she'd actually had it rougher than he had lately, and that was saying something. "No big deal. I have plenty of clothes upstairs. I'll be right back—"

She bounced back up so fast she nearly cracked his chin with her head. "Really, don't bother yourself. I'm fine."

"But I have a bag right upstairs."

"Honestly, I'm good . . ." She glanced around her. "No reason for you to have to go upstairs."

He took in the white around her eyes, the way she gripped him tight, as if maybe he was the lesser of all the evils of her day. "You're scared."

She let out a laugh. "No."

"Just say it. You don't want me to leave you alone down here."

"Ridiculous," she muttered.

"Ridiculous? You're afraid of the dark, remember?"

"Not afraid, exactly. Unhappy with it."

"And it was only my imagination that a few minutes ago you were looking at me as if I might be a murderer?"

"Or a serial rapist." Her lips were still blue as her teeth chattered from her chill. "B-but I've since decided you're probably neither."

"Gee, thanks."

"Now you're just the guy standing between me and my honeymoon suite." More bone-crunching shudders wracked her, appearing to start at her roots and end at her toes. "My w-warm honeymoon suite."

Once again he ran his hands up and down her arm, truly alarmed for her now. "You were up there," he said, maneuvering her closer to the fire. "You know it's not any warmer than the rest of the house. At least not yet."

She didn't answer that but looked horribly dejected at the thought.

"Okay, listen," he said. "You can come *with* me upstairs, or you can wait here. Either way, I'm going to get us both something more to wear."

She plopped back into the chair and sent her chin to the heavens. "I'm not budging."

God, she was stubbornness personified. And frustrating. And somehow, also, inexplicably adorable. "Suit yourself, but I'm going. I'm getting you a change of clothing and me some socks and a shirt, and then I'm starting a fire up there so I can hit the sack."

"Not my sack, you're not."

Had he thought her adorable, even for a second? "I'll be right back."

He left her and loped up the dark, dark stairs, feeling his way along the hallway toward the bedroom, thinking the only way he'd want her in his bed was with a gag over that lovely, full, smart-ass mouth.

The image alone began to warm him up.

Four

I'd tell him to go to hell, but it just so happens I'm stuck there and don't want to have to see him every day.
—Breanne Mooreland's Journal Entry

Breanne watched Cooper walk away and concentrated on breathing through her panic. There was also the fact that the firelight gilded his broad shoulders and sleek back, highlighting the worn Levi's that fell low on his hips, intimately cupping his tush, which she had to acknowledge was absolutely worth intimately cupping.

He had a way of moving, and a way of taking in his surroundings as he did. *Intensely aware*, she would have said. As if he was a predator.

And maybe he was.

Gulp.

Then he vanished entirely, was simply swallowed up by the dark house, the only person she really had in this Alice-in-Wonderland place. Too proud to speak up, she sat there, heart in her throat, staring into the dark, gaping doorway that she couldn't see beyond, wondering what, or who, else besides Dante was out there.

A loud thump came from nowhere, and she leapt to her feet. The vibrator fell to the floor. Sweeping up the still-glowing thing, she clutched it to her chest as the thug/butler came back into the room.

Dante's hood was low over his face, but he carried a tray

with two steaming cups of something, and suddenly she didn't care if the beefy, scary guy was Hannibal Lecter, he had something *hot*.

"Here," he said, and handed her one of the cups with surprising grace for a tough, built guy who looked as if maybe he wore a cape and wrestled in his skivvies for a living. Or whacked kneecaps.

She stared at the offering, thinking of every bad movie she'd ever stayed up too late watching. Not only was she the stupid heroine alone in the house with two potential bad guys, she was about to be poisoned—

"If I was going to do something to you," he murmured, "it wouldn't be poisoning your drink."

She looked up at him and caught a surprising flash of humor in his eyes. "Are you laughing at me?"

"Nah, that would be rude." He pushed her mug toward her mouth. "Drink. You're shivering so much you're making *me* cold."

"Fine." At least she'd die warm. She tucked the vibrator back into her waistband, grateful he hadn't made fun of her makeshift flashlight. Then her fingers closed around the ceramic mug, and at the blessed heat of it, she nearly burst into tears. "What was that noise before?"

"What noise?"

"I heard something bump. Or crash."

Dante turned away, his wide shoulders completely blocking the fire's warmth for a moment as he set the other mug down on the small table by the couch. "I dropped something. Drink before you freeze to death."

Or something to death, anyway. She sipped and, despite herself, moaned aloud at the frothy, thick, melting chocolate on her tongue. "Oh, my God."

"Good?"

"Amazing."

"Shelly made it, the cook here. She had water going on

the stove before the power went out, luckily. I'll tell her you like it."

Eyes closed, Breanne sipped some more, savoring the heat of it as it slid down her throat. Lifting her head, she went to smile at her mysterious butler, meaning to ask about the rest of the invisible staff, but he was *gone*.

Without a sound.

Yikes. Real or Memorex? She'd have sworn she'd imagined the whole thing—except she was holding the hot chocolate. Lord, she was losing it here. She looked around uneasily, the only sound the crackling of the flames and her own heartbeat echoing heavily in her ears. No sign of her hooded, right-out-of-a-thriller butler.

Or, for that matter, Gorgeous Naked Guy.

She sucked down more of the hot chocolate, wishing it was liquid courage, then stood and moved closer to the fire. She was tired of shaking, and damn tired of being wet and cold, so she tugged off her iced-over sweater. That left her in just a white tank top, and, crouching down before the flames, the warmth of the flames danced over her torso and arms, and she wished she could shuck out of her wet jeans, too.

"Miss me?"

Whipping around, she faced one tall, dark, and slightly attitude-ridden Cooper Scott. Still sockless and shoeless, he smiled grimly, and she did her best not to drool or stare.

His gaze touched on the sweater she'd spread across the mantel to dry, then swiveled back to her standing there in her little white tank top. She'd worn it because it sucked her in and pushed her out in all the right places, and because after competing with Dean's cell phone and long hours at work for months, she'd decided *no more*. She'd wanted to make sure he noticed her tonight, every inch of her.

Too bad Dean hadn't told her that *he'd* also decided *no more*. No more *her*. Now she was standing there, probably looking like a coed after a wet T-shirt contest.

Cooper's gaze lingered on her chest for a beat before lifting to her face. He didn't say a word, but jaw tight, dropped a duffel bag at her feet. In that oddly graceful and yet utterly masculine way he had, he hunkered down and began to go through it, the long, sleek muscles of his back and shoulders bunching and releasing with his every movement. "I couldn't see upstairs," he muttered. "Or I'd have—Here."

She reached for what he offered, a dark pair of plain sweat bottoms. Elastic around the ankles and the waist. He tossed her another dark item as well, a matching sweatshirt.

Her job in the accounting firm required her to dress up on a daily basis, which was amusing given that in school she'd never met a math class *or* a dress she'd liked, but years later she'd developed a taste for both.

Sweats hadn't figured much in her life. But then again, this wasn't her life, this was some alternate universe she'd stumbled into. So what if the sweats were going to make her look both short *and* fat; this was about survival, not looking good. Or so she told herself. "These are too long."

"Roll 'em up."

Spoken like a man who'd probably never given his appearance a single thought. And why should he—she'd seen him naked. He had *nothing* to hide, not a damn thing.

"Hurry up," he said, and for a split beat his gaze dropped, running over her body. Specifically, her nipples, which could surely cut glass. "You're turning blue." He straightened and took a step toward her, maybe even to do it for her, and suddenly hurrying seemed like a good idea. She pulled the sweatshirt over her head; then, with her arms still up, she paused. Holy smoke, the inside of his sweatshirt smelled good, like . . . like rough-and-tumble man. She stood there and inhaled some more, thinking they ought to bottle this smell—

"You okay in there?"

She yanked the sweatshirt into place. "Fine. Just got stuck for a minute."

"Uh-huh." His expression said he knew exactly what she'd been doing, but he sat on the floor without a word and pulled on socks, then running shoes, making her realize she wasn't the only one freezing.

And yet he'd seen to her comfort first. That did something she hadn't expected—it tugged at her.

Whoa. Stop the lust train. *Had she already forgotten?* No more men. Not even tall, built, bossy ones with an oddly thoughtful nature. *Especially* not even tall, built, bossy ones with an oddly thoughtful nature!

His hair, fawnlike with its myriad colors, stuck straight up in spots. Probably because she'd gotten him out of the shower and he hadn't had time to so much as comb it. His shoulders were still bare, and wide enough to withstand a lot, she'd bet.

He covered them up with a T-shirt he pulled from the bag, and then added a thick black sweater that looked deliriously soft and warm. "Better," he sighed, then leveled his eyes on her. The firelight gleamed over his chiseled features, reflecting in his eyes. There was so much intensity there. And heat. Looking at her like that, he seemed impossibly handsome, and far too sexy for her own fragile frame of mind.

"Change your pants," he said, and turning his back, jammed his hands in his pockets. "Hustle."

His sexiness forgotten, she shook her head even though he couldn't see her. "I'm not going to change right here."

"You're going to go somewhere else to do it? Into the dark house and maybe an even darker bathroom? You with your phobia of the dark?"

Damn. Good point. "Okay, but don't peek."

"Because you didn't peek at me?"

Did he always have to be right? "What about Dante?"

With a long-suffering sigh, Cooper moved around the couch to the huge double doors that led to the hallway and foyer. Shutting them, he turned back to face her, waggling his finger in a circle as if to say, *Go ahead.*

Breanne crossed her arms tighter over herself and shifted her weight from one frozen foot to the other. "Why can't you be on the *other* side of the door?"

"So you can lock me out and away from the flames? Don't think so."

Another good point.

"You're stalling, Princess."

Princess? She'd show him princess! If she could move without trembling like a baby, that is. Since she couldn't, she just stood there in a rare moment of indecision, feeling oddly close to tears.

"Just do it," he said, sounding tired. "This place is supposed to be some sort of exclusive hideaway, famed for its privacy." Pushing away from the doors, he came close again, but then turned and faced the fire, holding out his hands to the flames. "Plus, I don't think Dante's exactly eager to have us demanding to know what the hell happened, booking two guests at the same time. He's probably in hiding."

Maybe. Another shiver shook her body. Her jaw was sore from all the chattering her teeth were doing inside her head, and she felt so weary she could have curled up into a tiny ball in front of the fire and slept for the rest of the week.

"You done yet?"

"*No.*"

"*Jesus.* Just do it, would you?"

She reached for the zipper on her jeans. "You always this patient?"

"It's a special gift."

"Betcha it gets you a lot of women."

"Yeah, they're beating down my door."

In direct conflict with those confident, cocky words, he hunched his shoulders, stretching the sweater taut across the muscles there as he stared into the fire.

She didn't have the time, nor could she spare the energy, to wonder about him, but she did. "Are you married?"

A rather harsh laugh escaped him. "No."

"Committed?"

"No."

With or without the attitude, she imagined he did have women beating down his door. It was all that disheveled hair calling to a woman's fingertips, that come-sin-with-me expression, those drown-in-me blue eyes.

And then there was the rest of him, which would have a weaker woman begging him for a distraction from this cold.

But she wasn't weak, and she had enough problems at the moment. She didn't need to be courting more. Hitching his oversized sweatshirt up to her chin to see, she reached for the zipper on her jeans, trying like hell not to inhale the delicious scent of the soft material again. Eyeing him carefully, she began to peel the wet jeans off her hips, not an easy chore because they'd practically iced themselves to her skin. She had to do the shimmy shake, and finally, *finally* got them to her knees, stopping to adjust her wayward panties.

Cooper turned around.

"*Hey!*" she squealed, crossing her hands over her tiny scrap of white satin—worn for the rat bastard Dean.

Cooper ran his gaze from her undoubtedly wild hair to his own sweatshirt stuffed up to her chin, exposing her belly button piercing and the panties that hadn't been meant to cover much, and didn't. "I figured fair's fair," he said very softly.

Five

I've heard that men are like fine wine. They begin as grapes, and it's up to women to stomp the shit out of them until they turn into something acceptable to have dinner with. Me, I just want to do the stomping.
                              —Breanne Mooreland's Journal Entry

Literally caught with her pants down, Breanne stood frozen to the spot, unable to move or even breathe. In that horrible beat of time she became painfully aware of how she must look, sweatshirt high, pants at her knees, her barely there bikini bottoms askance . . .

Cooper's deep blue eyes sparked, *flamed*, and the oddest thing happened to her. In spite of everything, a little ball of heat swirled low in her belly.

She had to be delirious. From the cold. From exhaustion. From her life sucking big-time. Awkwardly she hopped again, trying to pull her jeans back up, but they weren't going anywhere. Then she made one too many hops and caught her boot heel on the hem of the jeans. Waving her arms wildly, she struggled for balance.

Cooper merely stepped forward and caught her.

Fine. He could help her and she could die of mortification later.

But he didn't help. He put a hand to the middle of her chest and gave her a little push, making her fall gracelessly to the couch. Once again, the pink vibrator hit the floor and rolled to a stop at his feet.

They both stared at it for one beat before Breanne tried to bounce back up.

"*Stay*," he commanded.

Oh, no. *Hell, no.* She scissored her legs, meaning to kick him, either in the chin or the nads, she didn't care; she was going to take him down. *Now.*

But he just laughed low in his throat, and then again when she struggled to karate-chop him with her legs caught together by her own jeans. *Laughed*, as he crouched beside her, a big hand on either of her thighs and said, "Give in, Princess."

"I never give in."

Holding her down with ease, he reached for the fallen vibrator, lifting it up. The obnoxious thing still glowed neon-pink. "Never say never." Then he grinned at her in the firelight, looking just like the devil must look in the dead of winter with no one to torture. "This thing keeps showing up. Maybe you should claim it."

"It's *not* mine!"

"I don't know . . . earlier you were gripping it like it was your long-lost best friend." With a flick of his wrist, he turned it on.

The low hum filled the air, and with it came a buzzing in Breanne's ear—the sound of her brain coming to boiling point.

"Ready for use," Cooper said, suggestively waggling it in her face.

"Good." She struggled to get free, trying not to think about the picture she was presenting him with. "You can shove it up your—"

"Oh, no," he said. "Ladies first." He dropped the thing to the couch next to her, where it rumbled against the soft, buttery leather while he slid his hands down her legs to the jeans pooled between her knees.

"Don't even *think* about it," she choked out.

But he wasn't only thinking about it, he was doing it, fisting his fingers into the wet denim and yanking them past her knees to her ankles, where they caught on her boots.

His gaze met hers, intense and raw, and along with it a heart-stopping heat.

Did he have to pack such a sexual energy? She felt her entire body clench with a punch of shocking yearning.

"High-heeled boots," he murmured. "Ever so practical out here."

She stared down at the top of his head as he worked on stripping her. Her little triangle of white satin had not only slipped sideways, it was now riding up into parts unknown. She'd had a bikini wax two days ago—again for the rat bastard Dean—and judging from the very soft, very rough sound that escaped Cooper at her movements, he'd caught an eyeful up close and personal. "If I wasn't so tired," she murmured, sagging back, suddenly exhausted, "I'd kick your ass."

"Next time," he said, trying to untie her boots. The laces were iced. "I guess you were all prettied up for the honeymoon."

No. She'd prettied up for herself, to feel sexy, but she was not going to argue with a man when her pants were around her ankles; when she had a vibrator bouncing on the couch next to her, taunting her; when she had bigger worries, such as her panties, and what they still weren't covering. Shoving the sweatshirt down as far as she could, which was to the tops of her thighs, she leaned forward to hurry the process along.

While she worked on one boot, Cooper continued to work on the other, his fingers managing to work faster and far more efficiently than hers. His bowed head was close enough to her thighs that he could have lifted his head and drunk his fill, but he kept his gaze on her boot, pulling it off, pushing her hands aside, then removing her other as well. Finally he hooked his hands into her jeans again and peeled them away. Her legs were pink and mottled from the cold, and when his knuckles brushed against her, she flinched. Without a word he stood, once again turning his back to her, staring into the fire, looking a little more tense than he had a moment ago.

"A little late now," she muttered, pulling on the sweat bottoms.

He didn't respond to that.

"Done," she said, and stood.

Only then did he turn back to face her, his gaze sweeping from top to bottom, taking in the way his sweats looked on her. The only sign of strain was a tic in his jaw. "You want the couch in front of the warm fire?" he asked. "Or the cold honeymoon suite? We can start you a fire there."

She couldn't concentrate with the vibrator continuing to hum and jump on the couch, but she knew she didn't want to go further into the depths of the dark house. With an annoyed sound, she reached for the vibrator, desperate to turn it off.

Cooper beat her to it, turning it off himself before handing it back. "Keep it. You never know when you might need a friend."

She rolled her eyes, but the thing provided a tiny bit of light so she grabbed it. Plus, given that she was off men, it might be sooner than later before she'd need a friend of the battery-operated variety.

"'Night," he said with an irritating, knowing smile. He began to walk away.

"Wait!" When he turned back to her, she had to come up with something to say. "We . . . can't both really stay here."

He just raised a brow.

"And I think you should be the one to leave," she said, lifting her chin.

"Why me?"

"You said it yourself—I had a bad day."

"Hell, Princess, I've had a bad year, and you don't see me whining about it."

She wondered how bad was bad, and if it could possibly match hers.

"You want to trudge out in the snow and try to get into town?" he asked.

With the coyotes, bears, and God knew what else? "No. I thought . . ."

"That I'd do it." He shook his head. "I was here first."

"That's gentlemanly."

He laughed. "Yeah, well, you're not stuck out here in the middle of nowhere, in the storm of the century, with any sort of gentleman."

For some insane reason, that caused another flicker of heat to spiral through her.

Which proved it, really. She *had* lost her mind.

"We both know the roads are closed by now," he said. "And I for one am not snowshoeing into town. In fact, I'm not going anywhere."

"This is not how it was supposed to be," she said softly.

"No kidding. But shit happens, and we deal with it. Now are you going to pick a spot, or am I?"

There weren't many people who'd argued with her. Not her four older brothers, or the father she'd long ago wrapped around her finger. Fact was, she'd been getting her way since birth.

Aside from her family, the other men in her life had also let her get away with just about anything. Her first fiancé, Barry, had spoiled her rotten. Even Dean, King of Rat Bastards— whom she hoped had choked on his own tongue—had never so much as crossed opinions with her, but that was probably because he'd been too busy.

So the fact that this strange man was not only quarreling with her, but telling her how things were going to be, surprised her into momentary silence.

"Nightie-night, Princess," he said.

She looked around and once again panicked at the thought of being alone. Damn him, but he truly was the lesser of two evils. "Wait!"

He turned back, propping up the doorway with a shoulder as if he didn't have a care. "Yeah?"

She opened her mouth, but her pride ran away with her good sense. "Nothing." She casually dropped to the couch but something must have given her away, whether it was the sudden panic pumping her heart loud enough to wake the dead, or the renewed tension that gripped her body, because he sighed. "Are you going to be okay?"

Was she? She wished she knew. Alone, she'd go back to obsessing about spiders and coyotes and bears, but if he stayed, she'd have new things to obsess about . . .

Still, he'd stuck by her side, even helped her when she'd needed it, and hadn't once thrown it in her face as any of her brothers might have.

Not that he was remotely brotherly . . . And yet he'd had her at every disadvantage and he'd not tried to press himself on her in any way.

"Breanne?"

Even more unnerving, she liked the sound of her name on his lips. "Seriously, I'm fine. Don't give me another thought."

"No?"

"No. I certainly won't be giving you one." *Liar, liar, pants on fire.*

He looked at her for a long moment, then pushed away from the doorway, moving toward her like a long, lean cat totally at ease with himself, confident that he was at the top of the food chain. He had a nice gait, the kind a woman could watch all day if she was admitting such things. Which she wasn't. *Besides, she'd given up men.* His toes touched hers, then he crouched down, his face level with her belly.

Push him away, her feminist brain demanded.

Pull him close, her body countered.

"You're not going to give me another thought at all?" he asked silkily, and she knew damn well he was purposely invading her space.

She managed to shoot him a smile that she'd perfected before she'd ever left her crib. It was an I'm-fabulous, I-couldn't-be-better smile, an I've-got-the-world-by-the-balls smile. "Nope. Not another thought."

Reaching out, he settled a long finger to the base of her throat, where she imagined her pulse was about to leap right out at him. "So then what's this?" he murmured.

Only a moment ago it had been unease, even fear about her situation here, until he'd touched her.

Now it was arousal, plain and simple.

What kind of a woman was aroused by a perfect stranger? "Nothing but a physical reaction," she informed him.

"Ah." His fingers stroked over her racing pulse and then again. In the glow of the fire, his expression was one of curious intent as he watched the path of his fingers. "Because you're scared."

"I'm not scared."

His lips curved slightly. "Then what?"

Damn it, he'd caught her. "I'm tired and hungry and still cold."

"And that's making your heart pound?"

"Sure." They were so close his exhaled breath warmed her breasts through the tank and sweatshirt, so close that she could see his eyes weren't a solid azure blue at all, but had flecks of midnight dancing in them, holding secret all his thoughts.

He shifted then, his big, warm hand lightly cupping her throat, skimming to her shoulder and down her arm before gliding back up again in a gesture that could have been meant to warm. And it might have, if he'd been her brother or her father.

And she did get warm. Hot, actually. But something else as well, something far more.

"Still cold?" he murmured.

"Um, no. Thanks."

"No problem." His gaze dipped once again to her pulse. "It's still racing, Princess. How come?"

"Don't know."

"Want me to guess?"

Her pulse sped up even more. "No!"

"Because if you were still cold, or even afraid, we have an easy solution."

"Really? What's that?"

"We share this fire."

"You mean with you on the floor and me on the couch?"

His gaze didn't waver. "No."

Damn if her nipples didn't go happy at his low, rough voice. And other reactions occurred as well: her thighs tightened, and between them came a deep tingle. "We're perfect strangers," she reminded herself as well as him. "I'm not sleeping with a perfect stranger. I'm supposed to be sleeping with my husband."

"But there is no husband."

"*Good night*, Cooper."

"Yeah." He sighed, then shot a hopeful look at her carry-on. "You don't by any chance have any food in that bag of yours, do you?"

"No." *Just two sexy nighties*. "But Dante brought you a hot chocolate."

"Great. Hot chocolate." With one last stroke of his finger over her throat, he grabbed the mug and left, shutting the doors behind him.

Breanne let out a slow, careful breath and sank back. The man was potent, she'd give him that. But he was also domineering, and just alpha enough to make her want to scream.

And yet . . . and yet there was more. She didn't know what, and told herself she didn't want to. Curling up into a ball on the couch, she stared into the flames while the weight of the day began to drag her down, along with her eyelids.

But the problem with relaxing, even marginally, was that everything came back to her, beginning with being left at the altar.

How could she not have seen that coming? Seriously, her radar should have at least blipped a warning, but she'd gotten nothing.

She'd met Dean at work. As an investor for one of the companies her accounting firm handled, he'd sauntered by her cubicle, stopping to smile at her. Other than his most annoying habit of humming Elvis tunes at inopportune times—such as when he made love to her—he'd had a suave sophistication she hadn't been able to resist, even knowing he was a player. Foolishly, she'd let herself go for it, and for some reason that had always mystified her, he'd reciprocated.

But everything he'd ever told her—such as those three words, I love you—had turned out to be a lie.

And here she was. Alone. She looked around the large room, into the far corners and the shadows there, managing to convince herself she was fine. She'd even started to relax, at least enough that her muscles didn't ache. And then—

SNAP!

At the loud crack, she fell off the couch and landed on all fours, eyes wide, heart ricocheting off her ribs as she searched the room.

Just the fire crackling. Forcing herself to laugh, she climbed back up on the couch and let her eyes drift shut again. Everything was good, she was going to stay good—

A soft creaking sound had her leaping to her feet. She tried to tell herself she was still fine, but that was hard to believe as she watched the handle on the double doors turn. "Who—who's there?"

The door slowly opened, revealing the large, dark cavern that was the foyer.

"Cooper?" Her heart hit her throat. "This isn't funny."

A small, blond woman appeared. Mid-twenties, maybe,

with a petite frame and a sweet, angelic smile. "Sorry. Did I wake you?"

Was she kidding? Who could sleep in the haunted horrors of the honeymoon house? "No."

"Oh, good. I'm Shelly, the cook. I came for the mugs I sent here with Dante." She came further into the room, passing Breanne's empty mug, heading directly toward the fire, where she held up her hands. "Darn, it's cold between the kitchen and here." She laughed. "Some storm, huh?" She wore dark jeans and a soft-looking white turtleneck, her blond hair neatly pulled back in a ponytail. "And welcome, by the way," she said with a smile when she caught Breanne staring. "I hope you had a nice trip here."

Her honest, hopeful expression seemed so completely innocent, Breanne found she couldn't say what was on her mind, which was *Are you kidding me?* "Uh, yeah. Nice."

With a sigh, Shelly moved away from the flames, scooping up the mug. "You're on your honeymoon, right?"

Breanne felt her smile congeal. "Yes. Alone."

"Oh." That startled her. "So the wedding, it went . . . badly?"

"You could say so."

"I'm sorry," Shelly said with true regret. "And now this huge, unbelievable storm . . ."

"Until you got here, I was trying to convince myself this is all a bad dream."

"You poor thing." Shelly sat down on the couch next to Breanne. "Did you get your heart broken?"

The question, coming from someone Breanne had known all of a minute, should have irked her. It should have, at the very least, brought her great pain. Instead, she leaned back on the sofa, nothing but exhausted. "Maybe it's been a little stepped on," she finally admitted. "But not broken, no."

"Good, then you can try to enjoy your trip in spite of him. You don't need a man to have a good time." Shelly laughed at herself. "That's what my mom always told us, anyway. I don't really have a lot of experience to go by."

Breanne blinked at the easy familiarity with which Shelly had spoken. Breanne had family, coworkers. Friends. But truthfully, most were men. Girl talk had never really been her thing. "I don't know what I was thinking to do this, to come here alone. It was stupid."

"Oh, you're going to enjoy yourself, I promise you. And someday you'll find another man. A better one."

Been there, done that, bought the T-shirt, thought Breanne. "Would you know where I could get a few blankets?"

"Of course—I'll get them for you. But first, I came to bring you into the formal dining room."

No way was she going to be lured anywhere in this dark, haunted house. "I think I'll just stay here, thanks."

"I was spooked when I first got here, too," Shelly said kindly. "This place scared me to death."

"But not anymore?"

"Well . . ." Shelly hugged her enviable petite body for a moment, running her hands up and down her arms as if chilled. "I got used to it," she finally said. And then smiled. "And anyway, you're not alone in your fears. We all feel a little off tonight."

"We?"

"Me, and the rest of the staff."

"How many of you are there?"

"There's five of us. Myself, Lariana, Patrick, Edward, and Dante." She stopped with a faraway look in her eyes and sighed dreamily. "You've met Dante."

This pretty, innocent little thing was sighing over the hooded butler?

At Breanne's baffled expression, Shelly let out a laugh. "He's thrilling, isn't he?"

How about terrifying? "He's . . . something."

"He doesn't say much, but when he does, he's just so smart,

so kind. And funny, too. I just think he's the sexiest man alive, don't you?"

"I didn't get to see much of him," Breanne said tactfully.

"I know, I'm sorry." Shelly's smile was tremulous, making Breanne realize the cook was just as nervous as she was. "All this dark is getting to me. It makes me talk too much. I should go finish my chores before I get myself into trouble with the boss."

"Speaking of that," Breanne said, "do you know where the manager is?"

"Edward?" Shelly lifted a shoulder. "I'm not sure, exactly. He's usually scarce at this time of day. You let me know if you want any of the extras, okay? We have massages and a few other spa treatments available. How about some mud therapy?"

Breanne could never relax through anything like that, not under these circumstances. "Maybe some other time."

"Aromatherapy? We use oils—it's lovely, really. Or you can swim in the indoor pool by candlelight. Oh! I could make you a lobster picnic when the electricity comes back on. And if you want me to book you for a helicopter tour when we get the phones back, or anything else like that, just let me know. For now I've got candles going in the dining room so it isn't dark there. There's food, too."

Breanne's stomach growled.

"See? You're hungry. Come."

"Will Edward be there?"

"Um . . ." Shelly fingered the mug. "I don't know."

At some point Breanne had begun to warm up, except for her bare feet. If she wanted food—which she absolutely did— she had no choice but to slip back into her high-heeled, wet boots. Ugh. "How come I didn't see any of you when I first got here?"

"Sorry about that. But food will help take the edge off your travels. Then, in the light of day, everything will be okay."

The travels had been the least of Breanne's worries. She would happily take yet another horrendous flight, seated between a *dozen* stinky fishermen this time, if only she could erase the entire day from existence. But there was no magic genie in sight, and Shelly held the doors open, gesturing Breanne out first.

She peered into the dark, dark hallway and swallowed hard.

"Come on," Shelly coaxed. "I met the other guest on the stairs and redirected him. Cooper, right? He's there already." Shelly said this as if his presence should entice her.

Instead her stomach took a little dip, though truthfully it might not have been fear but an unwelcome sizzle of excitement.

"He's waiting for you," Shelly said.

"Oh, goody."

"Have you spoken to him? He's really nice."

"I've given up men for Lent."

"Are you Catholic?"

"No." She shook her head. "It was a joke. A bad one, sorry. Truthfully, I've discovered I have questionable taste in the male species, and I'm taking a break until I better hone my judgment."

"Well, that's a shame. He's cute."

Cute? Puppies were cute. Babies were cute.

But big, bad, sexy Cooper Scott was not. In fact, he was the furthest thing from cute she'd ever seen.

Which didn't explain that sizzle of excitement one little bit.

Six

When life throws you a bucket of shit, duck.
—Breanne Mooreland's Journal Entry

Cooper sat in the vast formal dining room, at a table longer than his entire condo. He looked out floor-to-ceiling windows that revealed a black, endless night filled with the glow of white snow.

A small pixie of a blond woman named Shelly had seated him, after appearing out of nowhere when he'd been heading toward the stairs. Dante had lit the myriad white candles along the window ledges that she busily set out. She was pretty, with a sweet, giving, almost naive smile, and yet nothing within him revved like it had when he'd been sparring with Breanne.

As irrational as it seemed, given that she was the opposite of every fantasy he'd ever had, he was insanely fascinated by the irritating yet sexy-as-hell woman.

Maybe it'd been the way she'd looked at his naked body. Or how she'd reacted to the vibrator: like a starving student and a scared Bambi-in-the-headlights, all at the same time. Now all he wanted was to get her to look at him like that again.

Because that was an unsettling thought, he concentrated on Shelly, who was neat and tidy, cute, and smelled like onions and seasoning. She had his mouth watering at the promise of something good to eat.

While he waited, the snow kept falling in long lines of white that were mesmerizing. He'd been told by Shelly that in good weather, he'd be able to see all the way to the far shores of Lake Sunshine, though tonight he couldn't even see the dock that was supposedly only twenty yards from the house.

Nothing but snow and more snow, and he figured one thing was certain: the skiing would be out of this world. Assuming it stopped coming down long enough to clear the roads so he could get to the lifts.

He knew if Breanne had her way, he'd be leaving at dawn, but that wasn't going to happen. But then again, neither was her honeymoon, so she could just relax. This place was plenty big enough for the both of them.

He heard a click-click-clicking, and knew the sound. It came from a pair of ridiculously high-heeled boots, squeaking from all the water they'd absorbed.

Breanne.

A/K/A Princess.

And though he knew exactly what she looked like—good Christ, the thought of her with her pants around her ankles and those barely there panties giving her a world-class wedgie would most definitely highlight his fantasies for the rest of his life—when she entered the room, she stole his breath.

Her hair had dried in long waves around her face. Her makeup, if she'd ever worn any, was gone. And though she walked like a princess, she still wore his sweats. A princess in sweats and fancy, expensive boots, with her chin up, only the clasping of her hands giving her away.

"You're squeaking," he said.

She sent him a cool gaze, then looked around, taking in the exquisite ceiling molding and incredible casement bay windows. "I'm also underdressed for this room."

"Oh, no," Shelly said, coming in behind her. "No one has to dress for dinner. This isn't an inn—it's your private house for the week. You dress as you want."

"Not exactly *private*," Breanne noted dryly, her gaze cutting to Cooper. "But it's a good thing about the dress code, because my luggage is gone."

"Oh, dear. You *have* had a rough day," Shelly said in sympathy.

Cooper wasn't sorry. He had hopeful visions of her having to go all week in only her underwear—

"How about I see what I can round up for you in the morning?" Shelly offered, crushing Cooper's dream as she left them alone.

Breanne stood just inside the room, seeming as if she'd run if she only had somewhere to go. At the very least she was going to sit in the chair farthest from him, which was approximately miles down the room. To avoid that, he rose and pulled out the chair right next to him.

Breanne hesitated, but then came close, until once again he could see the wild, almost frantic beat of her pulse at the base of her neck.

"You still afraid?" he asked.

"Of course not."

"Cold?"

"Haven't we already had this conversation? No."

"Then . . ." He lifted his hand and stroked his thumb over her throat. He wasn't really sure why, except the strangest thing had happened when he'd touched her before. He'd felt a spark, from deep inside where he hadn't felt anything in too goddamn long. And he wanted another.

And another.

His brother had been fussing over him for months to get the hell out, take a leave, relax, just be, before he landed in the psych ward. Cooper had finally caved and gotten the hell out.

He'd quit.

And he still hadn't felt any better. Hadn't felt *anything*.
Until tonight.

Breanne encircled her fingers around his wrist and that
inner spark leapt to flame. "*Cooper.*"

"Breanne." *Don't shove me away. God, don't.*

Shockingly enough, she didn't, and for a long moment they
stood just like that, eyes locked, her fingers over his.

"You keep touching me," she whispered.

He knew it. He had her soft skin imprinted on his brain already.

"If you keep it up, I'm going to—"

"What?"

Still looking into his eyes, she chewed on her bottom lip.
"Something."

"Anything you want," he murmured, and smiled grimly
when, with a sound of great vexation, she tossed his hand from
her and stalked around the table—click, click, clicking—strut-
ting as if she wore something straight out of a fashion maga-
zine rather than his sweats. In fact, just the look of her hips
sashaying with attitude turned him on.

He was in bad shape if riling and baiting her like this was
the most fun he'd had in too long.

On the other side of the table now, she pulled out her own
chair, shooting him a smug, superior smile.

"I think you're crazy about me," he said.

She sputtered. "You're delusional. You—" She broke off
whatever insult she'd been about to fling his way as Shelly
came back into the room with a bottle of wine. She was followed by Dante, who set down a large tray at the head of the
table.

Shelly beamed at the butler-who-didn't-look-like-a-butler.
"Thanks, Dante."

He didn't smile back. "You're welcome."

Shelly arranged the plates between Cooper and Breanne,
one filled with an assortment of breads, another with luncheon

meats and cheeses, and a third with fruit. "I feel so bad," she said, her smile still in place, but a bit wobbly now as she clasped her hands in front of her. "Edward insists on a gourmet meal, and I really did spend the day making up roasted chicken with asiago polenta and truffled mushrooms, but then the power went out, the oven flicked off—" She sounded close to tears. "It didn't finish, and now . . ." She lifted her hands helplessly.

"No worries," Cooper said. "I'd eat anything tonight and be happy."

"Really?" Shelly asked anxiously.

"Absolutely."

"Me, too." Breanne gave Shelly a smile of her own, one Cooper hadn't seen, which meant it was real and full of warmth. He almost did a double take, struck by how it softened her face, removing all lines of sarcasm and bite.

Had he thought her not classically beautiful? He needed his eyes checked.

"Thank you for serving us at all," Breanne said sincerely to Shelly.

"Oh, but it's nothing like how it should be," the cook told them, still twisting her fingers.

"You did the best you could," Dante said. "We all know it. Stop worrying."

She shot him a tremulous smile.

Dante jammed his hands in his pockets.

Breanne got busy, sliding some cheese and grapes on her plate. "The best thing I make is reservations, so for me, this is great."

More relaxed now, Shelly laughed as she picked up the empty tray. "Then you just wait until tomorrow. I'm going to spoil you both rotten."

Breanne paused, a grape halfway to her mouth. She set it down and looked at Cooper expectantly.

He knew what she wanted him to say, that tomorrow there

wouldn't be two guests, because he was leaving. Instead, he just smiled. He wasn't going anywhere.

Dante moved to Shelly's side and took the tray from her hands. Shelly gazed up at him as if he were a god. Her god.

Cooper wondered what it'd be like to have someone look at him like that.

Not coming close to duplicating the expression, Breanne sent him the evil eye. "One of us is leaving tomorrow," she said to Shelly.

Dante shook his head.

"No?" Breanne asked. "Why not?"

"The roads aren't cleared and no one's going to be able to get to them until the storm passes, which is supposedly no time soon. We're all trapped here."

"Where do you sleep when you're stuck like this?" Breanne asked.

"Oh, don't worry about us," Shelly said quickly. "There are servants' quarters we can stay in. You won't even know we're here." Leaning in, she began to pour the wine, first for Cooper, and then for Breanne, who scooted her chair back to make room for Shelly. At the odd scraping noise, Breanne looked down, then carefully lifted a sliver of glass. "Yikes. Something must have broken in here."

Shelly stared at the glass without moving.

Dante reached in and took the shard. "No harm done," he said, then took the bottle of wine from Shelly's fingers, set it down on the table, and directed her from the room.

Silence reigned.

Cooper looked at Breanne.

She pretended not to notice.

"So we're stuck," he said, making her face it. "Might as well relax about it." He hoisted his glass of wine in a toast. "What do you say?"

She stared at him, then lifted her glass as well, downing the contents in a few gulps before reaching for the bottle.

"You might want to slow down, Princess," he warned. "You're at altitude now, and that's going to go straight to your head, fast. Drink some water so you don't get dehydrated."

She bared her teeth and growled.

He laughed but lifted his hands. "Just trying to help you avoid getting hung over."

"I could avoid a hangover entirely by just getting drunk and staying there," she said miserably, and when he laughed again, she picked up a grape and looked as if she was considering chucking it across the table at him.

Arching a brow, he silently dared her, enjoying being distracted by her frustration. The woman must burn up more stress calories a day than the president of the United States.

Or at least as many as he did at work when adrenaline was flowing and—and that no longer mattered because he'd quit. He'd walked away and had become unemployed. Funny that he'd forgotten, even for a second.

He was just getting into his cheese and crackers when another set of footsteps came down the hall—not light like Shelly's, nor rubber-soled like Dante's. These were heavy, hard, and clinked and rattled with every step.

"What's that?" Breanne whispered, eyes wide.

Step, clink. Step, clink.

"Not a what," Cooper said, "but a who."

"That isn't Shelly or Dante."

"No," he agreed.

The footsteps came closer.

Step, clink.

Step, clink.

With a sudden gasp, Breanne rose to her feet, running around the table in those silly heels, directly at Cooper. He reached to pull out the chair next to him for her, but as she reached the corner, her heels slipped and she flew into the home stretch.

It was all he could do to catch her, but catch her he did. Her hair stabbed him in the eye, caught on his jaw, and even went into his mouth, but his brain had locked on the fact that her warm, soft curves were trying to crawl up his body. Her breasts were mashed against his chest, her legs entangled with his. He liked it all, but then again, it'd been so long since he'd had any action, he'd have liked just about anything.

Then an extremely tall, extremely lean shadow filled the doorway with indistinguishable features. "Sorry," the shadow said in a heavy Scottish accent. "But has anyone seen me bloody flashlight?"

Still in Cooper's lap, Breanne froze.

The shadow stepped further into the room. The candlelight caught him, revealing nothing more than a mere mortal man, possibly thirty, wearing a tool belt from which swung a hammer, a wrench, and an assortment of other tools.

Hence the clinking.

Cooper threw an amused look at Breanne, who remained utterly still for one instant before she blew out a short breath and struggled like a wildcat to get out of his lap.

But because he was a sick, sick man, Cooper used his superior strength to hold her against him before craning his head toward the man in the doorway. "No flashlight, sorry."

"Well, fuck me," Scottish said, and scratched his head. His red hair stood straight up. "I'm trying to get the generator up and running, straightaway."

"That'd be good," Cooper said.

"Power lines are down all over the bloody place. It'll be days and days with no electricity if I don't get the generator running."

Breanne looked horrified. "*Days and days . . . ?*"

"Aye. Well, off I go, then." With another scratch of his head, Scottish walked out.

Step, clink.

Step, clink.

"If I call him back here," Cooper whispered in her ear, "will you crawl up my body again?"

"Oh!" she spit out. "You are so not a nice man!"

"Are you sure? Because a minute ago you couldn't get enough of me."

"Let me up!"

Enjoying not only the squirming, but the lovely, warm feel of her butt rubbing against his crotch, Cooper did no such thing.

"I said, let me go!"

Grinning down at her, he easily held her against him. "Not until you say 'thank you, Cooper, for saving my life.'"

"You didn't save my life!"

"But you wanted me to."

She stared at him. "I can't believe you can walk through a door with your head as swollen as it is."

And it wasn't the only thing on him swollen, either. Her fidgeting was having another effect on him entirely, and given the way she went suddenly still, she knew. "*What do you have in your pocket?*" she demanded.

He let his grin speak for itself.

She ground her teeth together. "You. Are. Impossible."

"You're the one wriggling around." But careful to mind her knees and where she put them, he let her go.

Jerking to her feet, she yanked down on the sweatshirt, which fell to her thighs and covered too much of her.

His own fault, but it didn't matter what she wore because he knew what lay beneath—a thin white tank top sans bra that outlined her breasts and mouthwatering nipples in such a way that he'd nearly swallowed his own tongue. And then there'd been those tiny panties—

"Whatever you're thinking about," she said shakily, backing away to walk back around the table to her chair. "Stop. Stop it right now."

"Why?"

She reached for her glass of wine, her hand shaking. "Because I'm on my honeymoon, remember?"

"You didn't get married today, remember?"

"Yes. I do remember that part," she said softly, face averted.

Ah, hell. He was an ass, especially since he knew how she felt. He'd also once had a woman walk away from him.

Only at least he'd seen it coming. Annie had chafed long and hard beneath the impossible hours Cooper had put in on his job. She'd broken under the strain only six months before he had, but she'd been long gone by the time he'd been free.

It no longer mattered, though, because he still deeply resented how she'd never accepted that part of him. In fact, few had. "Look," he said more gently, "consider it this way. The guy's an idiot for letting you get away."

She snorted her agreement and poured herself more wine.

"And anyway, in the long run, he did you a favor."

"Yeah? How's that?"

"He left you free to take advantage of the next best thing to come along."

She regarded him for a long moment, her bitterness and sadness draining away, replaced by a reluctant smile. "You know, just when I think you're part of my worst nightmare, you go and say something almost human. And definitely profound."

He smiled and lifted his glass in a silent toast.

"Days and days," she murmured again after another long sip. "Can you imagine?"

"It could be worse."

"*How?*"

"You could be stuck here with your ex."

She rolled her eyes. "You're very helpful tonight."

"I try." He dug back into the cheese and crackers, and was well on his way to filling his rumbling belly when something hit him on the nose and landed on his plate.

A grape.

"What was that?" he asked.

She looked it over. "I believe it's a grape."

"I can see that, smart-ass. I'm wondering why it was bouncing off my nose."

"Gee, I haven't a clue." Looking as if she felt a great deal better, she rose. "Good night," she said loftily, and grabbing her plate and the bottle of wine, headed toward the door, where she'd undoubtedly go sit in front of the warm, toasty fire while he climbed the dark stairs and had to light his own and wait for it to heat the room, hoping it did so before his balls froze off. "'Night," he muttered, watching her curvy little bod practically quiver with her superiority. "Sleep tight. Oh, and . . ." He paused for effect. "Don't let the monsters bite."

Her step faltered but she recovered, and with that pert little nose thrust high, kept going.

Seven

Don't expect a man with a hard-on to be able to think; he doesn't have enough blood to run both heads.
—Breanne Mooreland's Journal Entry

Breanne kept her nose in the air until she left the formal dining room and found herself in the dark with nothing to guide her except for a faint glow from far down the hallway.

The fire from inside the great room.

Or so she hoped, anyway. She wished now she'd brought that vibrator as a flashlight instead of leaving it on the couch. Standing there all alone with the huge mansion surrounding her, the corners and far reaches unknown, she felt her belly quiver unpleasantly. "You're a big girl," she whispered to herself, and holding her plate and bottle of wine, took a tentative step toward the orange glow. "A big girl who's calm in the face of adversity." Another step. "A big girl who doesn't believe in haunted houses or monsters—"

Something creaked, probably just the house, but she jerked as if shot, then thought, *the hell with this.* She burst into a run, her wet boots squeaking, wine jostling, grapes flying, skidding to a halt just inside the great room. Panting, she shut the doors, then leaned back against them.

In front of her, the fire crackled. The downy-soft leather couches looked inviting. Perfect for snuggling up on a night like this. She pushed away from the doors and headed toward them.

Halfway there, the doors opened behind her, and with a startled gasp she whipped around, dropping both the plate and the bottle of wine.

"Just me," Shelly said quickly. "Sorry."

Right, just Shelly. Because there were no boogeymen or monsters anywhere in this house.

Shelly crouched down to help pick up the dropped plate. "You okay?"

"Sure." Except now the wine had spilled. She really could have used the rest of that bottle. "Sorry about the mess."

"Don't worry about it. It's not my usual fare, anyway. Trust me, once the power comes back on and I feed you, you'll think you've died and gone to heaven."

"I'll look forward to that." She looked up when another woman appeared in the doorway.

"Breanne, this is Lariana," Shelly said. "She's the maid here."

Lariana was not petite like Shelly or average like Breanne, but a tall, curvaceous, exotic creature, the kind women envied and men killed for. She wore tight black trousers and a white Lycra satin blouse with the top and bottom buttons undone, emphasizing her tiny waist and huge boobs. These were thrust forward due to her five-inch stiletto heels that had Breanne both envious and wincing at the thought of being on them all day long.

"Welcome," Lariana said. She had a beautiful Latin complexion and dark hair piled up on top of her head, with long strands artfully drifting free. She was incredibly beautiful and yet somehow also incredibly intimidating at the same time. "I have a warm bedroom for you upstairs," she said to Breanne, her voice soft, cultured, and slightly accented. Though she couldn't have been more than a few years older than Breanne, she spoke with far more elegance and grace.

Feeling sloppy and out of place, Breanne tugged at Cooper's sweats. "Did the heat kick on? We have electricity?"

"No," Lariana said regretfully. "But I started a fire for you in an upstairs bedroom."

"Which means no freezing to death tonight," Shelly said. Her smile faded at a long look from Lariana. "What? That's good news, right?"

Lariana didn't roll her eyes, nothing so obvious, but Shelly still looked chastened. "Yeah, um . . . How about that snow, huh? Crazy stuff."

Lariana shook her head and moved through the room, scooping up Breanne's wet sweater and jeans, holding them up with two fingers as if they were dirty instead of just wet. "I'll get these washed."

"Oh, no, that's not necessary," Breanne said, feeling as if she should have cleaned up for the maid.

"It is part of your service." Lariana's expression was perfectly even, and perfectly lofty. "Where is your groom?"

"He's . . ." The hell with it. "He dumped me." She waited for some sign of superiority from Lariana.

But the maid dropped her icy expression immediately. "Men are such scum," she said with feeling. "Bottom feeders. Every last one of them."

"Not *every* last one," Shelly said quietly. "Some are good."

"Take off the rose-colored glasses, Pollyanna," Lariana said.

"So I'm hopeful—so what?" Shelly lifted her chin. "She'll find another man. A *better* one."

"No, thank you," Breanne interjected. "No more men."

"Ever?" Lariana asked, intrigued.

"Ever."

Lariana didn't look convinced. "They *are* scum, but once in a while, they are good for a *few* things . . ."

Breanne picked up the vibrator, waggled it. "Anything that this can't take care of?"

Shelly gasped, but Lariana burst out laughing. "I have extra batteries, when you need."

Shelly looked scandalized. And desperate to change the

subject. "I still can't believe Edward messed up and booked two of you for the same week." She tossed a big log onto the fire. "He never messes up."

Lariana snorted her opinion of that, and when Shelly looked at her, more unspoken communication passed between them. "I need to get back to the kitchen," Shelly said.

"You do that." Lariana moved to the fireplace. "You can't just add a piece of hard wood, Shelly—it'll die. You have to put in some kindling, too."

Shelly ignored her and joined Breanne by the couch. "Don't let her intimidate you while I'm gone," she whispered as they both watched Lariana handle the fire like a pro.

"She is pretty intimidating," Breanne admitted.

"It's all an act. You should have seen her the last time Edward yelled at her. She cried."

"Edward yells at you guys?"

Shelly laughed, but there was no humor in the sound. "Just remember, she's human. I mean, she's sleeping with Patrick, for God's sake."

"Patrick?"

"Our fix-it guy."

"Does he clink spookily when he walks?"

Shelly grinned. "Aye, mate, that he does," she said in perfect imitation of Patrick's accent.

Breanne looked back at the cool, classy-looking Lariana poking at the fire and tried to picture her with the tall, skinny, almost gangly, redheaded Patrick. "Are you *sure?*"

"Oh, yeah."

Lariana rose, and with Breanne's clothes over her arm, moved toward the door, picking up the carry-on as well. "Please follow me, Ms. Mooreland."

"Breanne," Breanne said, but Lariana was already gone.

Unless she wanted to say good-bye to her bag and everything in it, she didn't have much choice but to follow Lariana out into the pitch-black hallway. Ahead of her, the maid moved quickly and briskly, her heels tapping as she pulled a flashlight out of nowhere to light their way.

They came to a fork in the hallway.

"Down that way is the movie theater, with thousands of DVDs to pick from," Lariana said, sounding like a tour guide. "On the other side is the gym, complete with sauna and indoor pool, and if you want, Shelly is also an excellent masseuse."

"I don't think I'll be staying long enough to enjoy those things," Breanne said, not having missed Cooper's non-committance about leaving. If he didn't, she would.

"Are you going to let a bottom feeder ruin a perfectly good vacation?" Lariana asked coolly.

"It's not just that. I just... don't think I should have come."

"Did this almost-groom of yours cover the costs of being here?"

"Yes."

Lariana smiled coldly. "Then you should enjoy it."

They took the stairs, this time without the comfort of the light sconces casting a warm glow over the hardwood floor and interior walls. The flashlight lit the way but didn't do much for Breanne's mental health, as it created as many shadows as it chased away. At the top, Breanne was breathing erratically, and wasn't at all sure it was just the altitude bothering her.

Lariana opened the first door on the right. Her thin beam of light revealed an open-beamed ceiling and hardwood flooring with several throw rugs. There was a stone hearth, lit, crackling cozily. The four-poster, raw wood, tiered bed had a matching dresser and an oval mirror hung over it. Lariana moved to the dresser, on which was a tray with lit candles. She carried a few to the two wide-framed windowsills, the dark glass revealing nothing but black sky.

"There's a down comforter," Lariana said, pointing to the

fluffy cover folded at the foot of the bed. "There's also an attached bathroom that's shared by the bedroom on the other side, but that bedroom is empty."

They both looked at the closed door. Breanne was half hoping the maid would open it and check for the boogeyman, but she wasn't about to ask and apparently Lariana wasn't much of a mind reader. "There aren't any baskets of accessories in there, are there?"

Lariana didn't blink. "Did you want a basket of accessories?"

"No!" Breanne said, thinking about the pink vibrator she'd left downstairs. "I'm good."

"Well, then. I'm going to make sure our other guest is comfortable. Good night."

Their other guest. One sexy, irritating Cooper Scott, who was right now all cozy in *her* honeymoon suite.

The moment Lariana cleared the doorway, Breanne locked the door. Then she stood there, looking around. Feeling alone. It occurred to her that if Edward hadn't screwed up, Cooper wouldn't even be here. She might be even more alone.

She was glad she wasn't, a fact she'd admit out loud only upon threat of death, and maybe not even then.

Braving the bathroom, she brushed her teeth and moisturized her face. A silly thing to do while in the haunted house of terrors, but the routine made her feel better.

Moving back into the bedroom, she glanced uneasily at the candles. There were five of them, three burning very low already. Would the other two last until daylight, and if not, what would she do?

One thing was certain, the next time she traveled, she was leaving the sexy nighties at home and packing a flashlight. And chocolate. And alcohol.

Lots of it.

Even though the room had indeed warmed up nicely, she

climbed into the bed still fully decked out in Cooper's sweats. The bedding was lush, thick, and combined with the fire, she was cooking in less than two minutes. Swearing softly, she got out of the bed and went to her carry-on, pawing through it as if by some miracle she might find something else to wear. No such luck. She pulled out the siren-red teddy she'd gotten at her shower. See-through lace, high cut on the thighs, nearly nonexistent over the breasts, it hadn't been made for sleeping, that was for sure. It'd been made for her groom to say, "Looks great, baby, now take it off."

And just like that, self-pity welled up hard and fast, swelling her heart, filling her throat so that she could hardly draw a breath. She'd managed to keep it all at bay for hours and hours, but now there was nothing distracting her but her own pathetic thoughts.

Somehow she'd screwed everything up. Again. Truthfully? She'd blown just about every opportunity she'd ever been offered. With only so-so grades in high school—she'd thought grades didn't matter, she had Barry, ha!—she'd ended up at a junior college, with no idea of what to do with herself. She'd made her way through a string of go-nowhere jobs, and also a string of go-nowhere men, including fiancé number two.

And then Dean had come along.

She'd found him smart and cool under pressure, two traits she greatly admired because she wished she had more of each. With a single smile he'd swept her off her feet, despite the warning voice deep inside that said he wasn't the one, that said he didn't love her the way she wanted to be loved, that said she'd only get hurt in the end.

Her inner voice had been right. He *hadn't* been the one, he *hadn't* loved her the way she'd wanted to be loved, and she *had* gotten hurt.

Or at least humiliated.

Tossing aside the red lace, she reached for her Palm Pilot and made a new entry.

To Do list:

1. Live down expensive wedding that didn't happen
2. Find new job so you don't have to ever face Dean again
3. Hurry on #2 because you're broke due to #1

She read the words, then nodded and tossed the thing back in her bag. Now that she had a plan, maybe she could sleep. Sure, she'd have to face the mess that was her life in the morning, but not before then.

Still too hot, she pulled out the second nightie, a creamy white silky camisole and short set, made of staggeringly expensive silk. The top had spaghetti straps and dipped low between the breasts, and the bottoms uncovered more than they covered, but they'd be soft against her skin, and wouldn't itch.

Double checking the lock on both the bedroom and bathroom doors was a small gesture that made her feel marginally better as she stripped out of the sweats, and then her still-damp tank and panties. She put on the silk pj's that had been meant for show only, which was ridiculous when she thought about it. Surely women ended up being ditched on their honeymoons with some regularity. You'd think they'd make these things more practical.

She slid back into bed. Given how badly her life had gone today, and the new and unknown path she'd be taking from this day forth, she'd figured she'd lie there forever, stressing and obsessing, but the minute her head hit the soft, giving pillow, she sighed again, and drifted off . . .

She was standing at the back of the church wearing her gorgeous wedding gown as she peeked in at the large, restless crowd waiting for her nuptials. They were beginning to murmur, wondering about the groom's absence. Some pitied her, some merely nodded to each other, agreeing that she probably deserved what she'd gotten.

Her father, tall and stern and serious, looked at his watch for the hundredth time. Her mother's white, pinched face, strained with tension, forced a smile her way.

Breanne forced one in return, because a Mooreland never allowed a situation to get the best of her.

Even when that situation was seriously kicking her ass.

He wasn't going to show.

Crying in the church wouldn't do, so instead she turned tail, ran out of the church, and grabbed a cab. Mercifully, this was a dream, so it shifted forward then, in fast-forward past the horrendous plane ride, directly to the honeymoon house.

Suddenly she was dressed in her red teddy, walking toward a lovely four-poster bed. Only this time, a man waited in it, and her heart surged joyfully. She wasn't alone after all—she had a groom! How lovely of the house to come with a groom.

He sat up with a sexy grin, reaching for her, his eyes hot and hungry, his hands warm and sure. Cooper.

Cooper?

Whoa. Laughing at herself, Breanne opened her eyes and came back to reality.

Which was a dark face leering over her.

She stared at it for one heart-stopping moment before it sank in. *No longer dreaming.* Someone was actually leaning over her. With a terrified gasp, she fell out of the bed and scrambled toward the door—

And ran face-first into it.

Hitting her butt on the floor, she shook off the daze and the pain, and leapt up again. *Don't look back.* Fumbling, terror stuck in her throat, she yanked on the handle, belatedly realizing it was still locked. Somehow she managed to release it, then hauled the door open, heading down the hallway, her only thought being to get away—far, far away. She could have screamed and brought the staff running; logically she knew this, but there was no logic in her half-awake brain at the moment.

Besides, she didn't want Dante, with his beefy, scary mystique, or Shelly with her perpetual cheer. She didn't want Patrick with his spooky walk, or Lariana's quiet disdain—she'd had enough to last her a lifetime, thank you very much.

All she wanted was comfort.

The direction she ran for startled her almost as much as the scary face hanging over her bed had, but she'd face that later.

She sprinted directly toward the double wooden doors at the end of the hallway and burst into the dark room of the honeymoon suite, where a possibly far bigger predator lay than the one she was running from.

Cooper Scott.

Without pausing, she took a flying leap onto the high mattress. As she landed, bouncing twice, Cooper sat straight up with a muttered, *"What the hell?"*

Nearly sobbing with a relief she didn't quite understand and didn't want to, she launched herself at him, hitting him square in his gorgeous chest.

"Oof," he said, and caught her.

Eight

When climbing the ladder of life, don't let boys look up your dress!
—Breanne Mooreland's Journal Entry

Out of breath, Breanne burrowed in closer to a warm, strong Cooper as his arms came around her. "I was asleep—" she began.

"Me, too." He said this in a voice she hadn't heard from him before, rough and husky and . . . sweet. "But this is better. Much better. What are you wearing?"

"No, you don't understand—" Her words choked off when he slid his hands down and cupped her butt, squeezing, kneading. "I got too hot. I locked the door to strip—"

"Mmm," came from deep in his chest as he pressed his face to her throat. "I like the stripping part."

"And then I thought I was dreaming. Maybe I *was* dreaming—"

"About me?" he asked hopefully, opening his mouth on her neck, sucking on a patch of skin.

"Oh, my God." She fisted her hands in his hair and pulled his head back. "You're not listening!"

"Sure I am. You stripped."

"Is every single penis-carrying human the same?"

"Yeah." He went back to work on her neck.

Her eyes crossed with lust. "I'm having a crisis here!"

"Sorry," he said with dubious regret. "Go on."

"It's just that I don't know how he got in—"

"Wait." He tightened his grip on her and pulled back to see her face. "This isn't about you coming here for a slumber party, is it?"

"No!"

"Damn." He sighed, but sounding extremely alert now, he gave her one of those long, studying looks that did something funny to her belly. "Finish."

Somewhere in the back of her mind she realized he was once again shirtless, but as he was still holding her, that was only a bonus. "I saw a face leaning over me—" Just saying it brought it back. "*Leering*—" She squeezed her eyes shut. "I didn't know what to do, so I—"

"Jumped me." He held onto her when she might have wriggled free, but truthfully, she didn't want to get away.

Even awkwardly sprawled over the top of him, she could feel the easy strength in his body, the delicious heat, and then there was the disconcerting fact that he smelled better than the most expensive chocolate, better than coffee on a freezing morning, better than *anything* she'd ever smelled, which was really damn unfair.

The room had seemed pitch-black when she'd first entered in her blind panic, but her eyes had slowly adjusted. He had candles in a tray on the dresser, too, though there was only one left burning, just a small flicker of light in the huge room.

He brushed her hair from her face. "Did you really see a face, or did you have a dream about a face?"

"I really saw a face." At least she thought so. "When I opened my eyes, someone was leaning over me."

His sharp gaze swiveled to the door, which she'd left wide open. "Wait here."

"What?" She scrambled to her knees when he set her aside and rose out of the bed, wearing . . . *nothing.*

Absolutely nothing.

"Oh, my God," she said, staring, mouth open.

Perfectly at home in his own skin, he walked to his bag on a chair and took out a pair of sweats.

The man had the best ass she'd ever seen. She was still staring when he pulled on the sweats, and oh, baby, how they fit. Low on the hips, snug to his fabulous physique . . . if she hadn't been so afraid, she might have pretended to be. "You can't go! What if it gets you?"

He glanced back at her, and even in the dark, with the grim mood hovering over them, she caught his vague and brief amusement. "Don't worry, Princess. I can handle myself."

"But . . ."

Without bothering to tie the sweats, he moved to the door, ready to defend her world.

"Cooper? I'm sorry I called you a jerk earlier. You're not."

A brief smile touched his lips. "Yeah, I am." He nodded toward her. "Stay."

Right. Stay. Normally just the word would awaken every ornery, defensive bone she had, but she wasn't going anywhere. Not when she'd slid beneath his blankets and yanked them up to her chin, absorbing the incredible body heat he'd left behind; not when she'd been struck dumb and mute by the incredible protective gesture he'd just given her, whether he'd meant to or not.

Not when God knew what was out there, waiting.

At that thought, she clutched his blankets closer, frozen to the spot. *What had she sent him into?* If something happened to him, she'd never forgive herself. She should go after him, she should . . . do as he said and stay because he seemed more than capable of taking care of himself, and, in fact, more than a little dangerous in his own right.

Just the way he'd left the room, without drama or a need to show off, proved that.

She'd grown up with testosterone all around her, but typically her relationships with her brothers had been about torture. That is, their torture of her. The few times she'd needed any sort of rescuing or protecting, she'd done it on her own.

The men she'd been with had been more of the same. In the time she and Dean had been together, she'd rescued *him* quite a few times—from his boss, from other women, from his family.

He'd not returned the favor even once.

Which brought her back to her past decisions, and how she'd always made the wrong ones.

But no more.

It didn't matter how attracted she was to Cooper. When he got back—*if* he got back—she'd thank him, and then go back to sleep.

Temptation averted.

If only she could avert her tendency to screw up just as easily.

In another part of the house entirely, a shadow flattened against the wall as Cooper moved down the hallway.

Sweat beading.

Heart drumming.

Too close, way too close. If he'd so much as turned his head—

But he hadn't. No one had. No one saw.

No one ever did.

In the suite, Breanne waited. And waited. Going more and more crazy as the minutes ticked by.

Any time now, she thought. Any time now, Cooper would saunter back in, casually edgy, astonishingly sexy, laughing at her because he'd seen nothing. Yeah, any minute now.

And when he did, she was going to grab him and never let go—screw going to sleep. She was going to thank him, even though she didn't expect him to understand. She was going to—.

"Hi, honey, I'm home." Cooper swaggered back into the room, a vision in his sweat bottoms and nothing else, bringing life back into the place with just his presence.

"What did you find?" she demanded.

"Nothing." He crossed the room until his knees bumped the mattress. The candlelight danced over his sinewy chest, over that flat, rippled belly she wanted to touch, over his powerful thighs . . . and the intriguing bulge between them that kept captivating her gaze and holding it against her will.

"Nothing but a dark house," he said softly, in a voice that suggested he knew where her thoughts had just gone and liked it.

She forced her gaze up. "You went into my room?"

"I went down to the great room. Didn't see a thing." He frowned. "Not even your stuff. You weren't sleeping down there dressed like that," he realized.

She looked down at herself. The gossamer-thin silk clung to her breasts, just barely covering her nipples. Snatching the covers back up to her chin, she avoided his smirk that said it was too late—he'd already gotten an eyeful. "Lariana made me move upstairs to a bedroom," she murmured.

"And then you changed."

"I told you, I . . . got hot."

A fleeting smile touched his mouth at that. "Babe, you're always hot."

She was always hot?

"Which bedroom?" he asked.

She was always hot? "Uh, back to that *hot* comment. I thought I was a pain in your ass."

"Yeah, well, you can be both. You can be a hot pain-in-my-ass, how's that? Which bedroom, Princess?"

"Coming up the stairs, it was the first door on the right."

"Okay, hang tight."

"Wait!" No way was she getting left behind again. She leapt

out of bed, but a look at the way his gaze heated and she nearly dove back beneath the covers. She crossed her arms over her breasts. "Do you have a shirt I can wear?"

"No."

"Yes, you do. You have a big bag—"

"Do I look stupid enough to cover you up twice in one night?"

With an exasperated sigh, she tugged the sheet free of the bed. "Men are dogs," she muttered, wrapping herself up.

"Wuff, wuff," he said. "Come on, let's go find your boogeyman."

That slowed her steps, reminding her why they were doing this. Someone had been in her bedroom, someone had wanted to scare her or worse, and all she had for protection was a sheet and this man. She sneaked a sideways glance at his tall, leanly muscled form. That odd sense of awareness he had shimmering around him, coupled with the intensity he could get between the flashes of ridiculous guy humor, made her admit that low as her opinion of men was at the moment, if she had to depend on one even temporarily, she hadn't done too shabbily.

However, she'd long ago learned that the more good-looking a man was, the fewer his actual life skills. "You're not a pencil pusher," she guessed.

He looked startled. "Pencil pusher?"

"Accountant."

He let out a low laugh. "No. I'm not an anything pusher."

"What do you do?"

"Nothing at the moment."

Not exactly comforting. "But you think you can keep us safe if it comes right down to it?"

He gave her a funny look. "I think I can manage."

Glancing uneasily toward the door, she nodded, having no choice but to trust him. "'Kay, then." Her voice wavered only slightly. "Let's go."

"Hey." Stepping close until their thighs bumped, he reached out and slowly, purposely, stroked a finger over her hairline, across her temple, ostensibly to tuck a wayward strand of hair behind her ear. She didn't buy that, though, not with the way he was looking at her, as if maybe he was starving and she was a twelve-course meal, as if maybe he could gobble her up in one sitting.

Odd how that made her knees wobble, as did the way his own breathing wasn't any more steady than hers. "What are you doing?" she whispered.

"Comforting you." His fingers stroked their way over her throat, then further down, taking the sheet with them, to her shoulder. "Is it working?"

She slapped his hand away. "I'm fine."

"Sure?" he asked in that voice that melted her brain cells at an alarming rate. "Because I have a lot more comfort in me."

Damn her wobbly knees anyway. She locked them into place, along with her jaw. *No more men!* "Positive," she said through her teeth, afraid to let her mouth stay open for too long because God-knew-what would pop out of it, probably something like "Take me now, please."

"You can wait here, you know," he said.

"I'm going with you."

He studied her for a long moment, and she got the impression he saw far more than she wanted him to. "Suit yourself, then," he said.

"Oh, I will. I always do."

Wasn't that just the problem.

Nine

People who think they know everything are annoying to those of us who do.

—Breanne Mooreland's Journal Entry

As they left the bedroom together, Cooper surprised Breanne by taking her hand, leading the way. The hallway was every bit as dark as she remembered, and though she was no longer cold, a shiver shook her.

Cooper pulled her to his side, sliding an arm around her. She might have protested, but there was something incredibly protective, even possessive, in the gesture, and she was feeling just weak enough to need both.

She couldn't see a thing, but Cooper didn't seem to have the same problem, leading them unerringly to the bedroom she'd just vacated. Once inside the doorway, the glow from the candles on the dresser lit the room.

Cooper put a hand on her shoulder and gently squeezed, which she took to mean "stay," and then he walked through the room, checking the bathroom—which was *un*locked—the closet, under the bed, and even under the mountain of down bedding.

When he turned back to her she expected to see amusement, or perhaps even annoyance, but instead he looked quite intense. "I don't see anything."

He hadn't said she was crazy, or that she had an imagination she needed to turn off. He simply believed her. "Thank you," she whispered around a suddenly tight throat, fighting a sudden urge to hug him. "I'm just losing it. I can sleep now."

"Are you sure?"

"Very. Thanks."

Looking not quite happy with that, he again lifted the covers, this time for her, in a silent invitation for her to get back beneath them.

He was tucking her into bed. The sweetness of that didn't escape her, but her feet just wouldn't take her to the bed.

"Breanne?"

"Yeah. I'm coming."

"See, that's the thing," he said, watching her very carefully. "Your feet aren't moving."

"I know. Maybe if I give them a minute."

He dropped the covers and moved toward her. Reaching up, he entwined his fingers in her hair at the nape of her neck and tugged lightly, tipping her face up to his. "You don't really want to sleep in here, do you?"

She started to nod yes, but ended up giving a slow shake of her head. *No.*

"Back to the couch?" he asked.

Another shake in the negative.

"You can have the suite—you know that, right?" he asked.

This time she nodded.

"Is that yes, you want to switch rooms with me?"

She bit her lower lip.

His gaze dropped to the movement. "I'm going to need words here, Princess."

"I don't suppose you'd mind hosting a sleepover?"

His eyes flamed.

"I meant the platonic kind of sleepover," she said quickly.

"Ah."

The "ah" was loaded, and the air felt charged as he looked at her. "What if you can't control yourself?" he finally asked, his fingers still in her hair.

"I think I can."

An almost smile curved his lips. "Sure?" He had fine laugh lines fanning out from the corners of his mischievous blue eyes, and looking into them, she thought, God help me, *I'm not*. "Don't flatter yourself." She backed away from him and grabbed her bag.

Before she could sling it over her shoulder, he took it and slung it over his instead, then held out his hand. He waggled his fingers, waiting, and when she slipped her hand in his big, warm one, he smiled at her. It was a kind smile, not mocking her fear or her antics of the night, and she felt herself want to smile back.

No more men.

Oops. Almost forgot. Damn, how easy was she? One smile and she'd been just about to make another bad, *bad* decision. Good thing she'd caught herself. Good thing she was strong. *Hear me roar.*

They headed back the way they'd come, through the dark, cedar-fragrant hallway, the pictures and equipment on the wall unnerving now instead of quaint. Halfway, Cooper stopped at the third door on the left, his body tense and still.

"What—"

He broke off her question with a finger to her lips, his eyes dark and unreadable.

She heard it then, the soft scuffle from the other side of the door.

Goose bumps rose on her body as she turned to face the door, and so did the hair on her neck. Was it the person who went with the scary face? Just the thought had her letting out an involuntary whimper, but Cooper was right behind her, a hand on her shoulder now as from the other side of the door came an unexpected sound—an extremely female moan. It didn't sound sinister, it sounded—

"Oh, Patrick . . ." floated through the door in a sexy, familiar Latin accent.

Lariana.

"You like that, darlin'?" came an answering Scottish voice.

"Oh, my God, yes," Lariana gasped.

"Then how about this?"

"Yes! Yes, that, too. There. *There!*"

Breanne stared at the wood as a banging came next. "That's . . ."

"The headboard hitting the wall," Cooper said in her ear.

"Oh." She felt her face heat. "Right."

This was followed by some indescribable, embarrassingly earthy moans and more cries, and then the sound of wet flesh slapping on wet flesh.

Patrick and Lariana were getting lucky.

On *her* honeymoon.

If that wasn't just perfect, she didn't know what was, and she took a step backwards, right into the hard wall of Cooper's chest.

Just like that, the night changed. Or the darkness did, anyway, somehow becoming richer, deeper, encircling the two of them with an air of intimacy she hadn't counted on as the heavy panting on the other side of the door continued.

"Sounds like fun," Cooper whispered, stroking a finger over the back of her neck.

Now her goose bumps weren't from fear, but something else entirely. She began to heat up, and apparently so did things behind the door.

"Come," Patrick demanded of Lariana in a rough Scottish voice. "Come for me."

Breanne liked sex—sometimes she even loved sex—but she'd never had a guy tell her what to do in bed, or demand an orgasm from her. It sounded pretentious, rough, and . . . embarrassingly arousing. Her nipples hardened, her belly quivered, and her thighs tightened. Annoyed at herself for the reaction, not to mention desperate to hide it from the man behind her, she tightened her grip on the sheet wrapped around her. She was done with men, damn it, done, done, *done*. She did not want one in her life, she did not want one in her bed, telling her what to do or otherwise.

"*Come for me right now.*"

Oh, jeez.

"Yes!" Lariana screamed the word into the night, the rhythmic banging turning even more frantic; along with it came Patrick's low, serrated groan, and then . . . complete and utter silence.

Breanne whipped around to face Cooper.

His eyes burned as they held hers, and in a rare anomaly, she found herself speechless. Pushing past him, she fumbled her way down the hall and into the honeymoon suite. Stopping short, she stared at the large, lush bed and swallowed hard. Her body felt hot from the inside out, sort of achy and pulsing, and she didn't get it.

What had happened to her fear?

"It got to you," Cooper said softly, almost silkily, from right behind her.

She stepped away from him because she couldn't think when he was that close. "That ridiculous exhibition? *Please.* I've heard better on any number of porn flicks."

"It got to you," he repeated, then smiled. "But let's hear more about these porn flicks."

"This isn't funny." She hugged the sheet tighter to her body.

Again he came up behind her, not touching her in any way, but she couldn't miss that delicious body heat if she tried. Dipping his head low, he leaned in and inhaled her. "You smell so good," he murmured.

She'd powdered and lotioned and primped good before the wedding, but if any of it had held to her skin through all the fear and panic and humiliation of her day, she'd be shocked. "I do not."

"You're not supposed to argue when someone gives you a compliment."

"I'm not good with compliments." She turned to face him. "Do you think she was okay? He sounded a little rough. And a lot demanding."

Cooper's eyes lit with humor. "I think she's going to be just fine, yes."

Still hugging herself, she nodded. "Right."

"You know . . . you're all tough and cynical on the outside . . ." He still hadn't touched her, though she could feel his wanting. Or maybe that was her own. All she knew was that the anticipation was going to kill her.

Leaning in, he exhaled softly over her neck, making her shiver. "But so soft and sweet on the inside."

"I'm just as tough on the inside," she assured him.

"I don't think so."

She really, really wished he didn't smell so orgasmically good, or that he didn't radiate such confidence, such intensity. Or that he didn't look like he did, which was too amazing for her fragile state of mind.

For something to do, she grabbed her bag from him and strode toward a chair. There she pulled out her Palm Pilot.

"What are you doing?"

"I have to write something down." She brought up her journal and entered: *Either learn self-defense or start carrying a baseball bat. Do not—repeat, do not—ever ask a man to protect you again.*

There. She felt better already. Sort of. She flipped through the files and reread her earlier words:

No more failures.

No more men.

She underscored both two times and then repeated them in her head like a mantra until they blurred.

"What are you doing?"

"Nothing, I'm—Hey!"

He'd snatched the Palm Pilot from her hand. "No more failures," he read. "No more men." He eyed her over the digital unit. "Interesting."

"I always make myself notes," she said defensively, reaching for the Palm Pilot, but he lifted it over his head, and by the full-on, knock-'em-out smile he flashed, he was enjoying her efforts to grab it from him.

"What else do you have in here, I wonder." Turning his back to her, he began to poke at her files.

"Stop that." She shoved at him, but he was immovable, the ape. "Those entries are *private*."

"Whoa," he said with interest. "This one's good. 'Don't expect a man with a hard-on to be able to think. He doesn't have enough blood to run both heads.' Hmmm." He shot her a wicked grin over his shoulder. "I do. Want to see?"

"You are *impossible!* Give me the damn thing!"

But he was still busy having fun reading her private thoughts. "'Never agree to marry a man because he has potential,'" he read. "''Men are not like houses, they do not make good fixer-uppers.'" His gaze met hers. "You know I'm finding this insight into your psyche absolutely fascinating."

She was still struggling to nab her journal, her fingers touching his warm, hard chest and those yummy abs. She refused to let them do anything for her. "This is serious for me, okay? Someone was leaning over me while I slept tonight." Just remembering had a shiver running up her spine, and she hugged herself again. "It gave me the creeps. I know it's silly, but writing things in my journal calms me."

He went still, then sighed, the grin vanishing from his face as he handed her back the Palm Pilot.

"I know," she said, embarrassed. "I'm being such a wuss—"

"No." He looked disgusted with himself. "Fuck, no. Anyone would have been spooked, given what you saw, and I'm an ass for trying to tease you right now. Come here."

In the act of putting away the Palm Pilot, Breanne lifted her head. His eyes were dark, opaque, and filled with things that made her swallow hard. He was half-naked, she in nearly the same condition. Moving any closer to him would be like lighting the fuse and begging to get burned.

He simply took the matter into his own hands and stepped into her personal space again, stroking a finger over her cheek before settling his hand on her arm. "Could it have been Patrick?"

"I don't think so." She shook her head. "I don't know. What do you suppose he was looking for?"

Their eyes held, and all the possibilities floated through her mind, none of which was exactly comforting. His other hand came up to cup her jaw. "You're safe now," he said. "With me. You know that, right?"

She thought of sleeping in here tonight and knew that *safe* was relative. "Sure."

"We could sit around and talk if you'd like."

"Okay." She crossed her arms and tried to look casual. "So what's up?"

"Considering what you're wearing beneath that sheet, and what we just heard in the hallway, you might want to rephrase that particular statement."

Right. Feeling a blush creep over her face, she looked away.

He sighed. "Okay, so no talking. It's been a long day, anyway. You need some sleep."

They both turned to the bed.

"At least it's huge," she heard herself say.

He didn't say a word.

And Breanne did her best impersonation of a woman hiding her panic, because sharing a bed with him would be like sky diving. Exciting, thrilling, and dangerous as hell. "I'll roll something up between us," she decided shakily.

To show him, she unwrapped herself from the sheet and began to fold it in a long strip. When she was done, she crawled up on the high mountain of a bed and situated it right down the middle, moving around on her knees to place it fairly.

A rough sound escaped Cooper.

Blowing a strand of hair out of her face, she leaned back on her heels and craned her neck to look at him. At the expression on his face—an electrifying, sizzling expression—her stomach leapt as if she'd just taken off on the roller-coaster ride of her life. "Um . . . ready?"

He didn't answer right away, and when he did, his voice was husky. "Oh, yeah, I'm ready."

Ten

My life would be much more amusing if it was just happening to someone else.

—Breanne Mooreland's Journal Entry

Cooper looked at the incredibly hot woman kneeling on the massive bed wearing nothing more than a barely there silky camisole and shorts that were only called such because both legs went through them. He knew the outfit was one of her honeymoon sets that had been designed to drive her husband crazy.

The design worked.

She had one spaghetti strap slipping off her creamy shoulder, the other barely in place, the bodice of the silk dipping low enough between her full breasts to make his mouth water.

And she was cold.

Or excited.

He wouldn't have been able to tear his gaze off the hardened peaks of her nipples—perfect mouthfuls, both of them, poking against the silk as if begging for his touch—if it hadn't been for the shorts.

The shorts . . . those he could have stared at forever. Low on her hips, exposing the diamond twinkling in her belly in the front and the twin dimples at the base of her spine in the back, they clung to her like a second skin. The hem—God bless that hem—was so short it rode right up her ass, covering only a tiny strip right up the middle. That strip in turn outlined her to perfection, not to mention revealed a good portion of each cheek in a way that made him want to get down on his knees and explore every inch of her.

Ah, hell, with or without those shorts he wanted to get down on his knees and explore every inch of her, and that was just unsettling enough to have him standing there, staring at her like a horny teen. "Breanne?"

She swallowed hard. "Yeah?"

"I know you're trying not to freak out here, and that you want me to be the good guy, but with you in that position, I'm not thinking good-guy thoughts."

She sank to her butt.

Not much better. "You really think that sheet is going to work?"

She stared at it, then bit her lip and looked back up at him, her entire heart in her eyes—along with the fear of the evening, the stress of the day, all the hell she'd undoubtedly been through to get here.

Feeling like a pervert, he swore softly, shoved his fingers through his hair, and moved to the opposite side of the bed. "Forget it. It's going to work fine."

Looking grateful, she relaxed her shoulders. She tugged up on her loose strap and down on her wayward shorts, which might have adjusted her comfort level but then showed off more of the soft curve of her belly.

Jesus. "Get under the covers, Breanne."

She scrambled beneath them with more eye-popping moves that had his blood pounding thick and heavy, draining out of his brain, heading south for the winter.

Then suddenly she sat back up, the blankets slipping to her waist. "Wait. I forgot to—"

"Whatever it is, too damn bad." He slid beneath the covers on his side of the bed. "Lie down."

"Yes, but—"

"No. No buts. I hate buts." He lay back and closed his eyes but he couldn't relax to save his life, not with a nearly naked woman in his bed, the likes of which he hadn't had this close to him in . . . far too long. It'd been months since Annie had dumped him, and he hadn't been with anyone since. His family had all tried to set him up on dates. Hell, Jack had even given him his old black book, something his brother no longer needed now that he was married.

Truth was, Cooper hadn't had the energy to attempt another relationship, and while he could have had any number of pity fucks—his brother's old girlfriends were generous—he hadn't wanted that, either.

He must be getting old, but he wanted something real.

Too bad he was too screwed up for real.

Ah, hell. Sleep wasn't going to happen, not like this. Opening his eyes, he stared straight ahead in the dark and saw they'd left the door open. "*Shit.*"

"I tried to tell you."

Yes, but she'd effectively distracted him with that soft, honey voice and even softer body. Unbelievable. He got up and shut the door, then stalked back to the bed. He lay flat on his back and stared at the dark ceiling, watching the last of the candlelight flickering shadows across the wood.

On the other side of the rolled sheet, Breanne was tossing and turning, and though he didn't turn his head and look at her, he imagined those silk shorts riding up, her top slipping down, and he nearly groaned. "Can't you just pick a position and stay there?"

"Sorry."

But she kept moving, and he kept picturing her, until he couldn't stand it. "*Breanne.*"

"Do you really not wear underwear?"

A laugh choked out of him. "*What?*"

"I just—Never mind."

"No, this is a conversation I'm interested in."

"I saw your clothes earlier—there was no underwear. And you sleep naked."

"Yes. But I'm not naked now." Much to his annoyance.

She tossed around some more. "Sorry. It's just that every time I close my eyes, I relive my sucky day. I think about all the things that I could be doing right now."

"With your husband?" Odd how just the thought tightened his gut. He figured if she had said "I do," then she and her ex would right this minute be screwing every which way but Sunday. At least that's what Cooper would be doing if he'd married Breanne this morning. Hell, he wouldn't have waited until now, either; he'd have found a way to have her in the limo on the way to the airport, in the airport bathroom, in the airplane bathroom, on the ride into the mountains—

"Not with my husband," Breanne said softly in the night. "Because I'd have killed him by now." Her voice was steely. "The rat fink bastard."

"But if he'd shown up for the wedding, you wouldn't have had a reason to kill him," Cooper pointed out reasonably.

"Sooner or later he'd have shown me his true colors, and if he'd done it when I already had his name on my driver's license, I'd be even more pissed."

"Because hell, that's a damn inconvenience, right?"

"You're not kidding. You ever wait in line at the DMV?"

With another laugh, he turned on his side to face her. Holding up his head with his hand, he searched out her face in the darkness. "I'm sorry."

"Yeah." Her smile was sad. "Want to know a secret?"

"Sure."

"Today was my third time being ditched by a fiancé."

"Ouch."

She laughed unhappily. "Yeah."

"What happened?"

"The first time?" She sighed. "I'd loved Barry since . . .

well, since kindergarten. It seemed so natural, you know? Graduate high school, get married. But my parents thought we were too young. They offered him a chance to go to Europe to study foreign diplomacy as he'd wanted, paying him with a one-way ticket and a large stash of cash. Oh, and the edict that he not look back."

"Don't tell me he didn't look back."

"Okay, I won't tell you."

He swore softly. "You were better off without him, too."

"I did learn my lesson," she admitted.

"Which was what, not to date spineless assholes?"

"No. I decided no more engaging the heart."

"But you could still get engaged?"

She laughed a bit mirthlessly. "The second engagement, that was a favor. Franco just wanted to stay in the country, but he ended up getting deported anyway. So that one doesn't really count. Right?"

He stroked a strand of hair from her cheek. A mistake. Her hair felt like silk between his fingers, her skin just chilled enough that he wanted to leave his hand on her. "Did your dad get him deported?"

"No, overprotective dad and four brothers never found out about that one."

"Four brothers." He let out a low whistle. "You must have been quite the princess," he teased.

"You did call that one right."

"So do you get engaged to everyone you meet? Is that how that works?"

"Hey, I've resisted *you* so far."

"To my great consternation."

She smiled but looked away. "Obviously I have a terrible decision-making mechanism. I'm working on it. But believe it or not, there's a silver lining here."

"Yeah? What's that?"

"I won't be fooled again, not by another pretty face and

hunky body, not by sweet words, no way, no how." She shook her head, her eyes luminous in the dark "Love does not exist."

"You really believe that?"

"Yes. You?"

He shook his head.

"You've been in love?" she asked.

He lifted a shoulder. "I guess I thought it might become love."

"Did it?"

"Nope." He shot her a smile. "Got my heart crushed like a grape about six months ago."

Her gaze softened. "Oh, Cooper." She reached out and touched his chest over his heart. "I'm sorry."

"I'm over it."

Shifting up on her elbow so she could see his face, she left her hand on him and looked at him intently. "So you got hurt, and yet you'd give it another shot?"

The vulnerability in her voice made him ache. It'd been easier, far easier, to resist her when she wore her sarcastic edge like a coat, because this softer, kinder, caring Breanne tore through his defenses in a way he hadn't anticipated. "Hell, Breanne, I'm just saying it exists."

She flopped to her back, staring up at the ceiling. "Well, it can exist all it wants, as long as it stays far, far away from me."

Cooper lay back down as well, joining her in the study of the ceiling. He'd spent much of the recent past feeling exactly the same, but for some reason he didn't like to think that this vibrant, exciting woman, who had so much to offer, was going to hold back from love the next time it came around, simply because she'd been burned.

"Cooper?"

"Yeah?"

"Are you really unemployed?"

The sixty-thousand-dollar question. "I am."

"Where do you live?"

"In San Francisco."

"So what are you doing out here in the mountains? Alone?"

"My brother thought I needed to ski my brains out for a week and get over myself." *And get laid by a pretty, warm, sexy ski bunny.*

"Why?" she asked.

"Too many reasons to get into."

"We have all night."

"Maybe I'm tired."

"I thought guys liked to talk about themselves."

"Not this guy. Tell me about you. What do you do?"

"Bookkeeping for a big CPA firm." She frowned. "At least at the moment."

"At the moment?"

"I'm going to have to find another job."

"Why?"

"Because I'll have to see Dean there—that's rat fink bastard to you and me—and I still have an uncontrollable urge to kill him. That won't look good in my review, plus it'll be hard to get another job from prison."

He tried to see her in the dark. "You're not going to let him take that job from you, are you?"

"It doesn't matter," she said with a sigh. "You should see my resumé. It'd make you dizzy." She sighed. "Truth is, I don't sit still for long anyway."

"No? What jobs have you held?"

"Receivables, payables, payroll—you name it in accounting, I've done it."

"So you like numbers," he said, nodding. "Makes sense. You like order."

"How do you know that?"

"This whole setting makes you nervous because it's not what was planned."

"You can say that again," she said with feeling.

"And I've seen your journal. Very organized. Like an accountant's brain."

"I wasn't that organized when it came to staying with one job."

"Nothing wrong with that, as long as moving around makes you happy."

Now it was her turn to come up on her elbows and peer through the dark. "You really believe that?"

"Sure," he said, leaning in closer for a better look, because for a second he'd have sworn that her eyes went suspiciously bright with a sheen of tears. But then it was gone. "Breanne?"

"I'm tired," she whispered. She turned over, curling up into a tiny ball facing away from him. "'Night."

"'Night." He was confused as hell, but when it came to women, that was really nothing new. Nothing new at all.

He was just drifting off when he heard her soft whisper. "Cooper?"

"Still here." Maybe she'd changed her mind about the sheet. The thought made his body twitch. Yeah, she was going to toss that damn thing aside and roll toward him. She'd wrap that hot little bod tight to his, and he'd—

"Thank you," Breanne said very quietly.

He blinked. *Thank you?* He slid his hand down to cup himself. Still hard. Nope, he hadn't missed anything. "What are you thanking me for?"

"For chasing my boogeyman. For making me feel safe." Her smile broke his heart. "For letting me sleep with you."

Ah, hell. "No problem." But as he lay there, aching for reasons other than physical discomfort, reasons he couldn't seem to put words to, it was a very long time before he followed her into slumber.

Cooper was having the dream of his life, and he hoped he never woke up. In a bed of the softest down, surrounded by the gentle glow of dawn, she lay in his arms, the woman of his fantasies. She was scantily clad in silk that seemed to mold to her skin in an erotic, seductive way, and he couldn't keep his hands off her.

And because this was a dream, he didn't have to.

She was his. He couldn't quite remember how or why, but in dreamland, what the hell difference did it make? Around them, the air seemed thick. Spicy. Erotic. He dragged some of it into his taxed lungs and cupped her face, trying to see her through the haze all around him, but he couldn't quite—

A sound escaped her, a sort of breathy, wordless plea, and he smoothed his fingers along the line of her jaw, sinking into the lovely disarray of her hair, letting it drape over his forearms as he leaned over her, lowering his mouth toward hers.

"Mmm," she murmured as he swallowed her sigh of acquiescence. Her body seemed to melt against his like hot wax, and her mouth—God, her mouth was soft and warm and luscious, indescribably luscious.

She opened it to him, allowing his tongue to stroke hers, stroking his right back, both greedy and generous at the same time. His fantasy girlfriend was the best kisser he'd ever dreamed up. Not too wet, not too dry, but juuuust right. Her hand came up between them, opening flat on his chest. He took it in his, along with her other, and slowly dragged them both up over her head, palming them in one hand, using his free fingers to skim the hair from her face while he made himself at home between her thighs.

Eyes closed, hands captured by his, she arched up into his body with a soft, needy whimper.

In answer, he kissed her, and then again, sending shivers of heat and desire skittering to the base of his spine, pooling in his groin, where he was so hard for her he could hardly stand it.

"Nice," she murmured, sighing with pure, unadulterated

pleasure. Her full breasts pressed to his chest. Her hips cradled his. Her shorts were so minuscule his fingertips grazed bare skin as he reached down, the sweet curve of a cheek filling each hand. When he squeezed, kneading, she moaned and arched up, spreading her legs to better accommodate his, nestling his erection perfectly into the crotch of those skimpy shorts. Skimming his hand higher, beneath the silk now, he palmed her bare ass.

Not enough. Not nearly enough.

Deepening the kiss, he wrapped a finger around a tiny strap on her shoulder. Tugged.

A breast popped free.

A glorious, pale, perfectly rounded breast with a rosy, pouting nipple. Dipping his head, he very gently rubbed his jaw over the full curve, absorbing every hungry sigh. Then again, over the very tip this time, watching as it puckered up all the more as she writhed beneath him, her breath sowing in and out of her lungs.

Then her hands were fisting in his hair, and she was tugging his mouth back to hers. They kissed as if they'd been separated for years instead of seconds; he poured everything he had into that moist, hot, brain-cell-destroying connection, his heart and soul, because this was a dream, a glorious dream.

Even so, far in the back of his mind came the niggling truth: she wasn't really his. But the longer he kissed her, losing himself in the taste and feel of her, turning his head for a deeper fit, groaning with it, the easier it was to push all that out of his head.

She made it easy to do with those breathy little pants, her hands fisted on whatever part of him they could reach, stroking down his back to his butt, squeezing, pushing as she rocked to meet him with every thrust. They kissed as if it would be the end of the world to stop, as if they'd never get another chance to do this. With a low hum that reminded him of a happy kitten purring her pleasure, she slid her hands beneath his sweats. Squeezed. Cradled him all the tighter within her thighs. He could feel both her tension and his, could feel her tremble, could hear his own loud, labored breathing.

She whispered his name.

Unbelievably, his toes curled, his body tightening as he barreled down that narrow road toward climax. Given her own wild, delirious state, she was right with him. He kissed his way to her jaw, then her throat. "I'm going to taste every inch of you, Breanne."

Beneath him she went utterly still.

Abruptly he went from a blissful dreamland to brutal wakefulness. Lifting his head, he opened his eyes in the early morning light and stared down at her.

"*You*," Breanne said.

Yeah, him.

Just as in his fantasy state, he had her tucked beneath him, legs spread to accommodate his. He had one hand plumping up her bared breast for his mouth, the other gripping her butt, the very tips of his fingers dipping into heaven, his mouth wet from hers as he stared down at her.

For her part, she'd wrapped herself around him like a pretzel. "I . . . I thought it was a dream," she whispered.

"It was a hell of a great one," he said, half hoping she'd let him continue it.

She just stared up at him, hair tousled, eyes still sleepy, cheeks pink, looking like she'd just been fucked every which way but Sunday—and had thoroughly enjoyed it.

"I guess the sheet wasn't enough of a barrier after all," he said, wondering if he needed to apologize.

"Get off."

When he didn't, she shoved him off her in a sudden flurry of movement, scooting out of the bed, running into the bathroom, but not before shooting him a scathing look that might have shriveled another man's parts right off.

Not Cooper's. Nope, his part still bounced in his pants, the eternal optimist.

The bathroom door slammed shut with a finality that suggested he should go, and was going, to hell in a handbasket. Alone. "Uh . . . Breanne?"

Nothing from the bathroom.

With a heavy sigh, he got out of bed, looking ruefully down at his tented pants. "Down, boy," he murmured, and walked to the door. "Open up."

"Go far, far away!"

As if he could. "What are you mad at? That I was kissing you, or that you were kissing me back?"

She muttered something, some smear on his heritage, and then the shower came on. He hoped the water heater was powered by the propane tank he'd seen outside, or there wouldn't be any hot water.

"And for your information," she yelled through the door. "You were doing more than just sticking your tongue down my throat!"

"Same goes, Princess."

She replied with yet another unintelligible mutter, which for some sick reason made him grin.

It made no sense. Her late-night confessional warning that she was done with men still echoed in his ears. She wasn't interested in him, or at least she didn't want to be interested.

Fine by him.

But as he stood there in the early morning, getting chilled in nothing but a pair of sweatpants, a part of him wanted to prove to her that not all men were scum.

While another part of him entirely just wanted to sink into her body.

He heard the shower door open and then shut—yep, powered by the propane, because there was no way Princess was taking a cold shower—and he sighed yet again. No sinking, at least not today.

But there was always tonight.

Eleven

I hear copious amounts of chocolate solves all problems.
Someone send copious amounts of chocolate!
—Breanne Mooreland's Journal Entry

Breanne stared at herself in the mirror. Hot water rose from the shower, steaming the glass, but she could still see. Too much. Her hair was wild, her cheeks flushed, her lips plumped up from all the action they'd just seen . . . and there was a wet spot over the silk covering her breast—from Cooper's mouth.

She looked as if she was indeed on her honeymoon.

This was idiotic. This was dangerous. Just the *thought* of what she'd just done with that man scrambled her brain and made her squirm. He'd nearly sent her shuddering into an orgasm with just a long, languid kiss that had surprised her with its potent heat and shocking intimacy.

She looked away from herself—she had to. Lined up on the counter were an assortment of goodies laid out for the honeymooners. The condoms came in all shapes and colors, and she pictured lying in the bed, watching her man come toward her, erect penis dressed for the party in sunshine yellow, bouncing as it came closer—

Only it wasn't *that* image that made her slam her eyes shut, but the fact that the man in the vivid image had been one hot, hard Cooper Scott.

Bad. Bad, *bad* Breanne. She picked up a neck massager— uh-huh, right, she just bet that was used only as a neck massager—and then the scented body oils. The label said *edible*. *Chocolate*.

Her favorite.

No! No chocolate body oil in her near future, no way, no how. She needed to get a grip here, a serious grip. No parts of Cooper were going to be a chocolate-flavored dessert. It was not only fattening as hell, but incredibly wrong. Her life was in ruins, and she needed to remember that. She was on a mission to get the hell out of this place and back to civilization, where she could get to a Starbucks in three minutes or less, where she could hail a cab, *where her cell phone worked*.

She headed toward the shower, but on second thought stopped to drag the day couch from the far wall, pushing it against the bathroom door, protecting herself from any interruptions or boogeymen or voyeurs—never mind that she herself had been a voyeur only yesterday.

From the long, narrow windows on either side of the shower she could see only a sea of white. No depth perception, no landmarks visible, nothing but white, white, white.

Unbelievably, the snow was still falling. She turned the shower to scalding, stripped, and stepped in, and in spite of herself let out a little whimper of pleasure. My God, the showerheads were worth their weight in gold, aimed at all the good spots, hitting her already sensitized and aching flesh. For a moment she simply stood there absorbing the sensations. The soap smelled like—*Cooper*. Just the scent had her quivering, and by the time she rubbed it over her body she was aroused all over again.

Or still.

Ignoring it the best she could, she concentrated on her mission—getting out of Dodge. *Fast*.

She turned off the shower, and for lack of another choice, grabbed the lush, thick complimentary terry cloth bathrobe hanging on the back of the bathroom door. Only when it was on did she drag the couch away and open the door a crack. She had her chin up and was ready to battle wits.

Except she was alone.

Well, not completely. Lariana was making the bed. She wore black again, a snugger-than-snug, low-scooped black blouse, a pair of tight, cropped pants with a tiny white half apron tied in a perfect bow low on her spine, topped off with spike heels that sank into the thick carpeting of the bedroom as she tugged the sheets taut.

Breanne admired the strength and stamina it must take to work in those heels, and thought longingly of the suitcases she'd lost, filled to the brim with her favorite fashions. Hugging the white robe to her still-damp body, she thought of her choices— her jeans and sweater and ruined boots, or Cooper's sweats.

Ugh.

Lariana stopped nipping and tucking and faced Breanne with a holier-than-thou expression that was amusing, given that Breanne knew exactly how the maid had spent her evening.

Panting Patrick's name and giving in to his lusty demands.

"Sleep okay?" Lariana asked innocently, with only the slightest trace of sarcasm. They both knew Breanne hadn't started out in this bedroom.

"Gee, great," she said, just as innocently. "And you?"

Lariana's own superior smile didn't so much as falter. "*Fabulosa.*"

Yeah, she just bet. "So how often do you get stuck sleeping here?"

"Whenever there's a bad storm."

"Edward, too?"

Lariana began fluffing pillows. "Except him."

"Really? Where did he go?"

"I don't know—I'm not in charge of the man. He's in charge of me."

Breanne sat on the bed, so Lariana had no choice but to stop making it and look at her. "Someone came into my room last night."

"Yes. Apparently Cooper."

Breanne glanced at the scene of the "crime," the huge, luxurious mattress around her. She still couldn't get over what she'd allowed to happen. How stupid she'd been to think that sheet would possibly keep Cooper on his side of the bed.

But to be fair, it hadn't been him alone violating the imposed border. When she'd come all the way awake, she'd been on *his* side. Humiliating, really, that in sleep she'd been so desperate. "Not Cooper."

Lariana's perfectly waxed brow shot up. "No?"

"No. I fell asleep in that room you gave me and woke up to someone standing over the bed. After a near coronary, I came running in here."

Lariana frowned. "You sure? Very sure?"

"Sure about what?" Shelly asked, appearing in the doorway with a smile. Her petite frame was in another pair of jeans and a long pink angora sweater that fell to her thighs. She had her hair neatly pulled back in a ponytail and a flush to her cheeks as she looked back and forth between Lariana and Breanne. "What's up?"

"Breanne says she saw someone in her room last night," Lariana told her. "Standing over her."

Shelly gasped. "Really?"

"A dream," Lariana said. "On a night like last night, we probably all dreamed badly."

Shelly, eyes wide, nodded. "Yes."

"I wasn't dreaming," Breanne said.

Lariana and Shelly exchanged a wordless look that probably meant *humor the crazy guest.*

"Forget it," Breanne said with an irritated sigh.

Shelly patted her arm. "I made breakfast by getting creative with the fireplace. Cooper's already sniffing around the dining room, waiting. Are you hungry?"

She was starving, probably from burning up half a million calories just from trying to inhale Cooper's body a few minutes ago.

But could she face him? Another thing entirely. "I don't have anything to wear."

"Oh, I have plenty," Shelly offered. "I'll get you something."

Everyone looked first at Shelly's tiny frame, then at Breanne's not-so-tiny one, no one pointing out to Shelly the difference between a size one and a size eight.

Okay, a ten, damn it.

"I'll get you something of mine," Lariana said with a hint of martyrdom. "I brought a small bag with me to work yesterday because of the storm."

When she'd left, Shelly looked at Breanne. "You ended up here, huh?"

They both looked at the huge bed.

"I didn't sleep with him," Breanne said.

Shelly lifted a brow.

"Okay, I slept with him. But not *slept with him*, slept with him."

"Does he kiss as good as he smiles?"

Better. "Look, I'm not interested in him, okay?" *Trying not to be.* "I gave up on men, remember?"

"Oh, don't say that! You can't. You inspired me, you know." Shelly smiled. "Today is the day."

"The day for what?"

"That I get Dante to notice me." She twirled in a circle and laughed as she fell to the bed. "Any helpful hints?"

"You shouldn't take advice from someone who was dumped at the altar." *Three times.*

"I'm sure it wasn't your fault," Shelly said loyally. "Now, come on. Give me a pointer or two."

Oh boy. She thought of Dante's world-weary, old-before-his-time eyes, and then looked into Shelly's sweet ones. "Are you sure? Because—"

"He's the one for me."

"Well . . ." Breanne wracked her brain for any advice she'd ever read about and had thought sounded good but hadn't actually tried. "Maybe you should tell him how you feel. You know, go the honest route."

"Oh, I can't do that! He doesn't think of me as a woman!" Then she flashed that sweet smile. "Yet."

Breanne took in Shelly's lovely blond hair, her brilliant green eyes, her contagious smile. And then there was that cute, nifty little body any guy would go nuts over. "He'd have to be dead not to think of you as a woman."

Shelly blushed. "You're the sweetest guest we've ever had."

Breanne had been accused of being many things, but *sweet* hadn't been one of them. "I'm just calling it like I see it."

"You really think he'll want me?"

Breanne crossed her fingers and hoped. "I *know* it."

"Because men are complicated creatures," Shelly warned.

"Not true. They just don't think with the same head that we do."

Shelly giggled.

Lariana entered again. "No kidding, men don't think with the same head we do. You can tell a man that in order to get the best sex of his life all he has to do is pay attention to a woman and say a few nice words, and you know what he'll hear? Blah, blah, blah, sex, blah, blah, blah."

Breanne laughed. "So true."

Shelly looked like she didn't want to believe this.

Lariana held up a little black skirt and a siren-red, long-sleeved spandex top with metallic sparkles woven into the fabric. Matching high-heeled boots—twice as high as hers were—dangled from her fingers. "This is what I was going to wear on my date tonight, but I don't think I'm going any-where."

Oh boy. But Breanne took the hoochie-momma clothes with a combination of acceptance and good humor because there was nothing left to do but just live through this *Twilight Zone* episode.

"You change," Shelly said to Breanne. "I'll be waiting to serve you downstairs." She shoved Lariana out ahead of her while Breanne just stared at the outfit. "What the hell," she muttered, and dropping the robe, pulled on Lariana's clothes.

To torment herself, she looked in the mirror. Oh boy. For starters, the skirt barely covered her ass. The top nearly blinded her and plunged due south nearly to her navel, only an inch above the hemline, which exposed a strip of belly. She tugged at it, but only succeeded in exposing a nipple. Pulling the shirt back into place showed belly again. Settling for somewhere in between, she slipped into the boots and gained four inches in height. Now, *that* she could live with. But while Lariana would look beautifully ethnic and sensual dressed like this, Breanne felt vampy and oversexed. Not a good place to be while trapped in a house with a man who revved her engines with just a single gaze. Much as she didn't want to admit it, she needed Cooper's sweats back, damn it.

Hell, she needed a damn suit of armor, but the sweats would do.

She stuck her head out the bedroom door and checked to see if the coast was clear. It was. She ran/hobbled down the hall, tugging on the skirt as she did, all the way back to the bedroom she'd deserted.

No sweats.

In fact, the bed had been made, and any sign of her brief stay erased. Odd how such a small thing could defeat her, but she was considering crawling back into the bed when a heav-enly scent wafted up the stairs and into her nose.

Bacon.

Coffee.

Her stomach rumbled.

Fine. She'd go—what did she care? She took the stairs in the muted light of the early morning, gripping onto the handrail for all she was worth in Lariana's heels, hoping she didn't make an ass of herself and fall and break her ankle.

She couldn't afford such a thing, not when she planned to use her already-loaded Visa to get on a plane today headed for—

Where?

Aruba sounded good. "Or any island where there's no snow," she muttered. "And no mysterious hotties—"

Dante appeared at the base of the stairs in his usual way— without a sound, making her heart kick up into her throat. "Do you have to do that?" she asked, a hand to her chest.

"Do what?"

"Appear out of the woodwork! Walk without a peep! Show up out of midair!"

In the light of day, he still looked very much like a thug. He had a gray sweatshirt on over loose jeans riding so low on his hips she had no idea what held them up. Once again he wore a knit cap with the hood of his sweatshirt over the top of it, both nearly covering his eyes. His jaw was lean and square and smoothly shaven except for a goatee. His eyes were as dark as his hair, with no visible pupils. And he didn't smile. "Should I wear a bell?"

She paused, having no idea if he was kidding, until she caught the slight quirk of his mouth. "So you *do* have a sense of humor. Shelly mentioned it but I didn't believe her."

"Why?"

"Well, you're not exactly a barrel of laughs."

"No—I mean, why would Shelly mention me having a sense of humor?"

Because she wants to jump your bones. "Maybe because she thinks about you."

"Thinks of me?"

Were all men so innately dense? "You know, *thinks* of you."

At that he smiled, and Breanne blinked. Well, look at that . . . quite a transformation from scary punk to hunk, with those dark, dark eyes, tough body, and rugged face. She supposed if she'd been into the whole urban thing, she could see what about him might draw a woman.

If she hadn't given up men.

She really needed to remember that. Maybe she ought to have it tattooed to the inside of her eyelids. But Shelly *hadn't* given up men, and Breanne had decided to be a better person. Here came good deed number one. "At the risk of sounding like we're in high school, do you think about Shelly as well?"

He didn't answer.

"Okay, let's try this," she said, determined. "She's the sweetest, kindest thing I've ever met and she has a crush on you, and if you're at all interested, you'd better be good to her."

He just stood there, maybe breathing, maybe not.

"Hello, anyone home?"

"I don't answer trick questions."

"Trick questions?"

"Like when a woman asks 'does that skirt make my butt look big?'"

She clamped a hand on her butt and tried to crane her neck to see it. "I knew it! It's Lariana's, and—"

"It was a rhetorical question," he said, his lips twitching as if he were biting back another smile.

"Rhetorical question?" She stopped trying to see her own behind and looked at him, exasperated. "You know, for a man who seems to enjoy perpetuating a ghetto image, you sure don't talk like a thug."

He merely shrugged and began walking away.

"Right," she muttered. "Mind my own business. Got it." She pulled her cell phone out of her bag. Time to work on her own life. "Uh, Dante?"

He glanced back. "What, are we late for history class?"

"Ha, ha. Do you know if there's anywhere I can get reception on this thing?"

"Out the double French doors from the library. There's a deck there, facing west. It's the only place in the house where cell phones sometimes work."

Sometimes? "Point me in the right direction." She wanted to get her messages, mostly because she wanted to know if Dean had been hit by a bus—the only explanation she'd accept with grace.

"Shelly made breakfast."

"Okay."

"She's hoping everyone comes."

"Ah," she said smugly. "So you're not immune to her, after all."

His eyes narrowed. "It's my job to tell you about breakfast."

"Uh-huh." That this big, edgy, dangerous-looking man *did* care about Shelly's feelings made her take a good, long second look at him. And a third. In fact, something deep inside her niggled, something that said, *See? Maybe not all men are bad.* She squelched it. "Where's the library?"

He sighed. "That hallway there, third door on the right."

Grateful for the daylight, dull as it was, she moved along the beautiful hardwood floor past the curved staircase, past the great room, counting doors until she came to a large room with floor-to-ceiling shelves filled with books. In awe, she stepped in. There were overstuffed chairs and ottomans, bigger, cushier sofas, and beneath the huge windows, beautiful benches filled with pillows. A book-lover's delight. She was most definitely a book lover. She moved close to a shelf—all the Dickens classics. Another held Shakespeare. Yet another had five full rows of contemporary and historical romances by some of her favorite authors.

She could spend all week in this room and never regret spending her honeymoon alone. She picked up a personal favorite, an old historical classic. When she'd been thirteen she'd sneaked it home from the library, reading every dog-eared page beneath her blankets with a flashlight. The story had blistered her sheets.

"Breanne."

With a startled squeak, the book went flying out of her fingers. She turned around and faced the one man whose voice could make her quiver, make her ache.

Cooper looked at her from the bluest, sexiest eyes she'd ever seen. "Dante said you were around, talking to yourself about mysterious hotties. You did mean me, right?"

She rolled her eyes, but his had locked on her body. "Wow," he said huskily. "More honeymoon attire?"

"No. I borrowed some clothes."

"Hmmm." Wearing worn cargo jeans and a long-sleeved Henley the exact color of his eyes, he picked up the book she'd sent flying and looked at the cover—a nearly naked man, pulling a dress off a nearly naked woman. "Oh, goody," he said. "A bedtime story. You can read it out loud to me tonight."

"We are not sharing a bed tonight."

"Feel free to skip straight to the good spots." He opened the book to somewhere in the middle. "Right here, for example." He cleared her throat and read out loud: "'Elizabeth tingled at the thought of putting her mouth to his throbbing manhood.'" He lifted his head, sending her a lopsided grin. "Hey, *I* have a throbbing manhood."

Breanne crossed her arms over her chest, refusing to admit she felt his smile from her roots to her toes, and in every single erogenous zone between, of which she apparently had more than she remembered, damn him. "Get out."

"Sorry, Princess, there's nowhere to go. Come eat breakfast with me."

"Why? So you can turn that into something dirty as well?"

His grin went positively wicked. "You think sex is dirty?"

"Go. Away."

Of course, he didn't budge.

"You know what?" she asked, tossing up her hands. "Never mind. *I'll* go."

"You can run, but you can't hide."

"What does that mean?"

"Means we're still stuck, baby. Snowed in. With no cable services and nothing to do except—"

"Don't say it."

"Okay. I'll just think it."

She sent him daggers, refusing to allow him to see how much his thoughts were affecting her. "I'm going outside to make a call on my cell." Whirling away from him, she stepped to the French doors. Beyond them was a view that, under any other circumstances, would have made her sigh with pleasure. Surrounded by awe-inspiring, majestic peaks, they were nestled in a valley that lay under a glistening blanket. The snow was still falling in dinnerplate-sized flakes, coating everything in sight.

It boggled her mind.

Determined to check her messages, she bravely opened the doors and was immediately assaulted by the cold. Protected by a small covered deck, she stood a foot from where the snow came down in thick, blurry lines, falling eerily without a sound, piling into drifts. If she took a step off the deck she'd have sunk, vanishing from view.

Behind her she let the door shut so she wouldn't have to hear Cooper moving around the library. God only knew what the Neanderthal would find in there to read. She didn't care. Shivering, she kept her eyes locked on her phone display as she turned it on and waited with bated breath.

Two bars! And then the familiar beep, beep, beep, signaling that she had messages. Quickly she accessed them and laughed weakly when she heard "You have thirty-seven messages." A bunch were from her parents and siblings, and all were in a similar vein along the lines of *"Where the hell are you?"* There were more from friends, wondering if she was okay. The answer was a big, resounding *no*.

And then came Dean's voice, unusually subdued, and sounding as if he was in a vacuum. "Hi, Breanne—I realize you probably hate me by now."

"Give me a reason not to," she muttered.

"—and I know this will sound like some kind of joke to you," he said, "but believe me, it's not. I'm . . . in prison."

Breanne pulled the phone from her ear and stared at it in shock before listening to the rest.

"I was arrested for identity theft and fraud, and they say I'm looking at five to ten. Oh, and you should probably toss your Palm Pilot in the nearest ocean because I once used it for some illegal downloading." Then the sound of him hanging up. That was it, nothing more.

No good-bye, no I'm so sorry, no words of everlasting love.

There were more messages but she lost her signal. Hands shaking with the chill, she turned off her cell and tried to go back inside.

The doors wouldn't budge. She'd locked herself out.

Her mind went numb as she stood there and looked at the handle. Her vision wavered. Dean was a criminal. That meant this engagement had been nothing more than a sham. Of course it'd been. Hell, her entire life had been a sham.

Damn, she was done being a screwup, done just moving through life, going through the motions.

Things were going to change!

She tried the door again, but apparently her epiphany didn't have any impact on the fact that she'd locked herself out. Already frozen, she tipped her head upward in frustration, but there was no divine help to be had.

There was nothing but more bad luck as her eyes focused

on the eave of the house, and the shockingly huge web there. And sitting in it was the largest, fattest spider she'd ever seen. "Oh, God."

She really hated spiders. She'd hated them since she'd been five, when one of her brothers had put his pet tarantula in her bed. Frantic, she reached for the handle again, imagining she felt the spider drop to her head. Her breath clogged in her throat. "Oh, no. *No.*"

The doors were still locked.

She banged on the glass, and Cooper, at home in a large easy chair, reading the historical romance, lifted his head and smiled at her.

Waved.

"I'm locked out!" she yelled, banging on the door. "Let me in."

"Sorry." He shook his head regretfully. "Can't do that."

She would have sworn she felt the spider crawling in her hair and shuddered. *"Why not?"*

"You wanted to be alone, remember?"

Twelve

*Men exist because a vibrator can't change a flat tire. On second
thought, I should just buy a AAA card . . .*
                            —Breanne Mooreland's Journal Entry

Cooper waved again at a furious-looking Breanne standing out
there in the snow. She was glowering at him through the glass
in that outfit which made him extremely hot. Surprised to find
himself aroused at just the sight of her, he set down the book
and came to a slow stand.

She banged on the glass yet again, her extremely kissable
lips wide open in an O of vexation. Earlier he'd had them soft
and wet and open to his, and it had been shockingly good, but
now they were turning a lovely shade of blue. He felt bad
about that, but playing with her had proven to be more fun
than he'd had in far too long, and he couldn't seem to resist.

"Open up!" she yelled. "Can't you hear me?"

"Oh, I hear you. In fact, I think the people in China hear
you." He had no idea where she'd gotten that siren-red top
that glittered, or the tight, tight black skirt that hugged her
hips and showed off her legs, or those fuck-me boots, but he
was betting it was Lariana.

God bless Lariana.

"Open the door," she said through her chattering teeth,
craning her head upward, searching the roof uneasily. "*Please.*"

He moved to the glass. "What's the sudden rush?"

"There's a spider the size of my fist hanging over my head,

and it's going to get me. Just let me in before I start screaming and never stop." She looked up and let out a horrified squeak. "Ohmigod, it's gone!" Frenzied, she danced around in a circle, lifting her hands to her head, running her fingers through her hair. "It's on me, I just know it! Omigod, get it! *Get it!*"

Opening the door, he brushed her hands away and patted her down himself, enjoying the process immensely.

"Don't kill it," she cried. "Just get it off me."

"Hang on. I'm looking." He shifted his fingers through her hair, over her arms, her waist, brushing her breasts before streaking down her legs and back up again, briefly cupping between. "Spider-free," he promised.

"Are you sure?"

"Well . . ." Tongue in cheek, he searched her again, taking longer this time, noticing that when he stroked over her arms and neck, her breathing changed and her nipples went hard. So did he. But when he brought his hands up her legs and then between, she stopped dancing around and shoved at him, blowing a strand of hair from her face, looking furious and quite adorable with it. "You're just using this as an excuse to feel me up."

"And down," he said agreeably.

She growled, but he lifted his hands. "You really are spider-free."

"Thank you," she said through her teeth.

He cocked his head. "That didn't sound quite sincere."

Her jaw was so tight it looked as if it could shatter. "Look, it's freezing, all right? I don't suppose you could move your big, damn, hulking frame out of the way. I want inside."

"Maybe." He waited until she looked at him. "The truth is, I want something, too, Breanne."

She crossed her hands over her chest in an attempt to warm her body up, something he'd be happy to help her with. "Let me get this straight," she said. "In order to let me into the house, you *want* something."

"That's right."

A gust of wind blew in, topping her off with a layer of white powdery snow. Not him, though, because she'd been his wind barrier.

She shook the snow off. "Damn it, *what?*"

He didn't suppose she'd let him lick the snow off her body one flake at a time, which was a shame because he knew how good she would taste. Playing it safe—for now—he went for his second choice. "You have to smile."

She stared at him as if he'd grown a second head. *If she only knew.* "Are you insane?" she asked. "Just let me in."

"Smile first."

"I have nothing to smile about."

"This morning."

"Huh?"

"This morning," he repeated. "It was pretty damn fine. You could smile about that."

"Cooper—"

"Look, if smiling is too difficult, you can kiss me."

She practically had an aneurism on the spot. "*Kiss you?*"

"As a thank-you."

"For *what?*"

"For rescuing you."

"You *are* insane," she decided, tossing up her hands. "I'm trapped inside a house with an insane man."

"Actually, you're trapped outside," he pointed out helpfully.

"Forget it! I opt to freeze to death." Turning her back on him, she hunched her shoulders against the chill.

Ah, hell. He reached for her and put his hands on her arms, rubbing them up and down her chilled skin. "All right, Custer, you win. Come on, come inside." Stepping backward over the threshold, he pulled her with him, then reached around her to shut the door. Because she had goose bumps—his fault for playing with her the way he had—he put his hands back on her arms. He didn't know what it was, but he loved having his hands on her.

Lifting her head, she looked deep into his eyes, her own filled with a sadness that tugged at him. "You ever think that life just plain sucks?"

"Yeah." He cupped her cold face in his warm hands. "But right now isn't one of those times."

A shuddery sigh escaped her, but he took it as a good sign when she let him slowly pull her against him. Tucking her frozen nose up into the crook of his neck, she sighed again as he ran his hands up and down her back. And then, because he was a very weak man, he let his hand fall lower with each stroke.

She didn't object. In fact, she let out another breath, a hum of pleasure this time, and just like that, the embrace changed. Shifted. He was still holding her, touching her, but no longer for comfort. "Breanne," he said very softly.

"I know." Her lips moved against his throat. "God, this is crazy. I'm crazy."

"No." Another stroke of his hand down her back, slowly, curving his palm over the curve of her ass. *Ah, man.*

"Cooper?"

Don't say stop. Please don't. "Yeah?"

"I'm sorry you have to keep saving the stupid chick."

"You're not stupid." He let his fingers curl over the edge of her skirt, his knuckles brushing the back of her thigh now. Christ, she had soft skin. Her hair was damp against his cheek. The scent of the shampoo she'd used made him want to bury his face in it, or better yet, have the long strands teasing his bare chest as she rode him. Yeah, *that* would work—

"I went outside to get my messages."

He wondered if she knew that her entire heart was in her voice, defeated and sad, and with a breath of regret, he hugged her tight. "You heard from the missing groom?"

Still pressing her face to his throat, she nodded.

Something about the sudden tension in her body told him that whatever she'd learned had reinforced her no-more-men thing.

"He's in jail," she said. "For identity theft and fraud, and God knows what else."

"You were going to marry a helluva guy."

She let out a laugh that might have been half sob, and buried her face closer to him. "I didn't know he was a thief." She lifted her head, her eyes full of things, with anger and humiliation leading the way. "I would never have been with him if I'd known."

He stroked her cheek. "I know."

"How?" she asked, seeming surprised. "You don't even know me."

"I know you wouldn't kill a spider, even though it terrified you. I know you rushed to help Shelly feel better last night when she couldn't cook for us. I know that despite the whole kick-ass attitude, you're afraid of the dark."

"Those things don't have anything to do with dating a thief."

"You wouldn't," he said again.

She just stared at him as if seeing him for the first time. "I don't suppose you could call everyone I know and tell them that."

"Sure."

She laughed again, with a little more true humor this time. "You would, wouldn't you?"

"Yeah."

She shook her head, dropping her forehead to his chest. "It's my greatest fantasy to wake up and find myself in my own bed at home, this whole thing just a bad dream."

"Want to hear *my* fantasy?"

"No!"

He stroked her hair. "I'm sorry your week has sucked so badly."

"Thanks." Her fists had a death grip on his shirt. Slowly she loosened her fingers, and wound her arms around his neck. "That's the sweetest thing anyone's ever said to me."

"Don't take this the wrong way, Princess, but if that's the sweetest thing anyone's ever said to you, I don't think I like the people in your life."

"No, I don't think you would," she said solemnly. "And chances are, they wouldn't like you, either." Her fingers tunneled into his hair. "Cooper?"

She was looking at him with those whiskey eyes, and they'd filled with heat and desire. It took his breath. *She* took his breath. "Yeah?"

"Hang on for this one." She tugged his head down and captured his mouth with hers. It was his dream all over again, this morning all over again, and with a low groan, he hauled her up against him and dug in. She was right. On paper they didn't know each other from Adam and Eve, but in the flesh, their bodies knew enough. They stood there, straining together, dark sounds of neediness escaping each of them, and when she tangled her tongue with his, sucking him into her mouth, he nearly lost it. Her heart was slamming against her ribs, or maybe that was his, he didn't know and it didn't matter.

As long as it never stopped.

He clamped her head between his palms, inhaling her breathy murmur of pleasure as he changed the angle of the kiss to suit him. Only when air became required did he pull back a fraction, staring down at her. "I thought you were on a no-more-men kick."

"I am."

"Then what was that for?"

"Honestly? I have no idea. I just needed to." Her voice was satisfyingly thick, her eyes glazed over.

"Well, I need more." And he came at her again, settling his mouth more firmly over hers, moaning when her soft lips clung and her fingers gripped his face as if afraid he'd pull back.

Fat chance.

He had no idea how long he lost himself in the taste of her before he backed her to a set of shelves, slid his hands from her hair, down her body to her hips, which he squeezed, before gliding them both up, cupping her breasts. Her nipples were hard, pressing against the material of that eye-popping top, begging for attention, attention he was more than willing to give.

Breanne gasped when he dragged his thumbs over them, that same sexy little gasp she'd given him this morning when he'd bared one to the morning air and his own hungry gaze. Tearing his mouth from hers, he dragged kisses along her jaw to her ear. Touching the lobe with his tongue, he sucked it into his mouth in a desperate imitation of what he wanted to do to the rest of her.

Panting raggedly against his throat, she gripped him tighter, holding onto his chest in a way that would surely tear out each hair there, one by painful one, and he didn't care. He hadn't gotten enough this morning, and logically he knew he couldn't possibly get enough here, in the light of day, in the library, where anyone could walk in on them.

But she slid her hands beneath his shirt and stroked his bare back in a restless, desperate sort of gesture, and in the coup de grace . . . sighed his name, just a tiny whisper of a sound, but it was so endlessly, outrageously erotic he fisted his fingers in the stretchy, flashy red material at her shoulders and tugged. The top slid to her elbows, and her breasts popped free, exposing her for his viewing and tasting pleasure.

She wasn't wearing a bra.

"Lariana was still washing my clothes," she whispered, resting her head back against the shelving unit. "And I didn't fit into one of her bras—"

"Breanne." He stared down at her freed, bared breasts, at the way the nipples were tightening into two little buds right before his eyes, making his mouth water. "Are you somehow trying to apologize for not wearing a bra?"

"Yes, I—"

"Don't." This came out slightly more harsh than he intended, and panting for breath, he put his forehead to hers. "God, Breanne. You take my breath."

She shot him a tremulous smile, and with a ragged moan, he dipped his head and very gently rubbed his jaw along the heavy curve of her breast.

Her head thunked back against the shelf. A few books rained down over them. Not caring, he slid his hands down to the backs of her thighs and lifted her up, supporting her between the shelf and his body as he wrapped her legs around him. Her tight skirt got in the way, and impatient, he shoved that up, giving her the freedom of movement to hug his hips with her thighs.

He looked down, at her bared breasts, at the skirt gathered around her waist, which exposed the smallest pair of black lace panties he'd ever seen.

Wet lace.

Holding a warm, rounded cheek in each hand, he rocked against her, letting her opened thighs and the hot, damp spot between them cradle his aching sex. Then he bent and kissed her nipple, kissing, sucking, before nipping lightly with his teeth, gently tugging.

A sweet sound escaped her, rough and desperate, reaching out and grabbing him by the throat as he rocked against her again, moving in a tight circle, ripping more of those erotic murmurs from her as her breasts jiggled and made him so hard he was surprised the zipper on his jeans didn't split. She'd slid her fingers into his hair, doing her best to make him bald before he hit thirty-five as she brought his face back to hers to kiss him, her hips mindlessly thrusting to his.

More. He needed more. Dragging a hand down her body, he stroked a finger over that black lace, catching the edge, hooking it. Beneath he could feel her rose-petal-soft folds, hot and creamy.

For him.

He pressed against her and she writhed against him with an unintelligible whimper. With a matching groan, he rotated his knuckle in a slow circle, ripping another sexy sound from her before dragging the lace aside and drinking in his fill. She was so pretty there, all pink and glistening, her clit pouting for him the way her nipples had. He wanted to taste her, wanted to lick and suck until she screamed his name, wanted to watch her fall over the edge for him.

Lifting his head, he looked around them to see where he could get them out of plain view— "In the closet."

She let out a shaky laugh. "I don't think—"

He merely lifted her against him and began to walk.

"*Cooper.*" Her voice was grainy, her lips still wet from his, her hands shaking as she pushed his chest so that he stopped, having no choice but to let her legs slowly slide down his until her feet touched the ground.

"Sorry," she said, and touched his tight jaw.

That didn't bode well for getting behind the shelves and he knew it.

"I only meant to kiss you—I'm sorry." Without looking at him, she pulled the red shirt up over her glorious breasts, and if he wasn't mistaken, shuddered when the material stroked her nipples.

"Breanne—"

"Thanks for rescuing me over and over," she said as she shoved down her skirt.

"Thanks for rescuing you?" He stared at her. "What the hell is that?"

"You helped me last night. You unlocked the door for me just now."

"Jesus, Breanne. I don't want to be thanked for those things."

"I know," she said softly, covering her face. "God, don't you get it? Look at me, I make a living making bad decisions. I don't want you to be the next one."

"Breanne—"

"Seriously. Not going to do this." And then she walked away.

The story of his life.

"You gave up men," Breanne muttered to herself as she ran out of the library, body aching, heart skipping around like a jumping bean. God. The man could put her on the edge of an orgasm with just a single look.

Except nothing about him was simple. Nothing.

"*You gave up men*," she repeated, running blindly. In this hallway, the walls were lined with picturesque scenes of the Sierras in each of the four seasons, revealing a setting so glorious and innocuous that if one hadn't known *exactly* how isolating and dangerous winter could be out here, she'd believe she was in a fairy tale.

Turning a corner, she stopped to catch her breath. Gulping in air like she hadn't breathed in a week, she realized she'd ended up in a part of the house she hadn't seen before. She stood in the center of a wide arc that broke off in several directions.

And she had no idea where she was.

What a mess she'd made out of this. Hell, what a mess she'd made out of her life, getting dumped again, getting snowed in with no clothes and big spiders and strange characters and a gorgeous, amazing kisser she could really wrap herself around and *had*—except that *she'd given up men*.

She was an idiot.

Closing her eyes, she shook her head. When her stomach growled, she opened her eyes and drew a deep breath. One step at a time.

First up—breakfast.

If she could find it.

She went on the move again, turning down yet another strange hallway. This one had wood-paneled walls and a carpet runner on hardwood floors. At the end of it she found two doors on the left, two on the right, and a door straight ahead. From one of the left doors came the sound of someone ... humming?

Shelly? Relieved, Breanne knocked, thinking this must be where the cook had slept. "Shelly? It's me."

The humming stopped.

Breanne knocked again but now there was no sound at all coming from inside, nothing, just a charged silence, as if Shelly was on the other side of that door, holding her breath.

Breanne stared at the door in surprise for a moment, then turned the handle.

Locked.

She looked at the door straight ahead. Narrow, and not as glossed or pretty as any of the other doors in the house.

Not locked.

When she opened it, she faced a set of wooden stairs that led down into a cellar, dimly lit only from a high, narrow window that led outside.

A wine cellar. She could see racks and racks of bottles, and smiled grimly. If she didn't get out of here today, she'd be needing a bottle.

Or two.

There was an odd smell here, musty and closed in, but also something more. She moved down the stairs, and then down a row of labels, and because she wasn't watching her feet, tripped, landing flat on her face, her legs and feet still draped over whatever she'd caught her foot on.

Which was a crumpled body.

Thirteen

Men have it better than women; they're never required to wear panty hose, and they don't have PMS. On the other hand, they die earlier.
                        —Breanne Mooreland's Journal Entry

Breanne pushed up on her elbows and stared at the body. "Oh, my God! Are you okay?"

It was a man. He lay flat on his back, arms and legs sprawled, not moving. There was a gash on his forehead, the blood dried.

Surging up to her knees, she put her hands on his shoulder. "Can you hear me?"

When he didn't budge, a very bad feeling snaked through her. The thick, icky air seemed to close in around her as she stared at him, heart pounding in her throat. Who was he? Nicely dressed, he wore dark trousers and a dark, long-sleeved shirt. He was missing a shoe, she thought inanely. "Can you hear me?" she repeated.

Nothing. Less than nothing. "I was really hoping you'd blink," she whispered. "Or moan. *Anything.*"

He didn't blink or moan.

Or anything.

Oh, God. She got down low and tried to peer into his face. *Please be okay, please be okay . . .* Could she see a pulse in the base of his neck? As she leaned in, her hand slipped from his shoulder to his chest, which felt . . . stiff.

She pulled her hand back and stared at him in horror. "Oh, my God. You're not unconscious. You're . . ."

Dead.

Her entire body went as stiff as his. Her stomach sank, everything sank, weighing her down so she couldn't seem to move.

Dead.

The knowledge sort of seeped into her brain in slow motion, and when it finally landed and was processed, she did what any sensible city girl stuck in the mountains in a snowstorm without luggage, who'd found a naked guy and a dead guy within a few hours of each other, would do.

She scrunched up her eyes and screamed.

In what might have been an eternity or only a moment later, footsteps sounded above her. Cooper appeared. "Breanne?" He took the stairs two at a time, those always-aware eyes narrowing in on the body at her feet.

While Breanne's eyes narrowed in on the object in Cooper's hand.

A gun.

A gun.

It was hard to wrap her mind around much in the condition she was in, but facts were facts. She'd screamed and he'd come running, ready to slay a dragon for her.

"What the hell happened?" Cooper demanded.

"I don't know."

He hunkered down and put his fingers to the man's neck, then looked up at her, slowly shaking his head.

Breanne slapped a hand over her mouth to hold in another scream.

Rising, Cooper stuffed his gun in the waistband of his jeans low at his back and took her arms in his hands. "You okay?"

A few moments ago, he'd had her up against a wall, skirt shoved up to her belly button, hands in her panties, his fingers driving her straight to oblivion, and now . . . now he was this intense, cool, calm, and collected man.

With a gun.

"Breanne. *Are you okay?*"

She stared at him. He had his shirt loose and draped over the bulge of his gun. He looked rough-and-tumble. Badass.

Damn it, she had a serious weakness for badass.

"Breanne?"

"P-pretty sure I'm n-not okay." Her teeth were chattering again, though she wasn't cold. Or maybe she was and she couldn't tell because she'd gone numb.

With a low sound of empathy, he pulled her close, a protective gesture that felt amazingly seductive for its sweetness, so much so that she felt herself want to cling. *Just for a moment*, she told herself, and did just that: wrapped her arms around his neck and absorbed his strength, his heat.

How was she going to resist this? Him?

Didn't matter, she'd find a way. She'd promised herself a break from bad decisions, and anything she did here, while out of her element and scared and hurt, would be bad. Very bad.

Probably she should stay out of cellars, too.

Cooper pulled back, leaving his hands on her arms, and looked into her eyes. "Tell me why you're standing over a dead body."

"I got lost. I tripped over him."

"He was here when you got here? Like this?"

"Well, I didn't put him here!"

"Okay." He stroked his hands up and down her arms. "Damn. A dead body. I hate it when that happens."

She let out a hysterical laugh. "He's dead. Omigod, when did he get that way? Last night? When I saw a face over me? What if *I* was almost the dead body? What if—"

"Shh." He waited until she'd gulped in a breath and nodded.

She was okay. She was going to hold it together. She was. "You've got a gun."

"Yeah."

Was that his voice, all tight and grim, and so unlike the sexy, low, rough one he'd used only a few moments ago to murmur naughty nothings in her ear? "Cooper, why do you have a gun?"

"How about first we figure out why you have a corpse at your feet?"

She hugged herself and carefully didn't look down. "That's easy. Because I'm in the twilight zone. Or having a dream. Any minute now, I'm going to wake up."

"Sit," he said gently, and backed her to the bottom stair and pushed her down. "Hang tight."

Hang tight. Sure. She'd just do that while Cooper squatted next to the body about fifteen feet away, his eyes scanning the layout, taking it all in as he pulled out a cell phone. He looked at the display and swore at his lack of reception.

"Please tell me why you have a gun," she said as he shoved the cell back into his pocket. "And why you were holding it like a cop."

"I *am* a cop." He glanced up at her. "Or I was until last week when I quit."

More running footsteps sounded above them, then suddenly Shelly and Dante were crowding for space in the doorway above, peering down.

Shelly gasped, Dante swore, and they both came tearing down the steps.

From some dim corner of her mind Breanne realized that if Shelly had come with Dante from somewhere in the house, she couldn't have been in that next room humming, but then Shelly let out a shocked cry and lifted her apron to cover her mouth, her eyes wide and wild. "Oh, my God!"

Dante didn't say a word, just put a hand on Shelly's shoulder.

"Who is he?" Cooper asked them.

Shelly just stared at the body, her mouth still covered.

Dante lifted his gaze, hooded and inscrutable.

"Do you know him?" Cooper asked.

"Yeah." Dante's voice was like granite. "We know him."

"Who is he?" Cooper asked again, in an indisputable cop voice, one that demanded an answer.

"It's Edward," Dante said. "Our boss."

"Not missing," Shelly said into the apron. "But . . . dead."

Another gasp from the top of the stairs, and then Lariana practically flew down to them. *"Dios mio. Dead?"*

Cooper shot Breanne an inexplicable look, then gave a curt nod. "Yes."

"How? Did he fall?"

"Don't know," Cooper said.

"Hey, what's that?" Dante asked, reaching in to touch Edward's chest, but Cooper stopped him.

"It's a crime scene. Don't touch anything."

Dante gave him a long, measuring look. "There's a hole in his shirt."

Breanne hadn't seen it and though she didn't want to, she crowded closer to look. There did seem to be a hole in the material of Edward's shirt, a very small one, near his right pec.

"A bullet hole." Lariana's lips went thin as a line.

"A murder!" Shelly lost all the color in her face.

Cooper shook his head. "We know nothing without forensics, okay? Let's not jump to conclusions—"

"Oh, my God, we're stuck in the house with a murderer!" Shelly's eyes were huge, glassy with shock. "We have to get out, we have to—" She dissolved into tears.

Lariana wrapped her arms around her. "Shh." She looked up at Cooper and spoke calmly enough, though her hands were shaking. "What do we do?"

"Call it in," Cooper said.

Dante shook his head. "Phones are still down, roads still closed. No one's coming in or getting out."

Shelly sobbed against Lariana. "I can't be stuck in the house with a dead body. I can't."

More footsteps above them, and then Patrick stuck his head in the door. When he saw the crowd, he stayed at the top of the stairs. "No need to be hiding yourselves in the cellar for a snowstorm—that's for tornados."

"Patrick." Lariana's voice shook slightly. "We found Edward."

"Dead," Shelly wailed.

At that, Patrick moved down the stairs, his lean body in coveralls, his tool belt low on his hips. He inspected the body himself, then whistled low in his throat. "Well, fuck me. He *is* dead. Mean old bastard."

"What are we going to do now?" Shelly asked tearfully. "We can't all just stay here—we have to get out."

"We can't just leave him here like this—"

"Yes, we can," Cooper said. When all the faces turned in his direction, he added, "Nothing gets moved."

Everyone started talking at once but he lifted a hand. "Look, I'm a cop. Or I used to be. Either way, I'm aware I'm out of jurisdiction, but no one is moving the body or any possible evidence until the proper authorities come."

"No one's coming," Dante said. "No one *can* come."

Patrick agreed with that. "We haven't seen this much snow in all the years I've been here, and it's still coming down. I'm telling you meself it's going to be a while. Days."

"Breanne was able to get a signal on her cell outside the library a little while ago," Cooper said. "Someone needs to go there and try again."

"I will," Patrick said, rocking back on his heels. "But don't be holding your breath."

Shelly sniffed quietly.

Lariana stood still, pale.

Breanne's heart was still thumping.

"Everyone needs to get out of the cellar," Cooper said, rising, standing in front of Edward, standing for the dead. "And stay out."

"But—"

"No one comes in here," he said firmly. "No further contamination of the scene, period."

Dante turned to Patrick. "Let's get the ladies out of here."

"Will do." Patrick slipped an arm around Lariana, and Dante did the same for Shelly. With his free hand, he reached back for Breanne.

She allowed herself to be led up the stairs. At the top, she took a last look over her shoulder at Cooper.

Once again he was crouched by the body, expression grim, his big body gripped with a tension she hadn't seen in him before as he looked Edward over with careful precision.

He was a cop. *Had* been a cop. And though she had no idea why he wasn't one right now, she would bet it hadn't had anything to do with competence, because just watching him kneel on the floor and deal with a dead body—good God, a dead body!—with cool efficiency told her everything she needed to know.

He'd done this before. A lot.

It made her ache for him, not physically as she had in the library, but deeper. Odd how it felt as if she'd known him for more than just the one night. Odd how it felt as if maybe they'd known each other forever.

In that moment, he lifted his head. For a beat in time, his eyes warmed, and he gave her a small nod. *It'll be okay.*

She only wished she believed it.

Breanne sat in the great room, trying not to think about Edward. About her life being in the toilet. About Cooper. About anything.

Dante had stoked the fire, then left without a word. Equally silent, Lariana brought a tray with bagels, cream cheese, and fresh fruit, and after setting the food down in front of Breanne, moved to the door.

"Wait." She couldn't stand the thought of being alone. "Where's Shelly?"

"In the kitchen."

"Is she all right?"

"She will be."

"What does that mean?"

Lariana let out a breath but none of her tension. "Patrick couldn't get a signal on his cell phone. Shelly's upset at having to be here with . . . the situation."

No one wanted to say it. *Dead body.* There was a dead body in the house. Breanne's heart clutched as she remembered how Shelly had sobbed in the cellar. "I didn't get the feeling that she was close to Edward."

"Oh, no. We all hated him," Lariana said forcibly. "But because of the way she is—too sweet for her own good—she hated him less than the rest of us."

"I see." But she didn't. She didn't "see" anything about this crazy past two days. "What are those rooms on either side of the wine cellar?"

"Servants' quarters."

"Do any of you actually live here?"

"Honey, we're *all* living here. At least until Mother Nature decides to give us a break. Could you excuse me? I've got a long list of stuff I have to get to."

"Oh. Sure."

"Stay by the fire. No use getting cold if you don't have to," Lariana said, and left.

Breanne kept her eyes on the flames rather than look around her at all the shadows and corners. She really hated shadows and corners. She'd been afraid of them before Edward had been discovered. Now she was terrified. It was only midmorning, but with the snow still coming down, the light in the windows and skylights was muted at best. It felt like perpetual gloom.

In contrast, the fire radiated a nice, warm glow. She had nothing but those crackling flames for company as she contemplated the fact that she was entirely alone and a possible murderer walked around unencumbered.

A murderer. Her heart started pounding, and then a sound scraped behind her and the poor organ practically stopped.

Fourteen

Sometimes I just want to stop the merry-go-round that is my life and take a nap.
— Breanne Mooreland's Journal Entry

Breanne leapt to her feet and whipped around, nearly falling to the floor in a relieved pile of Jell-O when she saw Cooper standing in the doorway.

At just the sight of him, tall and big and sure of himself, she began to shake. Delayed shock, she knew.

He strode across the room toward her in his loose-legged stride, looking deceptively lazy and completely at ease. He always did, as if all motion was effortless.

Somewhere deep inside, she hoped he would haul her close. Instead he lifted her chin with a finger and peered into her eyes. "You okay?"

Since her teeth were rattling in her head, she simply nodded.

"I need you to hang in there a little bit longer."

No problem. She didn't need him. She didn't need anyone. Especially a penis-carrying human.

"The phones are still out," he said. "No cell service at all now, which means until I can reach the police, I'm it."

She stared into his set face, so determined to do the right thing, and felt something deep within her give. She was desperately afraid it was her pride, which meant that any moment now she was going to throw herself at him. "What do you have to do?"

"For starters, I'd like to know what happened. Tell me again what you know. You left me in the library and . . ."

"And I went running down the hallway. I made a couple of turns and got lost. I ended up in the wine cellar."

"You tripped over him?"

"Yes, I had my eyes locked on the bottles. I was going to take as many as I could carry to my room for a pity party."

"You didn't move him at all?"

"No. Did he fall down the stairs?"

He looked at her for a long moment. "The body's positioned just far enough away from the stairs that I don't see how that happened."

And then there was the hole in his chest.

"Have you seen any guns here?" Cooper asked.

She shivered. "Oh, my God."

He put his hands on her arms and pushed her to the leather chair. "Have you?" he asked more gently.

Her chest tightened and she moved her head in the negative.

"Have you seen or heard anything strange?"

A harsh laugh escaped her. "Are you kidding me? *Everything* has been strange."

He was still touching her, an oddly soothing gesture, considering she didn't want to need him. "You know what I mean," he said.

She sighed. "Well, yesterday I kept hearing odd noises."

"What kind of noises?"

"Odd bumps. Humming. Then there was that face over my bed last night. And then today . . ."

"Today . . . ?"

"Just before I went into the cellar, I thought I heard more noises, but I'm losing it, so what do I know?"

"What do you think of the staff?"

"Why, do you think one of them . . . ?" Unable to finish, she trailed off.

He looked at her for a long beat. "I don't know."

She saw the tension in the lines bracketing his grim, un-smiling mouth, in the dark shadows under his eyes.

"You're not making me feel better," she whispered.

"I'm not going to lie to you, Breanne." Their gazes locked. "Ever."

And she knew. He was telling her that despite what she'd learned from the men in her life, he was telling her the truth and always would.

She could believe in him.

But she just wanted to be far, far away, where there were no dead bodies, where there were no sexy-as-hell strangers now that she'd given up men.

"Can you think of anything else I need to know?" he asked.

"No."

"Are you sure?"

"No, I'm not sure! The only thing I'm sure of is I'm scared to death."

"Okay," he said, and pulled her against him. "Stay close to the fire," he murmured. "I'll be back when I can."

It took every ounce of courage she had not to cling to him when he pulled away. "Where are you going?"

"To talk to everyone else." With a quick stroke of his finger over her hairline at her temple, he was gone, leaving her to ob-sess over how she'd thought she'd hit bottom yesterday, but she'd been very, very wrong.

She was hitting rock bottom now.

So much for being on vacation, Cooper thought. He had a dead body and a houseful of possible suspects, including one hauntingly beautiful, high-spirited, and happy-to-hate-all-men Breanne Mooreland.

And nothing added up.

Because it didn't, he went back to the starting board—the cellar.

Edward lay exactly as he'd been left. He looked to be a man in his late fifties, and in prime shape for his age.

Except for the hole in his chest.

Several things were niggling at Cooper, the last of which was how Shelly had assumed at first sight that Edward was dead. In the dim lighting, Edward could have just been taking a damn nap, and yet she'd taken one look at him and had cried, "Not missing, but *dead!*"

A guess?

Or prior knowledge?

Another thing was that Edward lay on his back, sprawled out. Not a likely position for a person who'd fallen down the stairs and then crawled fifteen feet away to die.

Unless, of course, it hadn't been the fall that had killed him. *And what about the hole in his chest?*

Cooper pulled out a flashlight he'd lifted from the foyer closet and a pair of tweezers he'd gotten from the guest bathroom, and crouched before the body. "Sorry, buddy," he murmured, and lifted Edward's shirt, pulling it away from his chest to look at the chest wound.

A small, perfectly round hole. But not, as he'd first thought, a bullet hole. Or at least he didn't think so. The hole was too small, too inconsequential. In fact, he'd have sworn that it had come from a BB gun, given that he'd had many such wounds himself, courtesy of his brother, when they'd been kids.

Which brought up another unsettling point. A BB might hurt like hell—but it wouldn't have killed him, either.

So what *had?*

When Cooper left the cellar, he wasn't too surprised to find the house quiet as a mouse, with no sight of any of the staff. They'd scattered like wild seeds in the wind.

Funny how good they were at disappearing. He just hoped they weren't as good at being criminals.

He came to the main hallway, and heard a faint murmuring, which he followed to the dining room.

The empty dining room. "Hello?" he called out.

No answer, but he could still hear the voices, faintly but definitely there, coming from . . . the far wall? Odd, as there was no door there, no closet, nothing but drywall. Putting his ear to it, the voices became recognizable.

Dante and Shelly.

"Shelly, baby, *please*. Stop crying."

"I c-can't." Her voice was more muted than Dante's, as if maybe she had her face pressed to him.

Cooper pulled back and looked around the empty room. Where were they? Leaving the dining room, he strode down the hallway and into the kitchen, which shared the talking wall with the dining room.

The kitchen was also empty.

And yet the soft voices were still audible, coming from . . . the walk-in pantry.

"I just can't believe it . . ." came Shelly's voice.

Cooper lifted his hand to knock on the closet door, wanting to alert them to his presence, but Dante spoke again, his voice low and grim.

"He was cruel to you, Shelly. Christ, you feared him and you hated him."

Cooper's hand lowered.

"But I didn't want him dead!" she cried. "My God, Dante. I don't want anyone dead."

"Shh."

"I won't shh!" Suddenly her voice was no longer muted, as if she'd pulled away. "This is bad, so bad—"

"Shelly," Dante said again, softly, so gentle that Cooper had a hard time actually believing it was the tough-looking butler speaking that way. "Come on, come here."

The sound of clothes rustling drifted through the door, followed by a shuddering sigh.

Jesus, Cooper thought, *this house saw a lot of action.*

"I dreamed of you holding me like this," Shelly whispered. "But in my dream it was because you wanted to, not because you were trying to quiet the wigged-out chef."

"Maybe I do want to be holding you like this."

"But you haven't."

"You've only worked here a few months."

"Long enough."

"Shelly." Dante's voice was rough, gravelly. "I open the front door for a living."

"So?"

"So you came from a small town. You grew up with money. Hell, you went to that fancy cooking college—"

"What does *that* matter?"

"Goddammit, I grew up in Watts."

"I don't care."

"I was in a gang. I've done things—You know it."

"You said you left that behind you years ago, when you were still a teenager."

"I'm still ghetto."

"No, you're not."

"Shelly." Dante let out a disparaging sigh. "You have people who care about you deeply. I have no one who gives a shit, no one—"

"You have us here. All of us. We all give a . . . *shit.*"

"You said shit," Dante said, sounding both shocked and amused.

"I'll say it again with a bull in front of it if you tell me that our different social backgrounds is what's holding you back from being with me."

Dante stopped laughing. "That's what I'm telling you."

"Then you are a very stupid man, Dante. And not because you open doors for a living."

"Shelly—"

"Maybe I'm not who you think I am," she whispered. "You ever think of that? Maybe I'm less."

"Or more."

"Well you won't know unless you look deeper."

"But—"

"No. Dante, listen to me. I like you. I like you a lot, and idealistic as it sounds, that should be all that matters!"

"It *is* idealistic."

"And here I thought you were so brave—"

Her words were suddenly cut off, and if Cooper wasn't mistaken, they were cut off by Dante's mouth—that is, if the slurping, kissing noises coming through the door meant anything.

Cooper resisted thunking his head against the wall, though he knew exactly how Dante felt, as if he'd just been handed a winning lotto ticket. He knew because he'd felt that way last night when Breanne had flung herself into his bed and his arms, and had stayed there all night. He knew because he'd felt it again this morning, and in the library, so he really hated to interrupt. But there was a dead guy downstairs who hadn't died of natural causes and couldn't ask his own questions, and Cooper felt honor bound to get those answers for him.

"Oh, my God," Shelly gasped, not sounding like she was crying anymore, but breathless for another reason entirely. "Oh, Dante."

Dante murmured something back to her in his South American native tongue, and Shelly sighed dreamily. "That sounds so sexy," she whispered. "Say it again."

Dante obliged her, then let out a rough groan. "No, don't—" He swore lavishly in Spanish. "*Stop.*"

"Stop?" Shelly asked incredulously.

"Not in a closet." Dante sounded tortured. "Not with you."

"Why?"

"Because you're different."

"Different good?"

Dante's laugh was low. Baffled. "Yeah, different good. Jesus, Shelly."

"So we're going to be together?" she asked with so much hope in her voice that it almost hurt.

Did hurt. Cooper wondered if he'd ever been so hopeful. If so, his job, his world, had stomped it out of him long ago.

"We're going to be together," Dante said, sounding both fierce and shaky.

"Now, then."

"No." Dante let out another laughing groan. "Soon as we can get back to my place. In town."

"That might be days!"

"Shelly—"

"Come to me tonight. Please."

"Shelly—"

"*Please.*"

They were never going to come out of there, Cooper thought. He'd lifted his hand to knock again when Dante said, "Where's the guest?"

"Which one?"

"The cop."

Again, Cooper lowered his hand.

"I don't know," Shelly answered. "But he seemed . . . intense." Her voice hitched. "Didn't he?"

"Cops get that way over dead bodies."

A long silence followed, and Cooper's unease grew. What did they know that they weren't saying?

And would they tell him now if they thought he'd been eavesdropping?

Swearing to himself, he left them to their closet and went to find Lariana or Patrick. He just hoped they weren't in another closet somewhere knocking it out, because all this lusting in the house was getting to him.

As was one tough, soft, sweet-yet-hot Breanne Mooreland. She was *really* getting to him, but that in itself had just gotten complicated, very complicated.

Fifteen

You can't date a man and not plan on being disappointed.
It comes with the territory.

—Breanne Mooreland's Journal Entry

The house was quiet, almost eerily so as Cooper moved through it, looking for Lariana and/or Patrick. In the main hallway, he stopped.

A huge, round saw blade, about three feet in diameter, hung on the wall outside the great room. On it was a beautiful, incredibly pleasing-to-the-eye landscape of the house and the woods around it, so clearly, amazingly painted, right down to the ripples on the lake, that Cooper would have sworn that it was somehow lit from within.

Curious about who would hang something now, today of all days, he headed down the hall toward the sound of running water, and found Lariana scrubbing the already spotless floor of the bathroom off the foyer. She had a brush in one hand, a bottle of cleaner in the other, and was virtually attacking the tile just below the sink with a vengeance that spoke volumes about pent-up emotions.

As Cooper had already noticed about her, Lariana didn't look much like a maid. Even while scrubbing as if her life depended on it, she maintained some inexplicable sophistication and elegance. Oddly enough, she wore a different outfit than she had earlier, black jeans so tight they looked like barely dried, spray-on paint and a silver, long-sleeved top with slits in the sleeves, revealing her toned arms. Bent over as she was, with her jeans sliding south, he got a good look at a tattoo low on her spine.

TROUBLE, it read in cursive.

Trouble? He could believe it. "Spill something?" he asked.

With a startled scream, the brush went flying. Whirling around, she put a hand to her chest and stared at him, chest rising and falling with hummingbird-rapid breathing.

He nodded to what she'd been doing. "Scrubbing pretty hard there."

She narrowed her eyes. "Maybe *you* have nerves of steel, Superman, but the rest of us don't."

Leaning back against the doorway, he crossed his arms over his chest. "Meaning?"

"Meaning that after this morning's little surprise, I needed to keep my hands busy." Indeed, they shook as she retrieved the brush. "That's not a crime."

"Are you frightened, Lariana?"

"Only an idiot wouldn't be. If someone killed Edward—"

"If."

She nodded once. "If. Then it's one of us. Or one of you. Either way, we're all stuck here together. Not exactly comforting." She said this while continuing to scrub with a vengeance. "It's not like we often find dead bodies."

He noticed the more upset she was, the heavier her accent. "Why are you cleaning this particular bathroom?"

Her eyes narrowed and she sat back on her heels, swiping her arm over her forehead. "Just because you're a cop somewhere else, in another life, you don't get to ask questions as if I'm guilty of something." She went back to her frenetic cleaning, but when he just stood there, she once again sat back and glared at him. "*Dios mio.* Just do it. Ask. Ask me whatever you want."

"What do you think I want?"

"To know if I have an alibi."

"Okay," he said. "What were you doing between last night and this morning?"

"Sleeping."

Not exactly the truth, he knew. She hadn't been sleeping, she'd been doing Patrick. "When was the last time you saw Edward?"

"When he was screaming his lungs out at Shelly yesterday before either you or Breanne arrived."

"Why was he doing that?"

Lariana already looked as if she was sorry she'd said it. "I do not know."

"What was Shelly doing?"

She shrugged.

Cooper sighed. "Fine."

"Really? Because you don't seem like it's fine."

"Lariana, we have a dead man in the cellar. I just want to know everything there is to know."

"I suppose you cannot help yourself."

"I suppose not," he said with a ghost of a smile. It was true, he couldn't. Questioning, investigating, was just a part of him. Always had been. As a kid he'd sought to find the hidden mysteries in things. As an adult he'd gone into criminal science with a head for ferreting out the scum of the earth. He'd ended up in vice and had stayed there, even as it had slowly sucked the soul right out of him. The last case, a drug traffic ring, had taken him six months to crack, and at the end, in a fateful shootout he'd never forget, he'd had to decide which of two perps to shoot. The one he hadn't gone for had spun around and killed another cop.

That had been when he'd walked away before going under.

And yet, even now, he had no idea how to stay out of things. "Where's Patrick?"

Lariana's expression didn't noticeably change, though she

got up and turned her back to Cooper, rinsing her brush out in
the sink. Watching her, he hoped to hell she wasn't washing
away evidence.

"There's too many people in this house for Patrick,"
Lariana said. "He's off somewhere alone."

"But it's only you and the other staff, and two guests."

"Which for Patrick, the king of the unsociables, is five too
many."

"Six."

She blinked. "Excuse me?"

"It's six. You, Dante, Shelly, Breanne, myself. And
Edward."

Lariana said nothing, and he eyed the way her knuckles
had gone white on the brush. "You said he yelled at Shelly,"
he pressed. "Did he yell at you, too?"

She went back to rinsing.

"I'm trying to help," he said quietly. "Tell me about him."

She shrugged. "He hired us. He was the direct contact to
the owner."

"Go on."

"He dealt with the guests and the Web site, and handled all
the public relations and advertising."

"And?"

She turned off the water and shook her hands dry. "And . . .
what?"

"What aren't you telling me?"

She put her hands on her hips. "That he was a horrible,
crotchety old man universally hated by all of us. There. Is that
what you wanted to know?"

"No. I want to know who killed him."

Cooper found Breanne right where he'd left her, in front of
the fire. Curled up on the couch, she was entering something
into her Palm Pilot while nibbling on her lower lip, a lip he
happened to know was most excellent to nibble on.

It was insane how just seeing her made something within him leap. Definitely a physical reaction, but unsettlingly, it was more than that, a phenomenon that hadn't happened to him in a long time.

His job hadn't made it easy to meet women, much less keep one. There'd been Annie, and she'd been soft and sweet and giving—and had hated his job with a passion that had made it personal. From her, from countless others before her, he'd learned to hold a big part of himself back. He didn't want to do that anymore.

But he couldn't deny that just standing there, looking at Breanne, made him want to try again.

Hearing him enter, she lifted her head, eyes wide until she focused on him, not relaxing but no longer showing fear.

"Hey," he said.

"Hey back." She hugged her Palm Pilot to her chest. "Did you just hear that? A moment ago?"

"Hear what?"

Her shoulders sagged. "Nothing. I'm hearing things again. I wish I could say I'm also just seeing things, but I'm pretty sure there is really a dead body downstairs."

"Yeah," he said regretfully.

Behind him, the fire crackled loudly, and Breanne jumped as if she'd been shot, dropping her digital unit.

Scooping it up for her, he glanced at the screen. **Last will and testament.**

"You planning on needing a will?" he asked.

Snatching it out of his hand, she shoved it in her bag, her movements jerky.

"You're not going to die, Breanne."

"Yeah? Tell that to Edward."

She was breathing shallowly again, her pupils dilated to large black marbles. He locked his eyes on hers. "I'm not going to let anything happen to you."

Looking away, she nodded.

He pulled her back to face him. "Trust me on this one."

A slow shake of her head was his answer. "I don't do trust."

"This isn't a matter of the heart, this is a matter of life and death."

"Why aren't you a cop anymore?"

Now it was his turn to look away. "That's a long story."

"Right," she said. "And I'm so busy here that I can't possibly spare the time to hear it. Come on, Cooper. Tell me."

He sighed and sank to the couch next to her. "I was in vice. Saw a lot."

Her eyes softened as she turned to face him, sitting on a bent leg, her long, wavy hair around her shoulders. "You burned out?"

"Pretty much. But I still remember how to protect someone." He twirled a long strand of her hair around his finger. "I would tell you if I couldn't."

"So you really always tell the truth?"

"Yes."

Her eyes searched his for a long time. Then she stood up and put her hands out at her sides. "All right, then, tell me this truth. Does this skirt make my butt look big?"

He laughed.

She didn't.

Ah, he thought. A test. He stood, too, pondering her seriously. Then he lifted a finger, twirled it, gesturing her to turn around.

After a pause, she did.

He took a good, long look at her mouthwatering ass, so tightly encased in that black skirt he had no idea how she'd even gotten it on. "Hmmm."

She twisted around and tried to see her own behind. "*Does it?*"

"Can't tell. I'll have to feel out the situation." Sliding a hand down her back, he cupped her bottom.

A sound escaped her, one that he was sure did not relate to

distress. Her breathing quickened, and so did his, and from behind her, he rubbed his jaw along hers as he let his second hand join the fray.

"Cooper," she gasped.

He pressed against her through the skirt, feeling the heat of her as he set his forehead to her temple. "Christ, Breanne." Sliding his other hand to her belly, he held her in place while he dipped his fingers in as far as the skirt's material gave him.

A little whimper escaped her, and she arched her back, giving him better access.

"Nope. Not fat," he managed. "Not even close."

Her eyes were closed. Her tongue darted out and moistened her lips. "Okay."

He turned her to face him. "Okay—you trust me?"

Her breathing wasn't quite even, but she seemed to blink the sexual haze away faster than he could. "Maybe partially."

"Maybe?"

"Well . . . we *are* virtual strangers."

He slowly shook his head.

"We're not supposed to mean anything to each other. We're passing through each other's lives for one brief moment in time, that's all," she said, trying to convince herself.

"Which is why we practically implode on the spot whenever we touch," he answered, sounding ticked, and . . . *hurt?* "Christ, if we ever get to the big bang, it'll kill us."

"I gave up men," she whispered.

"You ever think that you chose the wrong men on purpose?"

She laughed over the vague unease his words brought forth. "Why would I do that? You think I *want* to be dumped all the time?"

"Probably easier than to be the one doing the dumping."

She stared up at him. "Let me get this straight. You think I choose men that dump me, on purpose? Because it's the easy way out?"

"Maybe."

"You know what? I don't care what you think." He wasn't right, he couldn't be right. "And I'm sticking to my plan."

"The no-more-men plan."

"That's right."

"Being careful is good, Breanne. But holding back entirely because you're scared?" He shook his head. "That'd be a damn waste."

"I told you, we're strangers."

"See, that's the thing." Again he stepped close, his broad shoulders blocking out everything but him, the azure color of his shirt emphasizing the clarity of his eyes, intent and frustrated as they were. "We're not strangers. Not anymore." His eyes captured and held hers, forcing her to face that truth, at least. "You have a passion for life. It's an attractive trait, and a sexy one. Don't waste it just because you're running scared."

"I make bad choices," she whispered, knowing it sounded like an old refrain. "You're not going to be the next one."

"But what if this is right?"

"How do I know that?"

"I think you'd just know," he said, and ran a finger over her jaw. "You'd feel it."

She gave a desperate shake of her head.

Disappointment flickered across his face, but he didn't press her. He wouldn't, she realized, and that was . . . oddly freeing and exhilarating all in itself. In her life she'd been pushed in one direction or another by a sibling, a parent, a boyfriend. Making her own decisions had been the best gift she'd ever given to herself.

Now she just had to stay on track and make the right ones. A powerful thing, really. "If I could just get out of here."

They both looked out the window, to the heavily falling snow.

"I guess wanting and getting are two different things," she said.

"I'd agree with you there." He was no longer looking out-side, but at her profile.

She turned to him and felt her heart squeeze at the look on his face. "This is crazy," she whispered. "There's a dead guy downstairs. *Dead.*"

"Yeah," he said on a sigh that spoke volumes about his ex-periences. To her this was a new nightmare, but he'd seen it all before, and had even walked away from it. She couldn't begin to understand how it must feel for him to go on vacation to clear his head and still face death. "Well, at least one thing's clear," she said very softly. "I have an alibi for last night and this morning." Her gaze dropped involuntarily to his mouth, her body even now remembering how good it tasted. "I was kissing the hell out of the detective working the case."

Sixteen

There are only two kinds of men: dead . . . and deadly.
— Breanne Mooreland's Journal Entry

By afternoon, Breanne needed a distraction. She figured food would do it. Moving toward the kitchen, she stopped short in the hallway and stared at a new painting. Or at least she thought it was new because this she would have remembered.

It was an antique, two-person saw blade, at least six feet long, maybe more, painted with the most beautiful landscape of a raging river surrounded by a thick forest, with a storm brewing on the left. Gorgeous.

But where had it come from?

She was distracted from that by the sound of Shelly talking in the kitchen. The cook had made herself scarce all day, and Breanne had been worried about her. Relieved now, she knocked on the closed door.

"Just a sec!" Shelly called out. Then, a minute later, she opened the door, looking rosy and rushed, but neat as ever. "Hey!"

"Want some company?"

"Uh . . ." Shelly took a quick glance over her shoulder, then flashed Breanne a smile. "Sure. Come on in."

Breanne looked around. "Who were you talking to?"

"What?"

"I thought I heard you talking."

"Oh." Shelly laughed breathlessly as she moved behind the island countertop. "Myself. I talk to myself. A lot. Have a seat. Are you hungry? I have hot water—I boiled it in the fireplace. Start with some tea while I fix something for you."

Breanne sat at a bar stool on the other side of the island counter, feeling the cool wood beneath her thighs thanks to the short, short skirt. She began flipping through a basket of teas to choose from.

Shelly unloaded an armful of things from the refrigerator, then began chopping carrots at the speed of light, defying gravity and all laws of relativity as her knife flew through the stack. When the carrots were gone, she moved on to celery. And then fresh broccoli.

Neither of them spoke. Breanne wanted to ask about Edward, but Shelly seemed like brittle glass, so instead she sat there shoving the chopped veggies into her mouth with the same velocity that Shelly wielded her knife.

When Breanne caught up with her, eating everything in front of her, she took her tea bag out of her mug and sipped Earl Grey.

"You know," Shelly said, breaking their silence, "women are a lot like that tea bag."

"How's that?"

"You don't know how strong they are until you put them in hot water."

Breanne laughed and it felt good. "Ain't that the truth."

"If men had to be half as strong as we are, our race would have died out." A sad smile crossed Shelly's face. "My mom said that a lot."

Jumping at the chance to think of anything other than Edward, she managed a smile also. "I have four brothers, so that statement would have started World War III in my house. Are you close to your family?"

"Oh. Yes." Shelly's smile softened. "It's just me and my sister now. More veggies?" She shoved the rest of the chopped broccoli toward Breanne. "I'd have made dip if the sour cream wasn't questionable. Damn the lack of power." She turned on a small lantern on the counter. It didn't light much. "Damn Patrick for the lack of a generator."

"A generator would be nice," Breanne agreed, glancing out at the fading daylight. Another night in the place. Another dark night, this time with a dead body in the cellar.

No one knew the exact time of Edward's death, which meant something even more disturbing. None of them had an alibi, not even her.

Did Cooper count her as a suspect?

Did she count *him* a suspect?

After all, what did they really know about each other, except that their bodies seemed to be predestined to yearn and burn when they were within sight of each other.

"He thinks it's one of us," Shelly said quietly. "The cop thinks one of us killed Edward."

It was still odd to think of Cooper as a cop. She'd not thought of him as one yesterday when he'd stripped her out of her wet clothes. Or last night when he'd held her close. Or this morning when he'd had his hands in her panties. She hadn't thought of him as a cop until he'd been standing in the cellar holding his gun, ready to take on the world for her.

Yeah, *then* he'd been a cop, through and through. And actually, given his world-weary eyes and ready awareness, she should have known.

Probably she would have at least guessed if she'd been thinking with her brain cells instead of with every fiber of her feminine being.

"He's walking around, you know," Shelly said. "Looking for answers." *Chop, chop, chop.*

Breanne marveled that the chef hadn't lost any fingers. "Maybe he's trying to clear everyone."

Shelly set down the knife and looked close to tears again. "I don't have an alibi or anything."

Join the club. "I saw you last night. I saw you this morning."

"But you didn't see me in between, or before you got here."

"No one saw me yesterday afternoon, either. It could be any one of us." An extremely disturbing thought.

Veggies done, Shelly moved to the refrigerator and searched the dark depths for something else to chop. "Dante told me he'd cover for me," she said into the crisper drawer. "Can you believe it? No questions asked."

"Maybe he cares about you and wants to prove it." *Illegally.*

Shelly shut the fridge and turned to Breanne, her cheeks two high spots of bright red. "He kissed me today," she whispered as if departing with a state secret. "I mean really, *really* kissed me."

"So I'm taking it that he noticed you were a woman," Breanne said dryly.

Shelly flashed a small smile.

"Was it good?"

She let out a shaky breath. "It was the best thing I've ever experienced, but he wouldn't make love with me because we were in the pantry at the time—"

"The pantry?" Breanne couldn't have imagined feeling like laughing, but she choked one out now.

Shelly looked uncomfortable. "So that's . . . weird?"

"Well—"

"Where's the oddest place you've kissed?"

Every time Breanne thought about that morning in the library, and what she'd let Cooper do to her there, her face burned hot as a fire poker. And other places burned, too. "For this conversation, I need something more fattening than vegetables."

Shelly went to a cupboard and pulled out a bag of BBQ chips. She opened the bag. "Tell me."

"Can't."

"That's too bad." Shelly dug into the chips with a heartfelt moan. "Yum."

Breanne could smell the salt, could practically taste it. "Damn it. In the library. Happy?"

"Wow. A public one?"

"No." Breanne snatched the bag of chips. "Here. In this house."

Shelly blinked. "You've been here before?"

"No."

"Then . . ." Understanding dawned. "Oh, my God. With the cop!"

"*Cooper.*" Breanne shoved another handful of chips down her throat. "And honestly, I don't know what's wrong with me. I was just dumped. *Again.* I swore off men. Also *again.* Can't believe I let him—Well."

They munched in companionable, stressful silence for a moment before a loud thud shook them.

"What was *that?*" Breanne whispered.

Shelly sidled closer. "Hopefully, Patrick fixing the generator."

"Or Dante digging us out of here?"

"He'd have to dig us to China to get us out of here."

Another thud.

Breanne and Shelly stared at each other.

"I'd feel a lot better if I knew what that was," Breanne said.

"Yeah." Looking around her uneasily, Shelly kept eating. "Up until this morning, I thought this house the most soothing, amazing place I'd ever seen. Now it's just . . . creepy."

"Agreed."

"It'll be different when the electricity is back." Shelly hugged herself. "Probably."

Another odd thump.

"That's it," Breanne said. She hopped off the stool and opened the kitchen door. "*Hello?*"

No one answered.

"It's getting dark," Shelly noted uneasily.

"Yeah."

"Wish we could make like a fat man's pants and split," Shelly whispered.

No kidding. "Where's Lariana?"

"She said she was taking a few hours off. I assumed she was having a late lunch," Shelly said.

"Wouldn't that be in the kitchen?"

They both looked around. No Lariana.

Thump.

"Come on," Breanne said.

"W-where are we going?"

"I'm tired of being scared. We're going to find out what that noise is."

"But it's nearly dark."

Was dark. Breanne tugged down the nearly obscenely short skirt, snatched the lantern, and then, on second thought, took a large butcher knife out of its block, handing it to Sherry before grabbing another one for herself. "Don't worry, we're going to be fine."

"Then why are we carrying butcher knives?"

"Just in case." She tugged Shelly out of the kitchen. The hallway was dark except for the lantern's glow, and she went still to listen. "What's down that way?" she asked, pointing with the knife past the dining room.

"A sauna, gym, Jacuzzi, and a small, indoor pool."

More thumps.

"Oh, God," Shelly said, swallowing hard.

"Come on." They tiptoed toward the area, their knives out in front of them.

The thumps got louder.

"Could you really use that knife if you had to?" Shelly whispered.

Breanne thought about the spider she wouldn't have been able to kill. "Yes," she lied. "You?"

Shelly's knife was shaking so badly it was in danger of

falling out of her hand, so she brought up her other hand to help support it. "Sure." She gulped. "No sweat."

They turned a corner and came to an open workout area, two of the walls lined in mirrors, the room filled with first-class gym equipment. There was a full-screen TV on one wall with an opened DVD case of *Friends: Season One* on the floor, and Shelly sighed in relief when the light from the lantern fell on it. "Oh, it's just Patrick."

"You sure?"

"He loves *Friends*. It's how he learned American slang. He must be around here trying to get that TV running on battery or something. *Patrick?*" she called out.

There was no response but the odd banging, which had become . . . steady. *Rhythmic.* "Oh, God," Breanne said and stopped, sagging in relief against a mirror. She couldn't believe it.

"What?" Shelly whispered.

Someone cried out, a woman.

"*Lariana,*" Shelly said, and ran for the sauna.

"Shelly, wait!" Breanne took off after her, catching her just before the door. "I don't think you want to—"

As they stood there, the door to the sauna opened and Lariana appeared in the doorway holding a flashlight, wearing only a towel and a cat-in-cream smile. At the sight of Breanne and Shelly, one carefully waxed brow shot straight up. Cool as ever, she shut the sauna door behind her.

"Ohmigod, Lariana." Shelly put her hand to her heart and nearly nicked her own chin with the knife. "You're not dead."

"Do I look dead?"

Breanne took in Lariana's dewy skin, the I've-just-been-screwed satisfaction swimming in her eyes. "Nope, you sure don't." Carefully, she relieved the still-shocked Shelly of her knife. "Sorry," she told Lariana for the both of them. "Overactive imagination."

Shelly blinked. "What were you—"

"I told you I was taking a few hours for myself." Lariana strutted past them. "Now if you'll excuse me, I'm going to get into the shower."

"Sure." Breanne didn't open the closed sauna door and peek, but she wanted to. She'd recognized those thunks. Lariana hadn't been in there by herself—she was sure of it.

"We heard you cry out," Shelly said, baffled. "We heard . . ." She trailed off when Lariana turned back.

"You're just spooked," Lariana said as she began to rein in her long, dark hair, piling it up on her head for her shower.

"You should be spooked, too," Shelly said. "And you shouldn't be alone."

For one beat, Lariana's eyes skittered back to the sauna. Then she smiled. "Don't worry about me. I can take care of myself." She vanished into the shower room.

Breanne watched her go, not missing the new love bite on the back of her neck.

"She thinks she's invincible," Shelly said. "But—"

"She wasn't alone." Breanne gestured to the sauna door.

"Oh?" Shelly's eyes swiveled to the same door as well. "*Oh.*"

Breanne transferred both knives to one hand and opened the sauna door.

Patrick jerked to a stand, hands holding his towel—the only thing he wore. "Uh, cheers, mates." Then he caught sight of the knives in her hand. "Christ Jesus, what's happened now?"

"We heard a strong noise," Breanne said. "We came to investigate."

"Oh, that'd be us—Me. I mean *me.*" Beet red, he smiled shakily and swiped his arm over his forehead. "No worries, then."

Breanne had never seen a man blush so hard that his face looked like a tomato. But the rest of his long, lean form . . . She'd imagined him like a stick, skinny and scrawny, but the opposite proved to be true. He was thin, but tough and ropey with strength. And quite attractive. In a very naked sort of way.

Shelly was trying not to stare and not having any success with it. "Um . . . yeah. We were just . . . Oh, Patrick." Closing her eyes, she covered her equally red cheeks. "You were . . ."

"*Shh!*" He glanced frantically around the workout room, relaxing only when he saw no one but them. "She'd kill me if she knew you saw me, no doubt about that." The shower came on, and he relaxed a bit more, hitching up his slipping towel. "Fuck me, but the woman's got eyes in the back of her head. I'm going to be screwed."

"You already were," Breanne said, and shocked Shelly into a horrified laugh.

"I'm sorry." Shelly once again clapped her hand over her mouth. "That wasn't funny."

Patrick moved past them and toward the showers where Lariana had vanished. That door was locked. "Bloody hell," he muttered, raising his hand to knock.

He lost his towel.

Shelly gasped but kept her eyes wide open.

Breanne tipped her head upward while Patrick swore and fumbled for the fallen towel, giving Shelly more of an eyeful, if her second and more audible gasp meant anything.

Still swearing, Patrick wrapped the thing back in place and knocked frantically. "Uh, darling? Open up."

Breanne was trying to look anywhere but at the flustered fix-it man, and while she did, her gaze caught on the doorway of the workout room and the man who'd appeared there, holding a flashlight.

Cooper.

He took in both her and the situation with one sweeping glance, and though he didn't so much as blink, she knew he grasped it all: the humiliated Patrick, the shocked Shelly, the unseen Lariana . . . and herself. He eyed the knives in her hand and arched a brow, but didn't say a word. He didn't have to—his expression said it all.

"We heard a noise," she said, feeling a little like Lucille Ball.

Patrick whipped around, and with a groan at the sight of Cooper, thunked his head on the door. Unfortunately, at the same moment Lariana opened it and he went stumbling in.

Lariana looked down at the man now sprawled at her feet, then up at the crowd watching. "You idiot," she said, and they all knew she meant Patrick.

"Aye," he agreed, still prone.

Lariana sighed, hunkered down, and patted his bare ass. "But you're my idiot, I suppose."

Patrick lifted his head and stared at her. "Am I?"

"Yes."

A slow smile replaced his worried frown. "You going to shut the door, darling, and give us some privacy?"

"Oh, yes," she purred, and did just that.

"That's so romantic," Shelly said with a sigh, and grinned at Breanne. "Isn't that just the most romantic thing ever?"

"You need to get out more," Breanne said.

"Yeah. So I've heard." Shelly turned to Cooper. "Is there anything I can get for you?"

"No, I'm good," he said. He looked at Breanne.

Breanne found she couldn't tear her gaze away, much as she tried.

"Well, then," Shelly said into the awkward silence. "I'm going back to the kitchen." She took the lantern Breanne offered and vanished, leaving Breanne and Cooper alone. Unless one counted Lariana and Patrick in the shower room, which Breanne didn't because she imagined they were very, very occupied.

In the dim room—lit only by his flashlight now—Cooper

just stood there, calm as can be, confident in his own skin and sexy as hell, apparently not feeling the need to speak.

Breanne looked around her at the shadows of the exercise equipment, at the smooth, clean floor, anywhere but at him, wondering how long it would be before one of them cracked. Correction—before *she* cracked.

Finally she ran out of things to look at, so she looked at Cooper again. Honestly, she could have looked at him all day long, with those jeans, faded to white in all the stress spots and worn like an old friend. His shirt was snug to his broad shoulders, untucked, and, she suspected, draped over the gun at his hip.

Which reminded her.

Dead body.

Unknown murderer.

Then, as if fate thought this whole thing funny as hell, his flashlight flickered and went out, leaving them in complete darkness.

Seventeen

Cheer up—I'm sure the worst is yet to come.
          —Breanne Mooreland's Journal Entry

Breanne's heart clenched and she let out an inadvertent whimper, but before she could really get behind a healthy panic, a hand settled on her shoulder.

She nearly swallowed her tongue, and with a terrified squeak, brought up the knives.

"Whoa, there," Cooper said softly, as if talking to a spooked horse. "Just me, remember?"

Right. Just him. The only man in her entire life that had—in less than twenty-four hours—made her feel precious, sexy, smart—

"What's up with the knives?"

"Oh, these?" She forced a laugh. "I thought I'd whip up some stir-fry—"

"It's going to be okay, Bree. You know that, right?"

See, now *that* should have rankled. The way he'd shortened her name was pompous, and yet . . . nice. No one had ever called her Bree before. No one had ever thought to.

But damn it, she was independent, fiercely so; she didn't need him. "How, exactly, will it be okay? I'm in a house with a dead body, and probably also the person who made him dead." She tightened her grip on the knives. "God, I hate this. I so really, really hate this."

She heard a click, and then there was a small beam of light. Cooper held up another flashlight.

She did enjoy a prepared man, but that usually applied to having a condom in his wallet, not being a flashlight carrier. "Were you an Eagle Scout or something?"

He laughed, a sound that scraped low in her belly. "Or something."

"A MacGyver type."

"A troublemaker," he admitted, leading the way to the door. "Come on, let's get to a warm room."

"Tell me about this troublemaking."

"You don't want to hear this now," he said, towing her along.

She had to run in the teetering heels to keep up with him, and tugged on the silly short skirt with the hand still holding the knives. "Yes, I do want to hear this now." She needed the distraction. This flashlight was smaller than the other, the beam of light small and narrow. Insubstantial, in her humble opinion.

"What are you doing back there?" he asked, pulling her up beside him.

Concentrating on not freaking out.

An arm slipped around her waist, and he snugged her to his side. "You hanging in?"

That was debatable. The pictures on the walls of the hallway seemed haunted, the eyes of the people in them following her. "I'd be better if you talked to me."

He glanced down at her. After a moment he said, "I was a rotten kid. I spent more time in the principal's office than class, and at home . . . don't even ask."

"Your parents had their hands full?"

"Just my dad, and yeah, he had his hands full. His answer for me and my brother's antics was his belt."

She looked up at his profile, but in the dark she couldn't see his expression. "Did it work?"

"Only momentarily. We were seriously rotten to the core. My brother and I still laugh that we ended up capturing the bad guys instead of being them."

It'd been one thing to resist him when he was merely a hot body and an unbelievable kisser. But now, with the picture of him as a kid with no mother to soften his father, she wanted to hug him. That, coupled with the knowledge that he'd grown up with a rebel heart . . .

No! She wasn't even going to go there. "We left Lariana and Patrick in the dark."

"I think that's where they want to be."

They were now back in the main hallway, between the foyer and the great room. "You ever been in any of those rooms just outside the cellar?" she asked.

"The servants' quarters?"

"Yeah, I heard someone down there right before I found Edward."

"Who?"

"I thought it was Shelly, but then she came running from upstairs, so it couldn't have been."

He studied her for a beat. "You didn't mention that before."

"I heard humming."

"You're hearing a lot of things," he said.

"I know." She rubbed her temples. "*God.* It gets dark at four o'clock here, and I *hate* the dark! I'm losing it completely, I can feel it."

"You're not losing anything. Let's go look."

She didn't exactly want to, but he had the light and the warmth, so she followed him, trying not to hyperventilate at the thought of what lay ahead.

When they stood in front of the closed cellar door, Breanne shuddered at the thought of Edward in there. Alone.

Dead.

The two doors on the right were open. In the first bedroom was a neatly made bed, a dresser, and a pair of strappy high heels on the floor—Lariana's. The second room had the same dresser, an unmade bed, and no personal effects.

Across the hall, the first bedroom looked untouched. The second . . . locked. This was the one from which Breanne had heard humming. There was no sound behind that door now, and no one answered their knock.

Cooper looked intrigued. "Wonder why that one is locked and not the others?"

Breanne thought about every cop show she'd ever seen and imagined him kicking down the door and drawing his gun to search the place. "Should we break in?" she whispered when he didn't move.

"No."

"Then let's get out of here." She glanced at the cellar door, glad when Cooper led her back down the hall.

Back in the foyer, there was a glow from the fireplace across the way, and Breanne breathed a sigh of relief. "I know you're probably used to this tense, overwhelming stress," she said, "but I'm not."

"I never get used to the stress."

When their gazes met, she could see that was true. He'd seen a lot, done a lot, and it got to him. He wasn't invincible, wasn't immune to the fear; reaching out, she took his hand.

He squeezed hers. "I know how we're going to get out of here tomorrow. Want to see?"

"Are you kidding? *Yes.*"

He turned and shined his flashlight around the foyer. The daylight had gone completely now, and from the long windows on either side of the front door came only an inky blackness, a fact that had Breanne's stomach tumbling hard.

Another long night . . .

Then she saw it, the door behind the reception desk that she'd never noticed before. Cooper opened it, and flashed the light inside.

It was a huge garage. They stepped in and Cooper shut the

door behind them. Breanne couldn't see much beyond a cavernous, dark, drywalled room, three garage doors, and several vehicles. She could smell oil, faint gasoline, and tires. Then Cooper held up the flashlight, highlighting the clean concrete floor, on which sat a Toyota truck, an SUV, and . . .

A trailer, with two snowmobiles on it.

Cooper walked toward them, stroking his hand along the hull of one. "They don't have any gas—I already checked. My guess is that it's early enough in the season that no one's used them yet. The engines look good, though."

She smiled. "What does a vice cop from San Francisco know about snowmobiles?"

He flicked open the hood of the first snowmobile and peered inside. "I know a little about mechanics."

The man fascinated her, no getting around that. He seemed such a contradiction, and she wanted to know more. "From what?"

"It goes back to that wild kid thing. I used to take everything apart." He fiddled with something in the open compartment. "It sort of stuck with me."

"What do you take apart now?"

"Cars sometimes. I rebuild them for fun. Or I used to. Haven't had time in a while."

"Because of your cop work?"

He shrugged, but she knew that was probably true. He'd worked so long and hard, he'd burned out. He'd probably desperately needed this week, and she'd wanted him to leave. She hated the selfishness of that. "I'm sorry."

Lifting his head, he looked at her. "For what?"

"For your time here being ruined. For me, for—"

He smiled at her. "I'm not complaining."

"Are you going to go back to being a cop?"

That got her another shrug.

"You know, you really talk waaay too much," she teased lightly.

His eyes lit with humor but he didn't respond to the bait as she would have. Instead he went back to looking in the engine compartment.

"How come you don't talk about yourself?"

"I'm just not into dwelling."

A throwaway comment, but she could read between the lines, and could well imagine how it'd been for him and his brother without a mom. With a tough-ass dad. With no softness.

And yet he'd taken any helplessness and channeled it into something worthwhile. He'd become a cop, of all things, a vice cop, where he'd seen things that she couldn't even imagine.

Maybe he was on to something. Maybe not dwelling was the secret to surviving not only this madness, but life in general. For instance, if she didn't dwell on her family and friends' reactions to what had happened to her yesterday, then she couldn't be mortified. If she didn't dwell on being left at the altar three times, she wouldn't have to have that *no-more-men* rule.

Dangerous thoughts here in the middle of nowhere, with no electricity and nothing to do but look at him.

And holy smokes, was he something to look at! He'd shoved up his sleeves now and was doing something there beneath the hood, and looking sexy as hell while he was at it.

She wondered at this insatiable attraction she had for him. Was it the sexy clothes she wore making her feel so . . . horny?

No.

Was it merely because she'd told herself she could have him?

No.

Was it because he was strong and smart and didn't seem to care what anyone thought of him? That he had no problem showing whatever he felt, whether it be frustration at their situation, hunger for her body, or a shimmering anger at the sight of a dead man?

Or how about the way he'd protected her without question, putting her safety ahead of his at all times?

Oh, yeah.

And damn if that utter selflessness of his wasn't the biggest aphrodisiac she'd ever experienced. It made her want to do things to him, things that involved a lot less clothing than they had on. She wanted to see him, lost in the throes of passion, vulnerable and open, and when she had him like that, she wanted to take care of him in a way she suspected he didn't often let anyone do. "Aren't the snowmobiles useless to us without gasoline?"

"Yep." Turning, he walked to a large wall shelving unit, randomly opening one, then going very still. "Shit," he said softly.

"What—" She broke off when she saw what he saw.

A shoe.

The matching shoe to the one Edward wore, just set innocuously on a shelf all by itself. "Oh, no."

Cooper stared at it, the muscle in his jaw twitching. "I'm not happy about this."

Neither was she. Her heart had leapt into her throat.

"Jesus," he muttered. "The whole fucking house is a crime scene."

She put a hand on his tense spine, felt the heat and strength there. "Cooper? I really, really want out of here."

"Tomorrow," he said tightly, and opened another cabinet. "Bingo," he said at the sight of the cans of gasoline. "Without power, we'll have to open the garage doors manually, and that's not going to be easy—I've tried. They're heavy from the large snowdrift that's probably up against it."

"We can shovel—"

That got a smile.

"What?"

"I'm seeing you shoveling in that shirt and skirt. With those knives tucked into your boots." His expression heated. "Nice picture, actually."

"Yeah?"

"Yeah," he said huskily, looking at her, really looking at her, as if he could see inside and hear her thoughts, which were pretty much going down a path to dangerous waters.

"This is crazy," she whispered, and backed up a step. She lifted her hand to swipe her damp forehead and nearly poked out her own eye with the knives. "This whole thing is crazy. The wedding, the storm, this house—the dead body."

His smile faded. "I know."

"I'm just so damned jumpy. And we both know I hate trusting you, but the truth is . . . I guess I do. A little, anyway."

He held out a hand. "Enough to give me those knives before you lose a body part?"

She held them out. "I can take care of myself." False bravado and they both knew it. She hadn't taken care of herself; *he* had.

He stepped toward her, searing blue eyes gleaming, invading her personal space in that way he had. Instead of annoying her, it backed the air up in her lungs and made her skin feel too tight.

Oh, and it also made her nipples go happy.

Damn nipples.

"You wouldn't kill a spider," he said softly. "So I'm guessing that if it came to using a knife on a real-life, flesh-and-blood person, you might have a hard time."

She quivered. "I'd be fine."

"That tough outer shell again." He traced her jaw with a finger, a gesture that might have been casual if he'd let his hand fall away, but he stroked that finger over her throat.

She shivered. A nice shiver. A goose bump-inducing shiver.

"I nearly had heart failure when I couldn't find you before," he said very quietly. "I thought you'd stay in the great room."

"I don't stay very well."

"I just want you safe."

She swallowed hard at that. This wasn't a game. This wasn't

about her pride. This was about far more than herself, and she wanted to stay safe, too. Very much. "I thought maybe there'd be safety in numbers. But then Shelly and I heard those noises."

"And you went after it."

"Not my finest decision, granted," she admitted.

His gaze flickered to the wall, where they could very faintly hear the water running through the pipes.

Lariana and Patrick in the shower.

"I do think it's sweet that they're using their fear for the greater good," she quipped.

"As long as it isn't murder that got their adrenaline flowing."

Suddenly Breanne needed more BBQ chips.

Cooper set the confiscated knives on a wooden workbench along the back of the garage. Then he straightened and looked at her, his eyes dark, his intent clear in that fierce, hot expression. Her knees wobbled, and she took a step back, only to come up against the wall.

His hands settled on either side of her head as he leaned in, trapping her within the confines of his body.

"Why do cops do that?" she asked, her voice steady even though her entire body reacted to his nearness—and not in fear.

"Do what?"

"Feel the need to intimidate with their superior bulk?"

He arched a brow. "You think I'm trying to intimidate you?" Bending his head, he ran the tip of his nose over her earlobe, a move that shocked her like a bolt of electricity. "Do you feel intimidated?" he murmured.

"Uh . . ."

"How about now?" he asked softly, and put his lips to the sensitive spot beneath her ear.

She'd expected a quick assault on her senses, a deep, intoxicating kiss—not this light, almost sweet, touch.

"Bree?"

"N-not intimidated," she gasped.

"Aroused, then?" He went after her other ear.

"Um . . . God. I can't think when you do that."

"I'm trying to remind you that we have a thing going on," he said in that voice, the one that melted her resolve—and far too many brain cells, while he was at it.

"Not a *thing*—"

"A thing," he went on, undeterred, "that you're afraid of—"

"I'm *not* afraid—"

"A thing that makes you soft and sweet, a thing that makes you hot for me."

"I'm not . . . hot for you."

His low laugh in her ear sent goose bumps dancing over her skin, and more than just her nipples did the happy dance this time. "Sure about that?" he murmured, and sank his teeth gently into her earlobe, lightly tugging.

She nearly slid to the floor in a boneless heap of desire. Instead she locked her knees and gritted her teeth, flattening her hands against the cold wall to remind herself to keep them off of his body. "Absolutely sure," she managed.

"I could prove you wrong." He nuzzled her some more.

Who'd have thought that little patch of skin beneath her jaw was a direct line to her erogenous zones, but she felt the tug all the way to her womb. "No need."

Another low laugh huffed out of him as he made his way down her neck now, with wet, open-mouthed kisses, and then—oh, my God—licked the spot where surely her pulse was going to burst right out of the base of her throat. "Stop."

"Say it like you mean it, and I will."

Damn it. "We're going to shovel," she said weakly.

"Not now. In the morning."

"But another night—"

"Even if we got out and I got one of these snowmobiles

started, I need daylight to find my way to the road and then into town."

"Dante or Patrick—"

"Even they'll need daylight. Getting lost out here at night . . . Bad idea. It'll have to wait until morning." He scraped his jaw over her collarbone, dragging the red stretchy material off her shoulder.

"Okay, but I am *not* hot for you."

"I know, baby. I know." He kissed her shoulder and her eyes crossed with lust. "It's all me."

"Yes, it's all you—"

He nipped at her as he tugged the shirt down further, baring her breasts. Her head thunked back against the wall, her body a quivering mass of need that she didn't understand. To gather herself and some desperately needed strength, she twisted around. Facing the wall now, she put her hot cheek to the cold drywall and dragged air into her taxed lungs.

"Say the word," he murmured, undeterred by her back as he slowly glided his hands down her body. "And I'll stop."

She opened her mouth to do it but nothing came out.

"Breanne?"

When she didn't answer, he dropped to his knees and kissed the back of a thigh. The feel of his mouth on her bare skin sent heat and desire leaping through her. Oh, God. She *was* hot for him, so hot she couldn't stand it, and she rolled her forehead over the cold wall trying to cool down.

Just sex, she told herself. *Just sex. Just sex*—

"You going to stop me?"

Yep, any minute now.

He slipped his hands around to her belly, which jumped and jerked like it was full of butterflies. Then he cupped her breasts, flicking his thumbs over her nipples, ripping a moan from her that was shocking in its neediness.

Still on his knees behind her, he lightly bit the curve of her bottom through her skirt; then, with his jaw, he pushed the material up out of his way, leaving her vulnerable in the most basic sense of the word.

"God, you take my breath."

She could have stopped him. He expected her to. Instead, she pressed her hot face to the cool wall, squeezing her eyes shut against the image she must have made with her skirt shoved high, revealing her skimpy panties, the do-me boots, knowing he was going to push her past her comfort zone.

Wanting him to push her past her comfort zone.

His hands slid down her hips, her legs, and back up again, palming her bottom. Leaning in, he kissed a cheek, then the other, and then his thumbs dipped between, ripping a gasp out of her.

"Just say the word," he murmured.

Say it, her brain commanded. *Stop him.*

But her body had taken over, and she thrust her butt out.

With a low, rough growl—the only word for the lustful sound that came from him—he skimmed the itty-bitty black panties aside.

Knowing what he could see, which was everything, she kept her eyes closed, her cheek to the chilly wall, and held her breath.

While he very slowly let out his, the warmth skimming over her exposed flesh, ripping a pathetic little whimper from her throat.

He didn't move.

She did. She squirmed, thinking if he didn't touch her soon she was going to be forced to beg.

"You're the sexiest thing," he whispered, running a finger over her. "And so wet." He dipped into that wetness. "Is this all for me, Breanne?"

Good thing the question seemed rhetorical, because she didn't have breath for an answer.

"Are you?"

"Yes," she panted when his finger stroked over her again. "I'm wet. For you."

He rewarded her with another stroke, and she nearly lost it right then and there. And then another while his mouth lightly bit the back of her thigh again, his callused finger still driving her right to the edge.

And all she could do was prop herself against the wall and let the sensations bombard her. Every time she sucked in a breath, her breasts grazed the cold wall, making her gasp in shock, adding to the sensations. "Cooper—"

"Are we stopping?" His voice was tight and strained, and though he went still, he didn't remove his hands—or mouth—from her.

She was so close to coming, her hips were still rocking, tiny little oscillations of movement she couldn't stop.

"Breanne?"

"No," she whispered.

The air left his lungs in a sigh of relief, but none of the tension left the hands that held her still and in place as he whipped her around. On his knees, he looked up at her, groaned at what he saw, then ran his hands from her breasts to her belly, to her thighs, and then between. His thumbs gently parted her, and he leaned in and kissed her.

There.

Something unintelligible left her mouth, though she had no idea what she'd meant to say because then he used his tongue. With a cry, she fell back against the wall, gone, just totally and completely gone. "I don't—"

"You had your chance to stop this," he murmured, using his fingers, his tongue, his teeth. "Shh, now."

"Ohmigod." She began to shudder. "Cooper—I'm going to—"

"Come," he said against her. "I want you to."

As if she could do anything else. Biting her lip, she let go and came hard, bucking against the hands that gripped her tight as he brought her to heaven and back, and then slowly eased her down, touching her as if he could read her like a book. When her knees gave out, he caught her. Mouth wet, eyes dark and hungry, he smiled, though his body was taut.

She put her hands on his shoulders and kissed his cheek, his jaw, his mouth. He immediately opened his and she dove in, but only for a moment before working her way down his throat, smiling when his Adam's apple bounced as he swallowed hard. "Your turn," she whispered, and licked at the hollow at the base of his throat.

Beneath her hands, his heart beat steady but fast. She kissed him again, or he kissed her. God, he was good at this, his lips brushing softly back and forth over hers, his tongue dancing to hers. When her tongue followed his, he sucked her into his mouth with a gentle, warm pressure that got her hot and bothered all over again, more so when a soft groan escaped him.

It gave her a rush such as she'd never known, rendering a man like this a trembling mass of need. On their knees, facing each other, she shoved up his shirt, kissing her way to a pec, flicking her tongue over his nipple, tracing her fingers along his amazing abs, then to the waistband of his jeans. A whole new rush of excitement at his quickened breathing. "Tell me to stop," she whispered, mirroring his earlier words as she unzipped him.

A choked laugh escaped him but he said nothing.

He wasn't wearing underwear. Just a most impressive erection right there in her face, very happy to see her. "Mmmm," she hummed, and tugged his jeans to his thighs. "Is this all for me?"

"Oh, yeah." His fingers tunneled in her hair. "Perfect way to get an in with the law."

Mouth open to take him in, she paused. Tipped her head up. "What?"

He smiled, sexy and lazy, more gorgeous than sin, and she

nearly pretended she hadn't heard him because she wanted his penis inside her more than she wanted her next breath, but she found she couldn't let it go. "You think that I need an *in* with the law?"

He grimaced. "Of course not. I—"

"Oh, my God." She pushed unsteadily to her feet. "You actually think I could have—" Voice shaking, she shut her mouth and shoved down her skirt, adjusted her shirt.

"Breanne. Don't be stupid. I didn't mean—"

Oh, now she was stupid. "Back off," she warned, her body still pulsing, and stepped clear. "You have got to be kidding if you think I'm going to let you touch me now."

She started to stalk off, but at the last minute whirled back and grabbed the flashlight. Let *him* be in the dark. She needed out.

When the door slammed, Cooper pulled up his jeans, wincing as he zipped them, sagging back against the snowmobile. "Genius," he muttered. "I'm a fucking genius."

Eighteen

Everyone makes mistakes. The trick is to make them when nobody is looking.

—Breanne Mooreland's Journal Entry

Cooper made his way through the dark house, his temper heating with each step. He could hear various sounds, someone walking upstairs, someone in the great room messing with the fireplace.

Normal house sounds. As if anything about this house had turned out to be normal.

There were candles lit in the main hallway, the glow making it easier to navigate the huge place but not taking away the chill or the flickering shadows.

He felt painfully alert, watching out for any little movement and sound. It was getting to him.

A dead body did that to a person.

So did all the sexual play without getting off. Damn, that was *really* getting to him. So was little Miss Fucking Attitude.

He had no idea where she'd run off to, the woman who'd actually thought he'd touch her the way he had and yet believe her capable of murder. Wherever she'd gone, he doubted he'd be welcomed anywhere near her. *Too bad*, he thought grimly, because he didn't feel comfortable with her wandering around here when they had no idea what they were up against.

He looked into the great room. Dante was the one stirring

up the fire. Breanne sat on the couch, her back to Cooper, laughing at something the butler was saying.

Laughing. His temper rose a notch.

Shelly stood off to the side, smiling dreamily at Dante.

Cooper let out a breath and entered the room, prepared to be universally hated. "Hey."

Everyone looked at him but no one said anything. Yep, universally hated. Breanne looked away first. He wanted to wring her neck. Instead he nodded to the flashlight she had on her lap. "I need that for a moment. Or your other one."

"Other one?"

"The Day-Glo pink vibrator," he said, being intentionally crude, but damn it she didn't have to look at him like he was a pervert. There'd been *two* people all over each other in that garage.

"Here," she said, shoving the flashlight at him.

He took it and walked out of the room. He decided that was the smart thing to do at the moment because he was absolutely not going to defend himself to her.

In general, people had two reactions to finding out what he did for a living. There were the "cop" groupies, the women who found his job an exciting adrenaline rush. And then there were those who clammed up and got suspicious of everything he said, as if he was getting ready to shove them against a car and cuff them like they did on *COPS*. The cop-haters.

The only person who'd ever accepted him as he stood was his brother, and that had been because they were two peas in a pod. But James was married now, and Cooper had gotten used to being alone. Good thing, since they were going to be here at least another night and he had a feeling he was definitely going to be solo for this one.

No warm, sexy Breanne, a woman he'd thought for a brief moment could maybe have gotten to know him, the real him. He'd been wrong. Again he made his way down to the cellar to make sure no one had messed with the crime scene, just for fun checking the locked bedroom door next to the cellar. Still locked.

He entered the cellar and hunkered down next to Edward, shining the light over him. Poor bastard. Then he eyed Edward's shirt and went still. Had someone adjusted the body? He leaned in closer. The smell was bad, but Cooper had smelled worse so he ignored that, especially as he realized something he'd missed before. There was a curious lack of blood around the hole in Edward's chest, as if the injury had occurred postmortem.

The body had suffered blunt trauma as well, a fact that had become more apparent with the passing of time. The body was bruised from head to toe, as if he'd been beat to hell, or . . . as if he'd fallen.

Cooper craned his neck and looked at the staircase, a good fifteen feet away. "Which came first, Edward? The fall or the shot to the chest?"

And why did Cooper have the gut feeling that neither had been what had killed him?

He scrubbed a hand over his face, frustrated and uneasy. Nothing added up—not the staff's reaction, not the lay of the body, and not the fact that he'd searched the house the best he could and hadn't come up with any sign of a gun, BB or otherwise.

He shouldn't care. He'd laid down his badge, ostensibly for good. At the time, he'd meant it. Even as late as this morning, he'd meant it. He'd worked his ass off and his soul into the ground, and he'd thought leaving the job had been the only answer.

But now, staring down at Edward, he wondered at his need to know what happened, at his need for justice.

The shadow flattened against the wall, heart pounding like a primal drum, watching Cooper.

Why did he keep coming back to look at the body?

Edward was dead already, dead, dead, dead, and no amount of looking at him could change that.

So why was there still so much fear?

Breanne sat in front of the fireplace in the spare bedroom where just last night she'd foolishly believed she could sleep. Shelly was pouring her a glass of wine.

Breanne figured she needed the whole damn bottle. But remembering what had happened when she'd oh-so-innocently gone into the cellar for a bottle, had her shuddering.

"There." Shelly pushed a tray of food toward her, a bowl of canned chili heated by the fire and some fruit. "I can't believe your bad luck. Missing out on my cooking for two of your days here."

"As if that's the worst of my problems."

Shelly let out a shuddery sigh. "Yeah. It's been a rough one around here, huh? First the break-in, then Edward—"

"What?" Breanne set down her wineglass and twisted around to look at Shelly. "You had a break-in?"

"Well, we're not sure exactly, to tell you the truth."

"What do you mean?"

"Last week Lariana went to town and cashed her check at lunch. That night after work, her wallet was missing from her purse out of the main hallway closet. Her entire paycheck, gone." Shelly lifted her hands. "Not that we get paid all that much, let me tell you, but still."

"Did she call the police?"

"No. Nothing else was taken that we could tell."

"Shouldn't the police have been notified?" *Or the future guests warned?*

"To tell you the truth, it wasn't my place to do so. And Lariana said it was her own stupid fault. We'd left the front door open that day for a big spring cleaning. Edward freaks when we leave the front door unlocked. If he'd found out—"

"But the front door was unlocked when I got here," Breanne said.

"Yeah." Shelly flashed her a guilty look. "See, the house is so big, and we all have so many chores because Edward's too cheap to hire a rotating staff. It's just easier to leave it unlocked rather than miss a delivery or a guest."

Breanne stared into the fire and remembered last night. The face hovering over her in bed. "But you make sure to lock the front door at night, right?"

"Always," Shelly promised, then winced. "Or at least I think so."

Terrific.

"It's just that I used to leave after I cooked dinner, so I don't know the late night habits."

"But last night you slept here. In the servants' quarters, right?"

"Yes."

"How about Dante?"

Shelly's smile congealed. "Him, too."

"And Patrick and Lariana?"

"Are you trying to get our alibis?"

Well, yes, but now she felt like a jerk for doing so. "I'm just trying to make sure I'm not scared out of my mind again tonight. If I know where you are, I just might be joining you in a slumber party."

Shelly laughed. "Dante slept on the floor next to me because I was scared and he's a sweetie."

"You mean before you got him in the closet today and showed him your feminine wiles."

"Hey, no wiles were shown." She moved to the door. "Sleep tight."

"Is Dante going to be on your floor again?"

Shelly turned back at the door. "Next to me would be better, but we're waiting until we get out of here."

"Good luck with that, because there's just something about this house that revs a person's energy."

"Maybe it's the altitude?"

"I meant *sexual* energy."

"Oh." Shelly grinned. "Right. I knew that. You're not the first guest to notice."

"It's not difficult when the staff goes around screwing each other at will."

"*Hey.*"

"I meant Lariana."

"I knew that, too."

"Just be careful."

"I should say the same to you. You're the one that ended up sleeping with the cop."

"Cooper. His name is Cooper."

"I know."

Oddly enough, Breanne felt a slight censure in her voice, which made no sense. Shelly didn't seem the type of woman to judge another soul on anything.

And yet Shelly didn't like Cooper, hadn't ever since she'd found out he was a cop.

The others were the same. Not only odd, but unsettling, and when Breanne was alone, she locked the door, then scooted her chair closer to the fire. Hugging her legs in close, she set her chin to her knees, staring at the flickering flames.

Did she like him? Even after what he'd said to her? Yeah, she did, because she knew she'd overreacted, just as she knew she'd done so as a self-protective gesture.

She was still pondering the why of it when a knock came at her door.

Leaping up, she whirled around and stared at it. "Hello?"

"Hey."

Just that, just *Hey*, but the unbearably familiar voice entered her system and jolted her out of her reverie and right into a high state of anticipation she didn't welcome.

Nineteen

When everything's coming your way, you're in the wrong lane.
— Breanne Mooreland's Journal Entry

Breanne stared at the door, her pulse drumming away madly, along with her resistance.

Cooper knocked again, just one light rap.

She could feel him on the other side of the door, his heat, his strength, and her body reacted as if it already belonged to him. Well, damn it, she didn't belong to anyone, especially a man.

"Let me in, Bree."

That'd be like opening the door to the big, bad wolf and inviting him in to blow her life down. As said life had been built fragile brick by fragile brick, she didn't dare.

"Please," he said.

Ah, hell. The magic word. Even knowing it was the mother of all bad decisions, she opened the door.

"About earlier," he said.

Turning her back to him, she moved to the fire and plopped down into the recliner, nonchalantly lifting her hands to the flames. "You mean when you asked if I was putting my hands in your pants because I wanted ... how did you put it ... to get an *in with the law?*"

"Yeah, that." He came close and hunkered down beside her chair. "You cannot think I was serious."

She studied the fire and didn't respond. She knew now he hadn't meant it, but just his voice alone was making her want to melt.

"Look at me, Breanne."

No. Looking at him would be like looking directly into the sun. Amazing but stupid.

But then his hands settled on the arms of the leather recliner and he whipped it around to face him. His face was grim, intense, and . . . still angry.

"I didn't mean it," he said. "You know I didn't. Now I want to hear you say it, damn it."

"Fine. I know you didn't meant it. End of conversation, please."

"Just like that?"

"Just like that."

He looked at her for a long moment, then let out a breath. "I'm a cop, Bree. Through and through, as it turns out. I thought quitting would change that, but apparently no."

Damn it, she knew that, but hearing him say it, knowing he felt as if he *had* to say it, got to her.

"I've seen and heard it all," he said. "And it's changed me, maybe even hardened me. I can't help that. But when I'm with you, I feel a little . . . clumsy." His eyes were dark and genuine. "I didn't mean to hurt your feelings. But you hurt mine."

"I'm sorry." She could admit it now. "I'm so sorry. "It's all me, I'm just . . . going crazy. Edward—"

"Was dead when we got here. Or so I think, anyway." His hands were fisted on either side of her, the sleeves of his shirt rolled up past his elbows, his forearms corded with strength as he leaned over her. "You sleeping in here tonight?"

Sleeping? Probably not. More like watching the shadows on the wall all night long. But she lifted a shoulder. "The bed's comfortable enough."

"I figured you wouldn't want to be alone."

"I'm a big girl, Cooper."

"Yeah, you are." He lifted her chin. "And you're running scared."

She jerked her chin free. "If I was running scared, would I be sleeping alone?"

"You're running scared of me."

She let out what was supposed to be a disbelieving sound, but it convinced neither of them.

"You expect me to believe you'd rather face another midnight intruder than sleep next to me?" His voice was heavy with disbelief. "I don't think so."

She shook her head. "How did you ever fit through the door with that big head of yours? Look, I'm going to be fine, okay? In fact, I'm quite exhausted." She made a big show out of stretching and yawning really wide, before putting her hands to his chest and pushing so she could stand up.

Only she didn't budge him.

"Excuse me," she said.

"You're going to sleep."

"Yep."

"Right now."

"That's right."

At that he backed up, leaning against the wall, arms crossed over his chest, the picture of an irritated, frustrated, sexy-as-hell man.

She made a big deal out of climbing up onto the high bed and tugging down the white down comforter. "Shut the door on your way out."

"You're going to sleep in those fuck-me boots and Lariana's clothes?"

Her own personal armor, and yes, she was going to sleep in them if that's what it took. "I'm sorry if the boots misled you today," she said primly.

"Trust me, it wasn't the boots. Though they are something—" Saying so, he moved forward and took hold of one.

Before she could kick him, he'd flipped her to her back, but instead of flattening her down on the bed with his body as she'd figured, he began to undo the boot with a quiet calm.

"Watch out," she warned. "Have you seen the heels on these things?"

"Shh." He'd bent his head to the task, and she might have melted at the unexpected sweetness of the gesture except he drove her crazy.

"If you shh me one more time . . ." she warned.

Lifting his head, he smiled grimly as the first boot came off and he tossed it over his shoulder. "You'll what?"

Damn it, she had no idea what.

"Come on, Breanne. Finish the threat—I'm all ears."

"Shut up," she said, utterly without rancor because he was looking at her with such genuine warmth and affection that her mad drained right out of her.

People she'd known all her life didn't look at her like that, yet he did. She didn't know what to do with him. "I wish you'd go away," she whispered, confusion and exhaustion, not emotion, creating a lump in her throat. She had no emotion left.

Or so she told herself. "*Please.*"

He went very still, staring at her for a long moment before lifting his hands from her and taking his weight off the mattress. "You know where to find me if you need me."

"I won't." With only one boot off, she turned over into a little ball and closed her eyes tight, not relaxing until she heard the door shut behind him.

"It's locked," he said through it. "Keep it that way."

Sleep didn't come as easily as it had the night before. For the longest time she lay there, muscles sore from holding herself so tense. The fire crackled. The walls creaked.

So did a floorboard.

Uneasy, she sat up, her gaze frantically searching out each corner of the room.

No floating face.

No boogeyman.

Nothing.

And yet she was in this house with a dead body. And some-one who'd made him dead.

She lay back down, but that lasted only until the next mys-terious creak.

Why had she wanted to be alone?

Damn bad time to have given up men.

Then, from somewhere in the house, came an odd, indis-tinguishable sound. Not the house creaking, but she couldn't place it. Again she sat up.

She'd definitely been hasty in sending Cooper away. Truth was, she didn't have to give up men as long as she did one thing—hold on to her heart and soul for all they were worth, never letting them go.

For anyone.

Hoping she was right, she slipped out of bed and slowly cracked open her door. The hallway was pitch black—not a sound, not even a whisper of air. She couldn't see all the way to the honeymoon suite where her salvation lay in one tall, hard, gorgeous package.

Couldn't see anything.

That's when the house creaked again.

Goose bumps rose over her skin, fear bubbled in her throat, and she ducked back into her room looking for a flashlight or a candle or something.

But the candles had burned down to stubs and Lariana hadn't replaced them. She'd had the fire for light and that had been enough. Stumbling into the bathroom, she went straight to the gift basket and fumbled for the vibrator that had reappeared. *Thanks, Lariana, for your obnoxious sense of humor.* Rushing back to the fire, Breanne held the thing up in front of the flames for a moment until it began to glow pink.

At the next creak of the walls, she gasped, gripped the

vibrator out in front of her like a beacon, and bolted for the honeymoon suite, limping in her one high-heeled boot.

This time she didn't jump Cooper in the bed. She didn't have to because he wasn't in it.

Shirtless, wearing only a pair of jeans low on his hips, he stood facing his own fireplace, hair rumpled, feet bare. For a moment she hung onto the doorjamb staring at him, a yearning welling up within her so strong she didn't know what to do with it.

What was it about him? Granted, he had an amazing body. His back was sinewy and sleek, broad and sculpted, tapering in at his waist and hips. And that butt . . . Lord, she just wanted to bite it.

Only it wasn't her body that tingled at the sight of him, but something deep inside. *Note to self: your heart and soul are locked up tight! Not accessible! Remember that!*

"You going to shut the door?" he asked without turning around.

With a sigh, she did, no longer surprised that he seemed to have eyes in the back of his head because she was getting used to that sense of awareness he had. She imagined he'd honed it over the years of being a cop.

Craning his neck, he finally looked at her, taking in her makeshift flashlight. "You need me to show you how to work that thing?"

"In your dreams."

"Oh yeah, in my dreams." He sighed and rubbed his forehead as if she gave him a headache by just being.

She had to admit it was entirely possible that she was a walking/talking headache inducer. "I, um, forgot to tell you something."

"Well, then." He turned toward her and slipped his hands in his pockets. The movement shifted his jeans even lower on his hips, gaping away slightly from his rippled abs that she always wanted to touch. "I'm all ears, Princess."

Actually, he was all solid, tough muscle, but she wasn't going to point that out. *Locking up the heart and soul and tossing out the key!*

He jerked a shoulder toward the fire. "Come here."

Yeah, colossally bad idea. "Don't you want to know what I forgot to tell you?"

"I want you to be warm."

His words made her realize she was hugging herself, and extremely chilled. "Getting close to you is bad for my mental health."

"And yet you're here instead of with anyone else in the house." He waggled his fingers. "Come on."

Her feet carried her, damn them, one boot on and one boot off, while he watched, calm and thoughtful. Coming to a stop next to him, she stared into the fire, ignoring his gaze, which she could feel running over her. "Better?" he asked softly as the warmth began to seep into her bones.

"Yes," she said so grudgingly he laughed as he bent down and helped her out of her single boot.

"So." When he straightened, he smiled into her eyes with that same confusing mix of heat and affection that felt infinitely terrifying to her. "What did you forget to tell me?"

"It's a deal sort of thing."

"Ah. Meaning you want something in return." Again he slipped his hands into his pockets and turned back to the fire, his smile gone, shoulders slightly hunched. "The question is, *what.*"

Too late, she realized the truth. As a cop, he probably got requests for "deals" every day. Guilt stabbed through her that she hadn't treated him any better than any of the criminals he'd dealt with, but there was no going back now. "I want to sleep with you."

That got his attention. Those eyes once again turned and locked on hers, blazing and filled with things that banished her chill. She swallowed hard. "That is, um . . ."

"Yeah," he said. "I thought you might want to clarify that."

"I want to sleep with you so I'm not the next body found dead on the cellar floor."

He let out a long breath. "Breanne, you don't have to make a bargain for that."

Her heart began to tumble but she bucked it up because, damn it, neither her heart nor her soul were involved here. They were locked up.

Tight.

"In return for letting me sleep here," she said, "I wanted to tell you what Shelly mentioned tonight. They had a break-in last week."

"A break-in?" He went from mere man to sharp cop in the blink of an eye. "What was taken?"

"From what I understand, just cash from Lariana's purse. Nothing else."

He frowned. "That makes no sense. There's a lot of valuable stuff here."

"I know."

"Only Lariana's money? Are you sure?"

"That's what she said."

"That sounds personal. What did the police say?"

"They didn't call the police."

He made a rough sound of disgust.

"They didn't want the owner to find out that they'd been leaving the front door unlocked."

"Anything else?" he asked.

"No."

He nodded. "Then there's only one thing left to do."

"What's that?"

"Go to bed," he said, and his hands went to the buttons on his Levi's.

Twenty

A conclusion is where you go when you get tired of thinking.
— Breanne Mooreland's Journal Entry

Cooper didn't miss the leap of emotion in Breanne's gaze. Except it wasn't *Oh, please take me to bed*, it was *Oh God, he thinks I'm going to sleep with him.*

With a harsh laugh directed entirely at himself, he ran his fingers through his hair and headed toward the mattress. "I'm taking it we need something bigger than a sheet between us this time." He snatched the folded comforter off the foot of the bed and stalked toward the overstuffed chair in the corner. The *small* chair. "'Night, Bree."

She stared at him as he sat and pulled the comforter over the top of him. It was a short comforter, and didn't cover both his chest and his feet at the same time. Perfect. Not only had he been stupid enough to give up the bed, he was going to be cold to boot.

Breanne was still staring at him. "I thought that you—that we'd—" Her gaze flickered to the bed.

"You thought what?"

"Nothing." She pulled back the big, thick down comforter that Cooper had reason to know was not only warm and toasty, but would cover him entirely, and slid beneath it, vanishing entirely except for the top of her head and her eyes. Eyes that were still locked on him.

Trying to forget her, he shifted to his side, aiming for some level of comfort. There was none to be had. His jeans were cutting off circulation to vital parts. With a sigh, he stood up and stripped them off, then wrapped himself in the blanket that came only to his shins.

Popsicles. His feet were going to be popsicles.

So were his balls. Good move, Ace. With another sigh, he stood up, put his jeans back on, and took a longing glance toward the bed. Looking considerably more comfortable, not to mention warm and toasty, Breanne lay there with only her hair and eyes showing.

Eyes which were closed.

He turned away, thinking, damn, she'd gone directly to sleep, peaceful as a baby, while he sat here chilly, frustrated, and—

"I have another deal," she whispered.

"The last one didn't work out too well for me, so no, thanks."

"This one's better."

He rolled back toward her, then was sorry. Her eyes were dark and haunted, her face strained, her fingers clutching the blanket up to her chin. Not wanting to be affected by her meant shit when his heart clenched without his permission every time he so much as looked at her. "What is it?"

"I'm . . ." She let out a breath. "I'm really scared."

He sighed. "Nothing's going to happen to you here, Bree."

"Yeah." Sitting up, she pulled her knees to her chest and wrapped her arms around her legs. "I keep telling myself that. The truth is, I'm a little shaky for a lot of reasons."

"You've been through a rough few days. Anyone would be shaky, even without finding a dead body."

"Yeah, makes that whole being dumped at the altar thing not that big a deal."

"It was a big deal for you," he said quietly.

"You know it's for the third time."

"Breanne—"

"Don't even try to tell me that's normal," she said firmly. "Face it, Cooper. There's something wrong with me. I'm not quite sure what, but there is."

"No."

"Maybe it's a sexual thing. Maybe . . ." She winced. "Maybe I'm bad in bed."

Christ, no man was strong enough for this. He pushed out of the chair and moved to the mattress.

She watched him, her eyes sad and shimmering. "About the deal. Do you think you could—I mean, would you—"

He put a knee on the mattress. "Don't say it."

"—have sex with me?" she whispered. "Make sure I'm not doing something really wrong?"

Definitely not big enough to walk away from that request, or the lingering hurt in her eyes, not to mention the offer of her sweet, hot body.

"I'll do all the work," she promised. "*Everything.*"

His knees actually wobbled.

"And afterwards, you can critique me—"

"*Breanne—*"

"And then tomorrow morning, we'll dig out and go our separate ways."

She was serious. She wanted to have him tonight, bare their bodies and souls, then walk away in the morning.

After he told her what was wrong with her.

"Think of it," she said softly. "A whole night of unattached, unemotional sex. Any guy's idea of Christmas, right?"

"Stop." Walking over here had been a massively stupid idea, because now he was inches from her, with a knee already on the bed.

She pulled her lower lip between her teeth. Stared up at him.

All he had to do was lean over her—

She tossed the covers aside.

On her back in that stretchy red top and painted-on skirt, both of which showed off her curvy body in a mouthwatering way, she smiled up at him—shaky, but a smile nevertheless. "Do you want me, Cooper?"

Only more than his next breath. He wanted to pull her beneath him, he wanted to slowly strip her out of those sexy clothes that were hot but not *her*, wanted to run his tongue and teeth over every inch of her.

But not like this. Damn it, not like this, not with her hurting, and vulnerable. Not with her trying to set it up so that for once she could be the one to walk away before she got hurt. It took every ounce of restraint he had, but he backed up.

"I know you want me," she said softly, and they both looked down at the unmistakable bulge behind the buttons on his jeans, offering vivid proof of that wanting. "Yes," he said hoarsely. "But—"

"No. No buts."

"*But* . . . not like this, Bree. Not because you're hurting and sad."

"*Cooper*—"

"I don't want you to wake up in the morning and regret anything. Especially me."

Her eyes were as luminous as the fire's glow while she digested this. "And I thought you said you weren't a gentleman."

A sound of deep need escaped him—he couldn't help it.

She turned on her side away from him and pulled the covers back over her head.

Was she embarrassed now? He didn't want that, anything but that. "Breanne—"

"Forget it."

He didn't move, couldn't get himself to walk away.

"Every minute you stand there," she said, her voice muffled by the covers, "you risk being jumped by the pathetic chick. I'd run if I were you."

Shit. He stalked the length of the room, heading back to the fire, even though he didn't need the heat; he was damn hot enough.

Craning his neck, he glanced back at the bed. The lump that was Breanne hadn't budged. Good. She was going to be a good girl and go to sleep.

He only wished he could, but as he was currently hard enough to pound nails, he doubted sleep would come any time soon. James would have smacked him upside the head for turning down the sexiest, hottest woman he'd ever seen. He couldn't believe he'd done it. He was truly an idiot.

Suddenly exhausted, he dropped into the chair, sprawled out his legs, and tipped his head back. Closed his eyes.

His mind did not turn off. Nope, it kept whirring and cranking out disturbing thoughts.

Wake her up.

Tell her you changed your mind—

Better yet, *show* her you've changed your mind.

"Cooper?"

He opened his eyes to find her standing right in front of him, his living fantasy in the flesh. "Thought you'd gone to sleep," he said.

Slowly she shook her head.

"You should go to sleep." He was sounding a bit desperate, even to his own ears, but damn it, he could only take so much with her standing there two inches from him, looking as if maybe she wanted to gobble him up whole.

He could really get behind that. "Breanne."

"I know. You want me to go far, far away, but I can't do that."

"Why not?"

"Because."

Her eyes held his, shadowed by insecurity. There was no use in pretending he couldn't see because he might as well try to stop breathing. Every part of him was focused on her, locked in some hypersensitive state. "You can't go back to bed because . . . ?"

"Because I want you in it with me."

"Breanne—"

"I need you, Cooper. Don't make me beg."

Ah, Christ. "Are you sure?" he whispered fiercely.

She straddled his legs and sat on his lap.

Okay, she was sure. "Breanne," he groaned. "We've taken this about as far as we can with our clothes on, and I don't want to stop again."

She shook her head. "No stopping this time."

"Good, because I've been hard since you got here. I'm going to damage myself if I keep it up." He shot her a lopsided grin. "Have some mercy."

She laughed, but her eyes shone with emotion as well, yanking at his heart, and his smile slowly faded.

"I need somebody tonight," she whispered, her hands going to his shoulders. "And I want it to be you. You, Cooper Scott, and no one else."

The promise was far more than he could have, or would have, asked for. He sat up a little straighter, running his hands up her body to cup her face, tugging her down for a kiss.

She obliged him in the sweetest, hottest connection he'd ever known, then pulled back, her lips leaving his with a little suction noise that tugged all the way through his body.

With a little smile, she got off of him and shimmied out of her skirt. God, he loved those black satin panties, the way the small patch of material barely covered her, how the stretchy fabric rode low on her hips, and though he couldn't see her ass at the moment, he knew the material was riding up, outlining her to perfection. "Breanne," he said hoarsely.

She crossed her arms in front of her, grabbed the hem of that red shirt, and pulled it over her head.

Leaving her in nothing but those panties, and suddenly he

wished he'd let her keep the boots on, because holy shit, that would have made quite the picture.

Not that he needed the boots at the moment. Hell, no. She made his mouth water without the boots. She made his mouth water, period.

Then she climbed back into his lap, tucking a knee on either side of his thighs. His hands went to his favorite part, her sweet ass. He squeezed, then slid inside her panties, cupping her bare skin before gliding downward—

She gasped.

He groaned, his fingers delving deeper, finding her wet and creamy, making him groan again.

She said his name in a rather strangled voice, having gone utterly still in what he hoped was anticipation. "Good?" he asked.

The sound that came from her was rough, low, and the most erotic thing he'd ever heard, and he slowly pushed a finger inside her.

This elicited yet another breathy cry, and he added a second finger.

"More," she whispered, squirming. "Please, more."

He'd give her more, and it would take all night. Even knowing that wouldn't be enough, he slid his fingers free, nudging her closer, then closer still so that her satin-covered crotch slid to his denim-covered one . . . oh, yeah . . . and those full breasts were only an inch from his mouth. He kissed the pouting tip of one and pulled back to watch it pucker up and darken for him. "You're so sexy, Bree. You're the sexiest thing I've ever seen."

"You don't have to say that." Her voice sounded strained. "I'm here. I'm willing. You don't have to say anything you don't mean. Just . . . take us to the finish line. *Please.*"

After all the teasing they'd done over the past two days, he wanted that more than anything, but not as badly as he wanted her to believe him, believe in this. He cupped her face, waiting until she lifted those whiskey eyes. "I never lie, Bree, remember? Never. This isn't just about the finish, spectacular as that's going to be. It's going to be about far more. Now do you still want to do this?"

She didn't take her eyes off him as she thought about that for so long he got worried.

"Yes, I still want to do this," she finally said. "But one of us is way overdressed." Saying so, she pulled back slightly, bending her head to the task of unfastening his jeans. Her hair fell forward, brushing against his bare shoulders and chest, and it was so much like his fantasy, he groaned. "There's no rush," he said huskily when she let out a frustrated cry, struggling. "We have all night."

"I like it fast."

Finally she slid her hands into his jeans, freeing him, humming with pleasure as she wrapped her fingers around the biggest erection he'd ever had. He tried to reach for her but she shook her head. "I'm doing all the work, remember?" She stroked him. Perfectly.

And then again.

At this rate, he'd last all of two seconds. Not wanting that to be the case, he captured her hands in one of his and held them at the small of her back.

Lifting her head, she looked at him from hot, hungry eyes. Flattering as hell, and he began to think maybe she didn't even have to touch him to get him off.

"Cooper." Frustrated, she rocked her hips, gliding that satin over his erection.

He saw stars.

"Mmm," she said, arms still trapped behind her, and rocked again.

And then again, her breasts jiggling so pretty and enticingly in his face, the little diamond in her belly button twinkling.

And again.

Her satin was wet now, causing the most delicious friction against him, and desperate, he squeezed her hip, trying to hold her still. "Don't," he said. Begged. "God, don't move."

"I can't help it." And she very purposely rocked again.

Abruptly he pushed her off him and stood up, shoving down his jeans.

She staggered back and stared at his body.

Staring right back, he kicked free of the denim.

And then she lost the last of the lingering doubt in her eyes and smiled at him, a real smile that he felt all the way to his heart.

Had she really believed he'd reject her? Was she really that unsure of her own appeal?

She was still looking at him. From head to toe, and back again, then zeroing in on the part of him the most happy to be having this special little sleepover.

"You're . . . big," she whispered.

Not that big, but hell, he wasn't going to argue the point. "Hold that thought," he said, and went to the little goodie basket, which amongst other things, had condoms. On the way back to the chair, he grabbed the vibrator she'd left on the bed, shooting her a grin that changed hers from anticipatory to . . . nervous.

He decided he liked that. He liked that a lot.

Twenty-one

If everything seems to be going well, you have obviously
overlooked something.
                    —Breanne Mooreland's Journal Entry

Breanne stared at the glowing vibrator in Cooper's hand, so
innocuous-looking—until he twisted the end and it buzzed to
life.

The sound of humming filled the air, making her body hum
as well. "Um . . ."

"Come here, Breanne."

Her feet stood rooted to the spot. He wasn't touching her,
nothing was, but her nipples were hard, and between her legs
she throbbed.

Then she lifted her gaze to Cooper's, and at the long, slow,
hot-eyed look he shot her, she swallowed hard.

He set the basket of condoms on the floor beside the chair
and sat, crooking his finger at her.

She went, and when she got close, he pulled her down on
his hips, his hands urging her thighs wide over his so that she
straddled him.

"Mmm," rumbled from his chest at the skin-to-skin contact. Holding her legs sprawled open, he leaned forward, put
his mouth on her throat, kissing his way over to her shoulder,
from which he took a little bite. She jumped when he brought
his other hand up, trailing the vibrator along first one inner
thigh, then the other.

And then between.

She felt the jolt clear to her toes, and put her hand over his. He lifted his gaze. "Too unromantic?"

Unromantic was exactly what she wanted here, to keep her heart out of the mix. "No. It's just that—" She felt herself blush.

"You've never used one of these before?" he guessed.

"Only for a flashlight," she admitted, sucking in a breath when the vibrator slid even higher, rumbling lightly, tingling her flesh, making her pulse leap with both excitement and trepidation.

"Ready?" he murmured.

"Um—" She broke off with a gasp when he sucked a nipple into his warm mouth at the exact moment he hit ground zero with the vibrator.

Her body tightened, strained, and the sound that tore from her throat was not a *no, don't* but a definite *oh, please.* An on-the-edge *oh, please,* to boot.

Slowly he circled the tip around, dipping into her own wetness, spreading it, and then back to her happy spot, just skimming lightly over her sensitive flesh.

She jerked again, let out another of those shockingly needy whimpers, and arched up for more. Suddenly her skin felt too tight, her pulse beat in her ears so loudly she could hear nothing but the rush of her own blood, heading south, pooling between her legs.

Another slow, purposeful circle of the vibrator, combined with a hot, wet glide of his tongue over her other nipple, and she was actually going to come without straining for it. In less than thirty seconds. "Cooper—"

"You taste amazing." Lifting his head a fraction, he stared down at her breast and lightly blew out a breath. "Do you know that?"

Luckily he didn't seem to require an answer, leaving her free to moan again.

And at the sound, he eased back, and she had to bite her lip rather than beg for more.

He was watching her. He knew exactly what she wanted, damn him. "Hurry," she managed, knowing she sounded too desperate, too impatient. She didn't care. She arched toward him.

His answer was another maddeningly slow circle of the vibrator, and just as she nearly tossed herself over the chasm into a glorious orgasm, he pulled back again, brought it to his mouth and licked the tip. "Amazing," he repeated huskily.

Staring at him, something within her snapped. Grabbing the vibrator, she tossed it aside, wrapped her fingers around his erection, sighing her pleasure at finding him both so silky and steely, and rubbed the very tip of him against her.

In. She needed him in.

"God, Bree." His fingers dug into her hips as he held her off, his expression tight. "Wait," he ground out.

No. No waiting. He was thick, even just the head of him— all she could get at the moment—stretched her. It felt glorious. She rocked her hips, wanting more.

He caved with a softly uttered "fuck," and thrust into her, making her gasp with pleasure.

"The bed," he ground out. "I want to—"

"Here. Now." Fast and hard. Just two bodies straining toward the same thing. No minds, and especially no hearts, no souls. She rocked again, running her hands down his damp chest. His body was tense and quivering, every muscle straining. "Please, now."

"Condom, then," he grated out, sweat breaking out on his brow as he struggled to remain still. "Get it."

Reaching down into the basket, she pulled out the first one her fingers touched. "Very berry," she read on the purple-colored prophylactic. "Grape flavored." She looked at him. "Yum."

This ripped a rough, laughing groan from his throat as he

took it from her fingers, tore it open, and stroked it down his length. He stroked a thumb over her throbbing flesh. "I wish you'd let me—"

"No, let *me*." And she guided him home.

"Slow," he said tightly, jaw bunched, his gaze never leaving hers.

"There's no *slow* tonight." She needed the oblivion, needed him to be the one to give it to her, and she sank down on him, almost melting at the feel of him gliding all the way home.

His quiet "Oh, yeah" mingled with hers. She would have moved on him, *had* to move on him, but his fingers dug into her hips, holding her. "Just for a second," he whispered, stroking a strand of hair from her eyes, looking at her so intensely, so sweetly, so incredibly deeply, she felt her throat tighten.

"No," she whispered, shaking her head. No *sweetly*. No *deeply*. No tenderness at all. Closing her eyes, she took his mouth in a kiss, entwining her hands with his so that she could lift up until he almost slipped out of her, then sinking back down. "Like this," she said, and as if she finally broke his reins, he swore lavishly and took over, arching up thrust for thrust, hips pistoning wildly as he took her. Hard. Fast.

She cried out, but he swallowed the sound with his mouth, one hand on her bottom, guiding her down as he arched up, his other hand in her hair, holding her head for his possessing, fierce kiss.

Hot.

Wild.

Out of control as they gasped for breath, damp flesh slapping against damp flesh, fingers digging into trembling muscles . . . and then straining toward that finish line she'd wanted, where a turbulent whirlpool of colliding sensations waited.

Breanne got there first; she felt it building, felt it sweep over her, an unstoppable freight train homeward bound. Through a kaleidoscope of lights going off in her head, she heard Cooper let out a low, guttural groan as he found his own release. Still trembling, she fell over his hot, damp chest, snuggling in when he wrapped his arms around her tight.

"Jesus," he breathed softly in her hair, his arms still trembling. After a long moment he sagged back and looked at her from beneath those sexy, heavy-lidded eyes.

Okay, no big deal, she thought. Sure, she'd broken her no-men rule, but she'd managed to keep her heart and soul safe and tucked in. But she hadn't accomplished that by meeting his see-all eyes and letting him warm her from the inside out. "Well." She smiled with forced cheer and didn't look at him. "That was fun." She tried to get up, but he held on.

He was still inside her, not hard but not soft, either. Sinking his fingers into her hair, he forced her head back so that he could look at her. Suddenly his eyes weren't so sleepy. *"Fun?"*

She swallowed hard at the indescribable expression on his face. "Yeah, you know. As in, let's do it again sometime."

"Fun is eating ice cream. *Fun* is having a day off. *Fun* is a walk in the fucking park, Breanne."

"Um—"

"What we did was pretty far beyond fun. What we did was off the fun chart." He narrowed his eyes. "You wanted to know what was wrong with you?"

"Uh . . . no. I changed my mind." The tension he'd banished with an orgasm was back.

"Did you, now?" he murmured. "Interesting."

Around them the fire crackled, the house creaked, all assuring her that this was real, not some sort of fantasy dream. It was real and she had a man, still buried inside her, staring into her eyes, seeing things she wasn't ready for him to see, trying to get to the bottom of something she didn't want to discuss.

So she cheated. She tightened her thighs, as well as her inner muscles, and hugged him.

Immediately his eyes went opaque. Almost helplessly, he thrust up with his hips. "No fair," he whispered.

Which is why she did it again.

This time he closed his eyes and groaned. "Let me guess. You want some more *fun.*"

"Good guess," she murmured, and leaned in for a kiss, squeaking in surprise when instead he surged to his feet, still holding her wrapped around him. With a hand on her butt, the other still fisted in her hair at her back, he headed toward the bed. "You're not going to rush me this time," he warned her, and before she could say otherwise, he let go of her.

She fell through the air and hit the mattress, bouncing twice.

She rolled to her belly to crawl away, just as a new condom landed right in front of her nose.

Lemon yellow. In spite of herself, her entire body tightened in anticipation.

"But first," he said silkily, holding her down with a hand low on her spine. "Back to that critique of your performance."

"No, I—"

"I'm not sure what you've been told before," he went on, unconcerned with the fact that she'd gone stiff and unhappy. "So we'll start at the beginning."

No way was she going to stick around for this. Surging up to her hands and knees to crawl away, she said through her teeth, "I told you, I changed my mind—"

Snagging her ankle, he held on with a grip she couldn't shake off, though she tried with the sudden strength of a samurai warrior.

He merely caught her other ankle and slowly dragged her back across the mattress, with her fighting the whole way. Kicking didn't help; he had a hold on her that didn't allow for it, though she gave it her best.

"Oh, go ahead and play dirty," he said conversationally, not even winded, the bastard. "I'm used to fighting dirty."

Gripping onto the covers gave her no traction at all as she was hauled closer and closer to her greatest source of stress. "Damn it, Cooper. Let me go—"

He simply yanked her the last few inches, then flipped her over, switching his grip from her ankles to her thighs, effortlessly holding her down, leaning over her to see directly into her face.

If he laughed, she swore to herself, she was going to kick his balls into next week.

He wasn't laughing.

Instead, he was looking down at her with a softened expression of tenderness that froze her limbs and sucked the breath out of her lungs, making her throat so damn tight she couldn't even swallow.

"Breanne," he said very gently.

"Don't." Somehow she managed to swallow the ball of emotion lodged in her throat, though it burned like fire. "*Don't.*" Though it was silly, she tossed an arm up over her eyes.

He simply reached up and pulled it away from her face, that much closer now, kissing first one cheek, then the other. Then her jaw, nuzzling the spot just beneath. "You are the sexiest, most amazing woman I've ever met," he said. "There is nothing wrong with you, nothing at all, except . . ."

She kept her eyes tightly closed. "Except . . . ?"

"Except that I missed a few spots the first time. I need to make sure I've thoroughly researched each area before giving you my full opinion."

She heard the rip of the condom packet and opened her eyes.

"Look at you," he murmured, staring down at her. "So sexy, so amazing. We're going to make love again, Bree, just so I can prove it to you. And then again, if need be. No task is too much for the cause—"

"Cooper—"

"Right here, babe." He slipped into her body, fitting like he'd been made just for her. "Feel me?"

Was he kidding? With his hands cupping her face, his body buried within hers, she could feel nothing *but* him. "I feel you." Closing her eyes, she escaped a little bit that way, a desperate attempt to bring this back to the purely physical act. And what a physical act it was.

Decimated from their lovemaking, Cooper watched Breanne sleep. A new experience. With Annie, he'd always gone home afterwards, to his own bed. With any others, he'd always run off before the condom even cooled.

Never in his life had he felt like *sleeping* with someone, as in actually closing his eyes and drifting off. Sleep was a personal thing, something one did alone.

Like jacking off.

But he didn't feel like sleeping by himself. Truthfully, he didn't feel like sleeping at all. He just wanted to hold her and look at her. Christ, he'd turned into such a sap.

Breanne hadn't gone easily into slumber. She'd tossed and turned until he'd hauled her back against him, her spine and butt snug to his chest and crotch—a very nice position because it left him a free hand to caress. Now he pressed his face into the crook of her neck to inhale her intoxicating scent, and rubbed his thumb over her nipple.

In sleep she reacted, the tip hardening.

He wanted to wake her up.

But he knew how exhausted she was, mostly from stress, so instead, he kissed her shoulder and listened to her breathe, with no idea what he was doing, because this sure didn't feel like a quick little ski bunny sort of thing.

It didn't feel like a quick little anything.

He wondered if it was still snowing, if they'd indeed be able to shovel out tomorrow and get into town. Then there was the matter of the dead body.

Even as he thought it, from far, far below, somewhere in the house, came a very soft thud.

Cooper's hackles rose. It was past midnight. Past the hour that Shelly would be making noise in the kitchen, or Dante would be doing whatever it was he did.

Maybe it was Lariana and Patrick with their habit of screwing in every room of the house. He didn't know, but there would be no relaxing now until he made sure. He slipped out of the bed.

Breanne rolled to her belly, spread-eagle, hogging all the space and the blankets, which made him grin. "Be right back," he whispered, but she didn't move.

He slipped into his Levi's, stuck his gun in the waistband, grabbed the flashlight he'd commandeered, and headed out.

The hallway was pitch black. He flicked on the flashlight, which didn't help much, but he knew his way by now. The noise had come from somewhere downstairs; he knew this, though as he searched, he found nothing in the great room, the kitchen, or the dining room.

Nothing anywhere.

He was halfway back to his bed and Breanne when he remembered.

Edward.

Swearing, he whipped around, making his way to the servants' quarters. The doors there were all shut, and silent. So was the cellar door. But the strand of his own hair he'd carefully draped across the jamb had fallen.

Someone had been in here.

Alert, he let himself in, shining the light down the stairs. "Hello?"

No one answered, but then again he hadn't expected anyone to advertise the fact that they'd gone against his command to stay out of there.

Edward was beginning to smell bad.

Bending down, Cooper tried not to inhale as he looked over

the body. Because of the cellar's icy temps, decomposition had begun slowly, but it had begun. "Your bruises are surfacing," he murmured, especially the long, dark bruise now accompanying the gash on the forehead. There was another bruise just below the Adam's apple. Cooper knew if he unbuttoned Edward's shirt, he'd see another across his chest.

The lines of the stairs, where he'd hit them face-first.

"Were you pushed?" he wondered out loud. "Or was it a terrible accident?"

And who'd moved him from the bottom of the stairs to his current spot?

And how had he gotten the hole in his damn chest?

Questions he really had no right to ask, but the cop in him just wouldn't let it rest. With a sigh, he rose, looking around.

There was no clue as to who'd come in here, or why, but at least the body didn't appear to have been moved.

He thought of Breanne asleep in the honeymoon suite, trusting him to keep her safe. He wasn't exactly sure when it had happened, but he trusted her, too.

Almost as unnerving as the dead body at his feet. "Hang tight, Edward," he said, and made his way back upstairs, to the warm woman waiting there for him.

Okay, so she wasn't waiting so much as snoring lightly into his pillow.

But he'd take that.

He'd take her.

She let out a soft "Mmm" when he slipped back into the bed, sleepily moving into his arms. "Cooper?" she whispered groggily.

Who the hell did she *think* it was? "Yeah," he said, tucking her beneath him, making himself at home between her thighs. "Me."

And then he set out to show her . . .

Twenty-two

Life is like a boner: long and hard.
—Breanne Mooreland's Journal Entry

The next morning—Cooper's second in the middle of his so-called vacation—was a mixed blessing for him. He'd slept all night with an incredibly hot, sexy woman, and nothing beat that.

But unfortunately, it was still dumping snow. And by dumping, he meant huge, fat snowman-sized flakes that accumulated in a blink of an eye. Not a good day for going outside, but it was a great day for being in bed with that hot, sexy woman. They had a whole basket of condoms left, in some extremely inventive colors and flavors.

But he was alone in the bed.

Damn bad luck for him.

He rolled off the mattress and stepped on an empty, lime-green condom packet.

And then a wily watermelon one.

Yeah, he thought with a grin . . . last night had been something. To his delight, Breanne had turned out to be a sensual, earthy, passionate lover. He couldn't believe she'd doubted herself. Kissing, licking, touching every single one of those doubts away had been his pleasure.

There'd be no more nights, though. Today they'd shovel out, then ride a snowmobile for help.

And go their separate ways, just as she wished.

Telling himself he was good with that, he hit the shower, then made his way down the stairs, noting there was still no electricity.

Dante appeared out of nowhere, dressed in black, oversized jeans and a football jersey, hat low on his head. "If you're hungry," he said, "Shelly's put together what she can for breakfast."

"Still no generator?"

Dante lifted a shoulder. "Patrick's on it."

"He's been on it a long time."

"To tell you the truth, Patrick's not all that great at his job."

Gee, Cooper thought, there's a news flash. "Then why does the owner keep him?"

"The owner doesn't know. Patrick was hired by Edward."

"And Edward never noticed that Patrick the fix-it guy isn't any good at fixing stuff?"

Dante lifted his shoulder again.

"Come on, Dante. By all accounts, Edward was a tough boss. Why would he keep Patrick on here?"

"Edward's sister made him hire Patrick," Dante admitted.

"Why?"

"Because she's Patrick's mom."

Yesterday, when a very dead Edward had been discovered, Patrick had had little reaction. *No* reaction, actually.

And yet Edward had been Patrick's *uncle?* An uncle who'd given him a livelihood? "How does Patrick feel about his uncle's death?"

"Why don't you ask him?"

"Did Edward give Patrick as hard a time as he did the women?"

"Yes."

"Sounds like the guy had some management issues."

Dante let out a hard laugh.

"And maybe some social issues."

"If you mean he was an asshole, you're dead-on." Dante's gaze never wavered. "No pun intended."

"We need to get him out of here," Cooper said. "You knew that. We need to get through to town."

"The generator—"

"Forget the generator. I saw the snowmobiles. If we all put in some effort, we can dig out. Two of us can ride until we get reception, or into town to report Edward's death."

Dante just looked at him.

"It has to be reported sooner or later," Cooper said.

"That's not what I'm hesitating over," Dante said.

"Then what?"

"The shoveling-out part."

"How hard can it be?"

Dante shook his head. "Spoken like someone who's never had to spend hours digging out his car. That snow is some heavy shit, man."

"Don't you have a snowblower?"

"Sure. But Patrick was a bonehead and left it under the eaves of the shed, which has unloaded about two tons of snow onto it since the storm began. That should take all day alone to shovel out—if it's not crushed, that is."

"You're exaggerating."

"You think so?" Dante's smile was grim. "I'll be happy to prove a cop wrong."

Cooper sighed. "I don't know what your beef is with cops, but—"

"Just go eat," Dante said. "Then we'll start."

"We'll get Patrick to help, too."

Dante nodded. "Sure. But just so you know, he's not much better at shoveling than he is at fixing stuff."

"Great." Cooper started to walk away, then turned back. "Hey, did you stay up late last night?"

Dante's expression closed. "Why?"

"I heard something, around midnight. Just wondering if you heard it, too."

Dante slowly shook his head. "Didn't hear a thing." With that, he turned and vanished.

Cooper stood there watching, thinking . . . *but I never told you what I heard.*

The lack of electricity wasn't nearly as disconcerting in the light of day—even though that light of day was so muted as to be nearly inconsequential. Cooper passed the foyer and stopped short. A huge mountain of snow stood in front of the open door.

Then the mountain began to move, turning into the outline of a man as he shook the snow off like a great big dog.

Powdery white flakes flew through the foyer, landing on every surface, including Cooper. That wasn't what sucked the air from Cooper's lungs, though; the shocking wind whipping through the open door did that.

"Bloody hell." Patrick looked around at the mess he'd just made. "Lariana will be killing me for this." Undeterred by the prospect, he stomped his feet, and more snow fell off him. He wore some sort of head-to-toe snowsuit, which still had snow stuck to every inch, his ever-present tool belt rattling as he stomped. "Sticky shit," he said conversationally in his Scottish brogue.

Cooper shivered. It had to be close to zero degrees. "Any luck with anything out there?"

Patrick shook his shaggy head regretfully as he shut the door, closing out the unbelievably bitter cold. "The generator is a no-go. The thing needs to be replaced. We actually have one on order but this storm came early. Didn't expect to be needing it so soon." With a rather absent smile, he walked past Cooper.

"Patrick?"

Lifting a hand to remove his beanie, which left his red hair standing up on end, the fix-it guy glanced back.

"Did you hear anything odd last night around midnight?"

"Not a thing, mate. But this place is haunted."

"Haunted?"

"By Edward's ghost." He said this utterly without a flicker of emotion one way or the other.

"I'm sorry about Edward, Patrick."

"Don't be."

"He was your uncle."

"He was a sorry excuse for a man." Then he turned on his heel and clinked off.

Cooper walked to the doorway and thunked his head on the wall.

"Is that like snapping your heels together three times and saying 'There's no place like home, there's no place like home?'"

Cooper lifted his head. Shelly stood there, watching him with a curious smile. Wearing whitewashed jeans rolled up to the top of her Ugg boots and a forest-green sweater with a small apron over the top of it, she looked like a melodious, euphoric little thing.

"There are whole days where I feel like bashing my head against a wall, too," she confided, and reached up to give him a little pat on the shoulder. "But not on an empty stomach."

"You look happy."

"I like it when there's guests here."

How about when there's a dead body? "I hope we're going to dig out today. You up for lending a hand?"

"Sure." She pushed up her sweater and flexed her arms. "I work out. You don't think it's easy lifting huge pots full of stew or chili, do you? I'm a snow-shoveling machine."

He felt her biceps and found rock-hard strength. "You *are* pretty solid."

Solid enough to have moved a dead body?

"Come into the dining room and get some food," she said.

Having burned every spare calorie worshipping Breanne's body all night long, his belly twitched hopefully.

"Oh! Breanne said to give you this." Shelly reached into her apron and pulled out a small piece of paper, folded in some complicated way that took him a minute to open. *Meet me in the theater room. B.*

"A love note?" Shelly asked.

He stuck the paper in his pocket. "Not quite. Where's the theater room?"

"Down the hall, right past the library, then left." She looked up into his face, suddenly serious. "She's a real sweetheart—you know that, right? Because she's been hurt, being stood up at the altar like that, I don't want to see anything else happen to her, especially out here where she feels alone and so vulnerable."

"Nothing's going to happen to her."

"You slept with her last night." She cringed. "I know, none of my business. Just . . . just be good to her."

And with that demand, she left him alone.

Cooper sighed—good thing so many people were worried about *him*—and left to find the theater room. Turns out he couldn't miss it with the two rows of luxurious red velvet seating, the huge screen, and last but definitely not least, the elaborate system on the right that rivaled any theater he'd ever been to.

But the room, however swank and sophisticated, was empty.

"Breanne?" His tennis shoes sank into the plush carpeting as he came to a halt just in front of a large sliding door on his right. The door slid open and a hand shot out, fisting on the front of his shirt, yanking him inside.

He smelled her just as the door slid shut again, that sexy combination of shampoo and woman, and because it was

Breanne, he let her accost him. "All you had to do was ask," he murmured, lowering his mouth as he slid his arms around her.

"Mmm," she said at the kiss, and then again as she touched her tongue to his.

Oh, yeah. Now *this* was the way to start a day. Pressing her back against something—he couldn't see a damn thing—he dove into the kiss as a few things fell down over the top of them. Probably DVDs. He didn't know, didn't care, as long as he had this woman and her body against his.

After they were both breathless, she pulled back, and at a small click, light surrounded them from the small lantern she'd turned on. They were in a closet, surrounded by shelves filled with DVDs, videos, and various electronic games. On the floor littered around their feet were the movies they'd knocked down.

And in front of him, gorgeously disheveled, stood Breanne, her mouth still wet from his.

She stared at his mouth as well, looking more than a little . . . flummoxed.

He knew the feeling, as he was currently bowled over himself, with the wanting of her; a wanting he was coming slowly to realize couldn't be sated by lust or even common sense.

She wore her own jeans today, and that pink, fuzzy sweater he'd first seen her in. It crisscrossed over her breasts and had a tie just beneath them. He itched to yank on it and unravel her.

"You came to me," she said, as if surprised.

He'd have thought they'd gotten past that, but if she needed reassurance, he could give it to her. His hands went to her hips and he brought her back against him, lowering his head, nuzzling her throat. "Soon as I got the note. I was hoping we'd still be in bed, but you vanished on me."

When he touched his tongue to her skin, she shivered, but put her hands to his shoulders and pushed back to look into his eyes. "Really?"

"Yeah, really." Leaning back in, he took a little bite out of her tasty skin, loving the way she trembled. "We could be having a great time right this very minute. Naked."

Her hands tightened on his shoulders, her fingers digging into him as his mouth cruised over her. "Is that . . . right?"

"Mmm-hmm." Letting out a slow exhale in her ear, he smiled when she shivered again. "I could be tasting you from head to toe. I'd start here—" He took a little nip out of her shoulder.

"That sounds . . . nice," she said, sounding as if she was having trouble getting air into her lungs.

"Nice?" He let out a choking laugh. "Trust me, it would have been a helluva lot better than *nice*."

She looked so intrigued he wrapped a finger around the pink angora tie beneath her breasts and tugged.

But she put her finger on the bow, preventing it from slipping out of its knot. "That's the only thing holding the sweater on."

"Is it?" He tugged again.

She held onto the bow. "Want to know a secret?"

"If it involves being naked."

"I've always had this closet fantasy . . ." She whispered this softly, as if she found the suggestion almost too naughty to bear.

But nothing was too naughty for Cooper, and though he'd been hard since she first yanked him in here, his jeans got even tighter.

"But if you'd rather go back to the bedroom—"

"No, let's stay in your fantasy." Taking her hands, he brought them down to her sides, urging them to grasp onto the shelf at her hips.

Both excitement and nervousness filled her eyes, but she held the shelf and let him pull on the string of her sweater until it popped free.

The sweater sagged in front where it was crisscrossed. A little nudge with his finger and it fell open, exposing a siren-red lace number that shot him from zero to sixty in one second flat.

"It's my other honeymoon number," she said softly. "It was my only fresh underwear."

He realized it was a one-piece, and the thought of following the lace all the way down between her legs made his mouth go dry. "It's amazing," he managed to say, tracing the edging between her breasts, watching her nipples react, poking through the material.

Letting go of the shelf, she slipped her hands beneath his shirt and laid them on his belly, making him suck in a harsh breath.

"What?"

"Cold hands," he whispered, tugging her sweater to her elbows.

With a breathless huff of laughter, she danced those cold fingers up his chest, then back down. "I love your body," she said, as if imparting another state secret. Her sweater was at her elbows, one narrow strap of her red lace off a creamy shoulder. "Especially your stomach." She stroked his abs. "Do you like to be touched like this?"

"More than breathing."

Again she laughed; then, holding his shirt up, she flicked her tongue over his nipple, making him thunk his head back against a rack of VHS tapes.

Stopping the exquisite torture, she glanced at him, then slowly sank to her knees.

His heart jerked hard. So did the rest of him, one part in particular.

"I, um, was wondering," she whispered as she set her mouth to his quivering abs. She kissed his belly button, then lower, at the edge of his jeans. "If you'd like it if I kissed the rest of you."

He undid his jeans so fast his head spun. "Kiss away," he said hoarsely.

At the first feel of her lips in the opened wedge of his jeans, he jerked again.

"Shh," she murmured with a seductive, knowing smile, enjoying finally being the one to shush *him*. Her hands fisted in the waistband of the denim. Slowly she pulled.

He moaned, and she smiled against his skin; then, in a move that made him yelp with surprise, she sank her teeth into his hip.

His reaction made her lose it. "I'm sorry," she gasped, sitting back on her heels, covering her mouth. "I don't know why, but I had to do that. I couldn't help myself." She went to lean forward again, leading with her mouth, but he stopped her.

"You got that biting thing out of your system, right?" he asked warily.

Her eyes were lit with humor and heat. An amazingly sexy combination. "Promise." Her hands brushed his away, then slid back into his jeans.

"You liked this," she murmured, stroking the length of him.

"It's pretty much a given I'm going to like anything you do to me."

"Sure?" She stroked him again, letting out a sexy little hum while doing it. Then she licked her lips.

Oh, man. He had to close his eyes. "So damn sure—*Jesus*."

She'd taken her hot, wet tongue on a happy tour. Gripping the shelves behind him for dear life, he did his best not to humiliate himself, but her mouth . . . Unable to keep standing, he sank to his knees and reached for her jeans.

In the charged air was the sound of their heavy breathing and the rasp of her zipper. They stared at each other as he pulled the denim down.

A pink condom fell out of her pocket.

"I'm resourceful," she whispered.

"I *love* resourceful women," he whispered back, tugging her legs out from beneath her so he could strip her jeans to her thighs. Reaching between them, he toyed with the snaps of her teddy while she sucked in a breath. With one pull, all three snaps came free.

"Now," she whispered.

"Yeah, now." But her jeans caught on her boots. They spent another breathless moment fighting their clothes, laughing like idiots, and finally, finally, she was in his lap facing him, her thighs opened and draped over his.

By the time she helped him roll on the condom, he was trembling and already on the edge. "Slow," he said, hands to her hips, lifting her up, guiding himself inside her.

"Fast," she corrected, then let out a gorgeous sound of helpless desire when he thrust up.

"Yes," she said fiercely, rocking her hips.

He'd wanted to take his time with her, draw it out, lose the both of them in the moment, but she didn't let that happen— she *never* let that happen. She wanted the kick and she wanted it now.

And buried so deeply within her that he could feel her heart beating in his ears, or maybe that was his own, he was in no position to slow them down. In a last desperate move, he gripped her oscillating hips. "Keep that up, and it's going to be over before we even get started."

"We started already. God, Cooper, I love to watch you lose it."

Just the words nearly accomplished that, and he tried to adjust his slippery grip on her hips. But she kept moving them, arching, rocking. Sweat beaded on his forehead. "Bree—"

"More," she panted. "God, please. More."

Ah, hell, he was a goner. All he could do was hold on and meet her thrust for thrust, closing his eyes to savor her clutching heat, quivering as he fought the orgasm building like a bus barreling down the highway. But he couldn't keep his eyes closed; he wanted to see her. Her head had fallen back, her skin gleaming. "Breanne."

Lifting her head, she opened her eyes, too, adding an unexpected intimacy Cooper hadn't expected. It hit him like a one-two punch. Her gaze was clear and open, allowing him to see more of her than she'd ever allowed him. *Trusting.*

His throat tightened. "Bree—God. I'm going to—"

"I know—" Her voice was tight. Strangled. "Me, too—" That was all she managed to get out as she exploded in a series of shudders that milked his own climax out of him. Vaguely he heard her cry out his name, and thought . . . *love the sound of that*, before the roaring of his own blood in his ears overtook all rational brain activity.

When it was over, they slumped together, breathing like misused racehorses. Breanne stirred, lifted her head from his shoulder. Her hair had rioted, sticking to her damp face, but her victorious smile said it all. "That was very . . . *nice*," she said mischievously, using the word he'd objected to. "Yes, *nice* just about covers it."

In answer, he lightly slapped her on the bare ass, making her laugh and hug him so tight he could hardly breathe.

But breathing was overrated, anyway, and he hugged her back. "Let's get the hell out of here and back into that suite so I can start all over again and do it right."

"No can do." She stood on wobbly legs. "We have to dig out."

Oh, yeah. They were getting out today. Going their separate ways, which she wanted.

He wanted that, too.

He just couldn't remember why.

Twenty-three

You have the right to remain silent. Anything you say can and will be misquoted and used against you.
          —Breanne Mooreland's Journal Entry

Breanne stood up in the theater closet, and, much to Cooper's consternation, began to look around for her clothes. "I really didn't write that note just so we could . . . Well." She laughed a little as she bent over at the waist to snap her teddy back into place.

Cooper's body twitched. Down, boy.

She shrugged the straps of her teddy back on her shoulders, then reached for the sweater. "You sidetracked me."

Watching her toss back her hair, he thought about side-tracking her again. And again. "Who sidetracked who?"

She smiled but it didn't quite meet her eyes, and then she turned away entirely to work on her jeans.

Uh-oh. Taking her arm, he pulled her back around to face him. "What's wrong?"

She shimmied her jeans up her hips. "You mean besides my life being a shambles? Besides being stranded here, hearing mysterious humming that no one else does, and oh, yeah . . . finding a dead body?"

"Yeah." He tucked a loose strand of hair behind her ears. "Besides all that."

She stared at him for a long moment, her eyes dark and un-readable. "Nothing."

He nodded, started to let it, and her, go, because really, what did it matter? But it *did* matter. At least to him, he was discovering, and he pulled her around again. "Did you know you wrinkle your nose when you lie?"

"Do not."

He touched the tip of her wrinkling nose. "Do so."

She clapped her hand over her nose and made a disparaging sound. "You can't know that about me—you don't know me."

Contemplating her, he pulled up his own jeans. "I might not know every little thing yet, but I'm getting a pretty good start."

"No," she said with a denying shake of her head, her eyes unhappy. "You aren't. You can't be. Don't be."

"Too late. Want to hear what I know already?"

"No—"

"You tend to jump into things heart first—"

"I'm changing that."

"You're sweet when you're tipsy—"

"I wasn't *that* tipsy that first night—"

"I know that you hate the dark and spiders, that you have a thing for incredibly sexy lingerie—"

"Circumstantial."

He curled his hand around the back of her neck, stroking his thumb over the soft, sweet spot of her nape. "I know that you're intelligent, funny, and incredibly passionate. You care about others, sometimes too much, and you care about me. None of that is circumstantial."

"It's too early to care."

"Yeah? Then why did you come to me last night?"

"I was scared."

"I didn't see you crawling into bed with Dante, Patrick, Lariana, or Shelly."

In a telltale gesture, she looked away. "So I care too early. Another fault."

"I think you also trust me, at least a little."

"*Trust* is a bad word, Cooper."

"Doesn't have to be."

"Maybe you missed some of my background," she said. "Three failed engagements, remember?"

"I can't help but remember. You wield them around like a shield."

"*Three* engagements," she repeated. "That's a helluva lot of wielding. A lot of failures."

Which was what was getting to her, he guessed. "You didn't have your heart in at least two of those engagements, Bree. I think you *wanted* to, you *meant* to, but you didn't, not really." He kept his hands on her hips when she would have turned away. "I know that first one messed with your head, but not every serious relationship ends in pain. I promise you."

She let out a soft breath. "I don't know."

"But I do. Getting engaged was a way to make a great showing. You could hide behind it, holding back all you want, especially with the particular men you picked."

"I don't follow you."

Yes, you do. "You picked men who weren't going to love you, not the way you want to be loved."

She stared up at him.

He stroked her silky hair. "Am I close?"

"No." But she swallowed hard. "*No.*"

"I'm different, Bree. What we could have is different."

"It's a chemical attraction. Period."

It was so much more than that, but she was standing there, arms tight around herself, breathing a little ragged, her poor bruised heart in her eyes, and he found he couldn't tell her. It was something she had to see herself.

Unfortunately for him, she wouldn't see it, because willing as she was to share her body, she wasn't willing to share much else. She shied away from true intimacy, and apparently that bothered him more than he would have thought possible.

"I'm still trying to wrap my mind around the fact that this

was supposed to be my honeymoon," she said, closing her eyes. "I didn't count on meeting you, Cooper."

"Yeah, well, you weren't on my calendar, either. But I'm glad it happened."

This brought a ghost of a smile to her lips. "I wanted to talk to you about Edward."

He sighed. From lovers to spies.

"They were all afraid of him."

"I know."

"I think he was rough."

"Physically?" he asked.

"I don't know, but he yelled at them. A lot."

"Even Dante and Patrick?"

"Patrick, yes," she said. "Lariana said he totally demeaned him at every turn, and he only put up with it because—"

"Because they're related."

"Yes." She sounded surprised. "How did you know?"

"Dante told me that much. What else?"

"Patrick has trouble keeping jobs. He's sweet and kind, but not all that great at what he does. Apparently he really wants to be an artist, but he needs the money from this job. He's a painter. That's how he and Lariana got together—she bought one of his paintings as a gift for her father. Shelly said that Patrick was late for work the morning before we got here because he'd been up all night painting, and he and Edward had a terrible fight about it."

"A physical fight?"

"I don't know."

"Did Shelly tell you what Edward yelled at her for that morning?" Cooper asked.

"No. That she didn't mention."

"I can picture Edward yelling at the women," Cooper said. "Possibly even Patrick. But Dante?"

"Supposedly none of them escaped the wrath."

He shook his head. "The problem is, I just can't see Dante standing for it, job or no job."

"And you know what else I can't see," Breanne said slowly, "is Dante standing idly by while Edward treated either of those women badly."

"Me, either."

She tipped her head up to his. "So what does all this mean?"

It meant that there were too many motives, and too many suspects. It meant there were going to be lots and lots of questions once the authorities got here. It meant unpleasant times ahead for all of them. Exhausted at the thought, he leaned back against the door and sighed. "We need to round everyone up and start digging."

"It's still snowing."

"I know, but we should do it now, while we have lots of daylight hours left. I don't know how long it'll take to reach town."

"You really think someone can get that far on the snowmobile without a problem?"

"I'm counting on it," he said grimly.

"Yeah." She let her arms fall to her sides and stepped close. Reaching up, she touched his face, her fingers warm now. Her touch was so unexpected and sweet, he closed his eyes to savor it.

"I'm glad we happened, too," she whispered, making him open his eyes again in surprise.

For her, it was equal to a shouted declaration of her feelings, and he felt his chest tighten, more so when she set her head against his shoulder and let him hold her.

"There's two snowmobiles," she said. "Who's going?"

"Hopefully, Dante and me. I think he'd be more capable than Patrick if we got stuck out there."

She slowly fisted her fingers in his shirt, staring at them as she said, "I dreamed about you."

"Yeah?" His hands squeezed her hips. "Tell me."

"I was running through the dark hallways here. Something was chasing me." She frowned. "Or someone."

"You should have woken me up."

"You had me wrapped up in your arms tight and snug, and I knew I was safe."

"You are safe."

She'd been watching her fingers move in little circles on his chest, but now she lifted her gaze to his, and he could see her uncertainty, her fear. "Once you leave on that snowmobile, no one left here is safe."

"Bree." He sank his fingers into her hair, leaning in, but just as his mouth touched hers, the doors slid open.

Lariana stood there with a DVD in hand, staring at them.

"Whoops," she said, and handed them the case. "Just found this and wanted to put it back. Uh . . . carry on." With a smile, she slid the door shut again.

Breanne winced. She knew the staff was probably used to such indiscretions, but she sure wasn't. "Well, that was . . . awkward."

Cooper just lifted an *oh, well* shoulder. His shirt was wrinkled, from her. His hair stood up on end. Also from her. And he was wearing one of those after-sex expressions that there was no hiding. He looked thoroughly debauched, and so rough-and-tumble sexy that she wanted him all over again.

Oh God, she wanted him all over again.

But that had to stop. Sex was sex, and they'd just had it. The end. But wow, he was potent. And something else . . . with Cooper, it never felt like just sex.

At her nod, he slid open the door, and together they stepped out.

"I'm starving," she admitted. "I need something before digging."

He followed her down the maze of hallways to the kitchen. At least she was no longer getting lost. She figured if she didn't get lost, she couldn't find another dead body.

In the kitchen, she beelined directly to the refrigerator.

Cooper grabbed a glass from a cupboard and moved to the sink for water. Hands wet, he looked around for a towel, then finally opened the door beneath the sink. "You need to drink, too," he said. "Before you get dehydrated—"

When he broke off so suddenly, Breanne turned from the drawers to look at him.

He was hunkered before the open cupboard, mouth tight, body tense. Absolutely still.

"Cooper?"

Turning only his head, he looked at her from eyes that were no longer lit with sexual prowess or good humor, but flat with concentration.

A cop's eyes.

"What is it?" she whispered.

"Beneath the bathroom sink in the foyer there's a brand new pair of rubber gloves, still in their packaging. I saw them yesterday when Lariana was in there cleaning. Can you go get them for me?"

She was so startled by the odd request, not to mention his cool, calm but utterly badass expression, she simply nodded and turned on her heels to do just that.

She encountered no one in the hallway on the way there or back, and when she re-entered the kitchen, Cooper was no longer by the sink.

"Here," he said from behind her, startling her into a gasp as she whirled to face him, a hand to her chest as he took the gloves from her. "What—"

His finger went to her lips. Then he pulled a chair in front of the double doors, so no one could come in on them unannounced.

She could only stare into his extremely tense face. "What's going on?"

He looked at her for a long moment, and she knew she wasn't going to like it. "Cooper, you're scaring me."

"Not as much as this is going to." He put an arm around her shoulders and walked her toward the kitchen sink. "Take a deep breath, but don't scream. Promise me you're not going to scream."

"Okay." She gulped in a deep breath, then crouched down with him and looked beneath the sink. At the towel shoved behind the pile, covered in something dried a brownish color. They both stared at it for the longest moment of Breanne's life.

"Fuck," Cooper finally said on a sigh.

Yeah. Her thoughts exactly.

Twenty-four

I suppose the word "calm" would lose its meaning if it wasn't sandwiched between moments of terror.
                    —Breanne Mooreland's Journal Entry

"Gee, that's funny," Breanne heard herself say. "It almost looks like a bloody towel."

Cooper didn't say a word, just began to put on the rubber gloves.

"Shelly probably cut herself chopping vegetables," she said through the roaring in her ears. "You should see how fast she chops. And then she probably shoved the towel down there and forgot about it. Probably."

Cooper flicked on his flashlight and stuck his head in the cupboard, carefully not touching the towel but trying to see around it.

"Or it could be ketchup," she said inanely, her mouth running away with her thoughts. "Maybe she spilled ketchup. That could have happened, right?"

Cooper pulled his head back out of the cupboard and looked at her. "Are you breathing? Because you don't look like you're breathing."

"Oh." She gulped in a few breaths and tried a smile, which quickly wobbled. That's not ketchup, is it?"

Cooper slowly shook his head.

"Something really bad happened here."

"Something," he agreed. He turned off the flashlight and

shut the cupboard door. Then he removed the rubber gloves
and reached for her hand.

"What are we going to do?" she whispered.

"Shovel. Shovel like hell."

They'd found the towel.
That was bad. They shouldn't have found the towel.
What would happen now?
If only it would stop snowing. If only they could all get out, get
away from here.
If only, if only, if only . . .

For Breanne, getting outside felt like a culture shock, not to
mention an actual physical punch to the chest. Her poor lungs
weren't adapted to the altitude, much less this biting cold.

At least inside the house, though sometimes equally icy,
she'd been in somewhat of a cocoon. There she could see the
snow, but had been distanced from it by the huge, frosted windows, buffered by the warm fires.

But standing on the front porch, the ramifications of their
situation, with the storm still dumping more precipitation
every passing minute, hit her hard. Twelve feet of snow had
fallen, setting records, shutting down airports and businesses,
closing roads, breaking electrical and phone lines.

The Sierra mountain range, spanning some two million acres
of national forests and wilderness land, had come to a screech-
ing halt.

Terrific time to almost honeymoon.

Way out on the outskirts of civilization as they were, this
unbelievable storm was apparently accepted as a part of the
life here. People were prepared for it with extra food, water,
and gasoline for their generators and snowblowers. They'd become an independent entity.

Everything had taken on a whole new meaning these past
few days, and it wouldn't have been a problem but for two

things. One, the occupants of *this* particular house weren't as prepared as they should have been, and two—and this was the biggie, in Breanne's opinion—*there was a dead body.*

Dead bodies changed everything.

No longer did the house feel cute and quaint—if it ever had. And getting out of here, storm of the century or not, had become a requirement. She stood wrapped in a borrowed stadium-length down coat, a leftover from some forgotten guest. She also had on one of Dante's beanies, and wool socks courtesy of Patrick.

Ever so helpful, her staff.

Huddled in her borrowed gear, she let out a breath that crystallized in front of her face as she took in the scene.

White as far as the eye could see.

And more white.

From here, the humongous mountain peaks that surrounded them in a three-hundred-and-sixty-degree vista looked innocuous and breathtaking. The flakes fell with an odd gentleness, and utterly silently, stacking on top of the banks of snow that had already fallen, piling up against the house, against the shed, against the garage, so that the three-story log-cabin house appeared to be only a little more than one.

Thanks to the lack of electricity, the house itself was dark. No sparkling lights shining from the windows, no scent of cooking food, nothing but a rather disconcerting hollowness that made it seem lifeless. There was four feet of snow on the roofs despite the fact that they'd unloaded themselves at least twice, leaving huge drifts stacked alongside of each structure, some more than eight feet high, making it impossible to get close to the shed or the garage until they moved the snow.

There were two power lines along the driveway, coated in white and sagging nearly to the ground. The trees were completely covered, and swaying from the weight as if alive. Four of the pines in the front yard had split or collapsed under the tremendous weight of the snow, and would undoubtedly have to be removed. The windows on the north side of the shed had shattered inward.

And still the snow came.

They all shoveled. Or rather, Dante, Patrick, and Cooper shoveled, while Breanne, Shelly, and Lariana watched. Mostly because there were only three shovels, but also because it was damn hard work, and Breanne for one wasn't very good at hard work.

"Look at that sky," Shelly breathed.

Lariana and Breanne both looked up. In San Francisco, Breanne had rarely ever noticed the horizon. In fact, the last time she'd looked up at all had been on one of her first dates with Dean, when he'd taken her to the roof of his building to show her the summer constellations.

What he'd really wanted to do was impress her, and then get into her pants. Damn it, she *had* been impressed, but she hadn't let him into her pants.

Not that night, anyway.

The point was, though, she wasn't an anal person, or rushed for time on a daily basis, and still, she'd never really spent much time sky-gazing.

Leaning back now, she staggered back a step, found her balance, and stood there in awe as the flakes fell onto her face, cool to her heated skin. It was like an explosion in a mattress factory the way the white flakes, not round, not any particular shape, really, drifted down from the sky like fluffy pieces of cotton in no particular hurry.

Cotton that sure piled up into not-so-innocent drifts that needed to be moved.

By them.

"It's making my mascara run," Lariana said. "I'm going in."

Watching the guys work, Shelly nodded. "Me, too, but wow, look at 'em. They're all . . ."

"Hot," Lariana agreed. "Very, very hot. But even the hottest of the hotties is not worth freezing to death. Let's go."

Breanne stayed behind. The cold temperature speared right

through her but the guys were sweating. Dante wore a black sweatshirt nearly coated over in snow now. Patrick wore his Abominable Snowman outfit. He wasn't as effective a shoveler as Dante, taking smaller shovelfuls and half the time dumping the contents in his own way, swearing with gleeful abandon as he did.

Cooper moved with a steady, easy precision that made it look extremely easy. He wore the blue sweatshirt he'd given Breanne that first night, now also crusted over with snow, but he didn't appear to notice as he labored. Breanne felt entranced watching him, mesmerized by the way his body worked as if poetry in motion. He was like that in bed, too. She figured he was like that in everything he set his mind to, and for a moment, her mind wandered.

What would it be like to see him outside of here, in the real world? Before the answer could come to her, Shelly came back out with bottles of water for the guys.

Breanne looked at the shovel Cooper leaned against a post. Feeling extremely aware of his gaze as he drank, she lifted the shovel. Wow. All by itself, the thing was heavy. But he was watching her, so she dug in, filling the bucket, then attempting to lift it.

It didn't budge.

Okay, no problem. She tipped half of the snow off. That worked.

By the third shovelful, she was panting. By the fourth, she couldn't lift it one more time.

A big hand closed over hers. She raised her gaze to Cooper's. "I'll get it," he said.

She could see the exhaustion in his face. "I'm sorry," she murmured. "I wish you didn't have to do this."

"You feel bad?"

"Very."

That seemed to perk him up. "Enough to make it up to me?"

She had to laugh at the teasing light in his eyes, but as he turned back to work, her smile faded. Because she found she *did* want to make it up to him. She wanted to do that, and more.

A lot more.

Breanne went inside to get more bottles of water. Shelly would have gone but Breanne insisted, needing a moment alone. In the kitchen, she set the tray on the counter and loaded more water bottles onto it. As she did, her eyes strayed to the cupboard beneath the sink.

Was the towel still there?

Heart in her throat, she nudged the door open with her toe. Yep, bloody towel still in place.

Her stomach lurched sickly, and she considered staggering weakly back to a chair but heard something behind her.

She spun around fast enough to get dizzy but realized the sound had come from beneath her.

Beneath her.

Whirling back, she peeked out the kitchen window. Dante, Patrick, Cooper, and Lariana were there. Shelly, too.

Everyone was outside.

Every single person.

At least every single *alive* person.

Oh God, don't go there. This wasn't the movies. There had to be a perfectly good explanation for that noise, and she was going to find out what. Yes, she was. She grabbed a flashlight, and on second thought, another knife from the butcher block.

Just in case.

Just in case what, she had no idea.

The hallway to the servants' quarters was going to give her nightmares for the rest of her natural-born days. Halfway down it, her heart was pounding so hard and fast she couldn't have heard a tornado ripping through over the sound of her own pulse drumming in her ears. She actually had to stop and breathe for a moment to be able to hear at all.

Nothing but silence greeted her, and then . . . a faint thud.

It'd come from behind the one locked bedroom door, naturally. Forget evening out her pulse now—the best she could do was gulp in a breath. She knocked once. "Hello?"
Nothing, though she imagined she heard panicky breathing. On *both* sides of the door. "Anyone in there?" She knocked again and told herself she was fine. Nothing could happen to her; she held a butcher's knife, for God's sake.
No one answered. Of course not, because the only one down here was Edward, and his answering days were long over. Turning, she peeked into the room where Lariana had been sleeping. Neat and tidy as a pin.
The bedroom next to it—Dante's, she could tell by the beanie on the foot of the bed—wasn't nearly as neat. He hadn't made his bed, and he had yesterday's clothes on the floor.
But from under the bed peeked out a hand.
Oh God.
In some kind of trance, her feet took her inside the room, and then to the mattress, knowing if she found another body she was going to truly start screaming and never stop. Cringing, she bent down, then let out a short, rough breath as she realized the truth. Not a hand, but a glove. A rubber kitchen glove stained with the same dark brown stuff that was on the towel upstairs beneath the sink. Desperately she wanted to believe what she'd told Cooper, that she was looking at dried ketchup, but she knew better, and had to shove a fist against her mouth.
And then she heard the one sound she hadn't wanted to hear. *Footsteps.* Wildly, she looked around her. No time to get out; oh God, no time to do anything but flatten herself to the floor and scoot beneath the bed, which she managed just as someone came into the room.
Two black boots and two white Keds. *Two* someones.
"We only have a few minutes," Dante said, sounding out of breath. "The cop is determined to get out of here."
"I know. I'm sorry." *Shelly.* "Dante, I lied to you."

Breanne, already frozen in place beneath the bed, stiffened in shock. *No, Shelly.*

"Tell me." Dante's voice was low and gruff, and yet infinitely gentle. "It's okay, just tell me."

"Oh no, it's not what you think!" Shelly rushed to say. "I meant I lied just now, upstairs, about having to talk to you. Because really what I wanted was . . ."

"You wanted what?"

The two Keds shifted until they were toe-to-toe with the black boots. Breanne didn't dare move but the gloves, the bloody gloves, were too close. *They were really beginning to get to her.*

"It's all so complicated," Shelly whispered.

Yeah, yeah, it's complicated, Breanne thought, trying not to look at the gloves right at her cheek. *Get back to shoveling!*

Then the unmistakable sound of a wet kiss floated down and Breanne scrunched up her eyes. Surely they weren't going to—*No.* Not here, not now—

"I know you said you wanted to wait until we got out of here," Shelly said breathlessly. "But everyone's outside and will be for a while. Haven't we waited long enough?"

"Shelly—" Dante broke off with a low groan. "God, Shelly, don't do that."

Helluva time for Shelly to find her sexuality, thought Breanne.

The mattress sank as the two lovebirds fell upon it, and Breanne wished for a large hole to open up and swallow her.

"Oh, Dante," Shelly whispered.

Dante whispered something back in his native tongue.

Breanne resisted thunking her head on the ground. She made the mistake of opening her eyes then, focusing in on the bloody gloves before slamming her eyes shut again and doing the only thing she could—stick her fingers in her ears and silently sing at the top of her lungs. *Lalalalalalalalala.*

"Oh!" Shelly cried out louder than Breanne's silent singing. "Oh, Dante."

Something fell to the floor. Shelly's sweater.

Her jeans came next.

Breanne shifted from singing to pretending she was on a beach. In the Bahamas. It was hot there, and cute cabana boys were bringing her drinks. Nice, big *alcoholic* drinks—

Something else hit the floor. Dante's shoes.

Then his jeans and sweatshirt. And his beanie.

Then his BVDs.

And finally, an empty condom packet.

Oh, good God.

The springs began to squeak as the mattress began moving in earnest.

"Dante—" Shelly cried. "That's—do that again. Please do that again!"

Squeak, squeak, squeak.

Breanne tried not to look at the bloody gloves. Instead she studied her fingernails. Oh, look at that. She needed a manicure.

"Yes, yes, *YES!*" cried Shelly.

Breanne decided she was going to need a vacation to recover from her vacation.

Scratch that.

She was never going to vacation again.

Finally the bed stopped moving, and there were more kissy-face noises and soft murmurs.

Breanne had long ago left the Bahamas and moved to the moon when four feet—bare now—hit the floor.

It took forever for them to dress—laughing and kissing— but finally, finally, they were gone. Breanne didn't know what she'd have done if they'd stuck around for round two. One time had been bad enough—*what was it with this house?*

She eyed the gloves. She needed Cooper to see them, needed anyone other than her to see them. Touching evidence was bad, she knew this. But . . . what if someone moved them before she could show Cooper? Not wanting to take that chance, she slipped them beneath her top, then cringed—

gross!—before sliding out from beneath the bed. She got to her feet, carefully not looking at the mattress. Sheesh. Tossing back her hair, she turned to the door.

And came face-to-face with Dante, who barely arched a brow—his only concession to his surprise at finding her here.

"I, um . . ." She hugged herself, hopefully hiding the bulge of the gloves beneath her shirt. "This is really a very funny story."

He leaned back against the doorway, blocking her way out, waiting for her to go on.

Oh boy. He had that scary face on, the one that assured her much of the ghetto still lived within him. "I heard a noise down here, and I thought it was Shelly—"

At that, he smiled all the way to his eyes. "You just missed her. She's back upstairs."

Oh, my God, was it possible he hadn't seen her coming out from beneath his bed? "Oh. Okay, well, then I'll just—"

Go tell Cooper you had bloody gloves beneath your bed.

"Sorry," he said, still smiling. "I'm just realizing something."

"What's that?" she asked bravely. *Please don't say you're wanting to kill me, too. Please—*

"—I'm in love with her." He sighed and shook his head, rubbing the spot over his heart. "Imagine that."

Yeah, imagine that. "Well, that's . . . sweet. But I've got to—" She gestured to the doorway and, miracle of all miracles, he didn't kill her, but moved aside for her.

With a last smile that was shaky to the core, Breanne scooted past him. It took every ounce of control she had not to run, run like hell, but she controlled herself until she was out of sight. Then she couldn't hold back any longer and she burst into a full gait, looking back over her shoulder—

Only to plow directly into someone.

Before she could open her lips to scream, a hand settled over her mouth and she was yanked into a dark room and held against a hard, warm body.

Twenty-five

The right lover is like a good bra: supportive, close to the heart, and damned hard to find.
            —Breanne Mooreland's Journal Entry

Cooper held a struggling Breanne against him. "Hey. Hey, it's me," he said in her ear as she fought him like a wildcat. "Breanne, it's me."

"Oh, my God." Snaking her arms around his neck, she burrowed in close, as if she wanted to climb inside him.

He stroked his hands up and down her back, trying to soothe her. "What happened?"

When she didn't answer, he reached into his back pocket and grabbed the flashlight, running it over her to make sure she wasn't hurt.

"I'm okay." But she gulped in air like water, clearly making an effort to get hold of herself. Pale, still shaking, she looked around them, saw they were in the workout room, and said, "I'm really tired of this house."

He had a feeling that was a huge understatement.

"I want noise," she said. "Airplanes. People yelling. I want a traffic jam on the bridge, *anything* but this quiet mountain, you know? Anything but more spiders and bloody gloves, and—"

"Bloody gloves?" Cupping her face, shocked at how icy cold she was, he looked into her still-glossy eyes. "What bloody gloves?"

"These." She reached under her shirt and pulled out a pair of cotton garden gloves, light blue with white trim, and stained with what could have been blood.

She shivered wildly and thrust them at him. "I can't believe I had those against my skin. *God.* I need a shower." She pulled her shirt away from her chest. "Now."

Gingerly holding the gloves by just his thumb and forefinger so as not to further contaminate them, he snagged her arm when she moved to the door. "Where did you get these?"

"I heard a noise that I thought came from the cellar, but you guys were all outside, so I—"

"Damn it, Breanne. Don't tell me you went to investigate."

"I, um . . ." She winced. "Took a knife with me."

He groaned.

"But I left it under Dante's bed because—"

"Dante's bed?"

"Yeah, I was stuck there while he and Shelly were bouncing it so hard I thought I was going to be squished like a pancake, and—"

"Whoa. Wait." He shook his head. "Start at the beginning."

"I can't." She was pulling at her sweater. "I need to scrub first." Shoving free, she ran out of the workout room and into the hallway, moving with remarkable speed through the house, up the stairs, as if she wanted to lose him.

Not going to happen.

At the honeymoon suite, she stepped inside, then tried to close the door behind her, nearly catching his nose in it.

"Maybe I wasn't clear," she said, her breath hitching. "I'm showering. By myself."

She hadn't gotten her color back, nor her breath. Her eyes sheened with emotion and much more. If he wasn't mistaken, she was an inch from losing it completely. "Thought you might like some company," he said.

"In the shower? Gee, what a shock."

"Breanne."

"So you don't want to see me wet and naked?"

"Well, yes, but that's because you look great wet and naked. Right now, however, I just want to make sure you're okay."

She hadn't taken her gaze off the evidence in his hands so he shut the suite doors, hit the lock, then very carefully set down the gloves.

She stared at them and then shivered again.

"Go shower," he said gently. "I'll wait in here."

She nodded, then covered her mouth with a hand. "I think I'm going to throw up. I really, really don't want you to see me do that."

"You're not going to be sick." But just in case, he slid an arm around her waist and nudged her toward the bathroom. There, he leaned her against the counter. "Keep breathing."

"I'm trying."

"Good." He opened the shower, flicking on the hot water; when he turned back to her, she was still concentrating on breathing. "Okay?" he asked.

"I'm peachy. Really. Just peachy."

Steam was rising from the shower, fogging the mirror and glass. "Come on, get in."

Nodding, her hands went to her sweater. She pulled on the tassel, let the material slip off her shoulders. She unzipped her jeans and shimmied out of them, doing a little dance on first one foot, then the other as she stripped down to her birthday suit.

A personal favorite of his, but he didn't say a word, just opened the shower for her.

She stepped to the door. One of her breasts brushed the sleeve of his shirt, the nipple puckering into a hard knot. "Get in," he said again, his voice a little thicker.

Nodding, she stepped in; then, before he could shut the door, she fisted her hand in his shirt, yanking him in with her. "I don't want to be alone," she said. "Distract me, Cooper, like only you can."

Water rained down over his head, soaking into his clothes, dropping off his nose. "Breanne, I—"

His words were cut off by her mouth. Pressing him up against the wall, she tugged his shirt up, leaning in to kiss him right over his heart. "Please?"

She wanted fast, hard, casual sex. She wanted to disengage her brain, if only for a few minutes. He got that.

But he wanted more than mindless when it came to the two of them. And yet, as always when faced with her gorgeous nude body, he couldn't hold back. He shucked out of his shirt while she tugged his jeans to his thighs. "Good enough," she said, and hopped up.

He just managed to catch her, all slippery and wet, and when she wrapped her legs around his hips, arching the hottest, slickest part of her to the hottest, neediest part of him, he staggered back against the wall and groaned. "I don't have a condom in here."

She bit his neck. "Are you safe?"

He had two handfuls of her perfect bottom, her breasts mashed against his chest. He had a hard-on that could pound nails, snugged up to her sex, which was hot and creamy. His mind was befuddled, to say the least. "Huh?"

"Because I'm safe." She attached her mouth to his neck and sucked, making his vision swim. "And I'm on the pill."

"Me, too," he managed to say as she arched up and let the very tip of him slip inside. Christ, she felt good. "I mean, I'm not on the pill," he corrected as she snorted. "But I'm safe—"

Her rough, breathless laugh was cut off with a low moan as he thrust into her.

Bare skin to glorious bare skin, Breanne thought, and for her, what happened next was as wild and unpredictable as the storm outside. She felt a blinding need, a desperate ache that had to be assuaged. There was more, too; it was as if she had a hole deep inside her that only he could fill, but she didn't want to go there, not now. Later, when she was safe and back home, she could dwell; later she could relive all that had happened, even what she'd lost, but for now she'd live in the moment.

And the moment was about this. She fisted her hands in Cooper's hair and took his mouth in greedy, hungry bites, while the hot water continued to rain down over them. "Hurry, hurry, hurry."

"Always a five alarm fire with you," he murmured.

"*Please,*" she heard herself whimper.

"We can hurry," he assured her. "But I'm not going anywhere." He cupped her face until her eyes met his. "Do you hear me? I'm not going anywhere, Bree. I'm here, right here."

Her throat closed up, and she couldn't speak.

He didn't seem to mind. Instead, he held her still, buried deep within her, and gave her a kiss as gentle, as tender as any kiss she'd ever known, a kiss that brought her to a new level of desire that boggled her mind.

And still he hadn't moved within her. God, she wanted him to move. She slid her fingers into his hair, along his scalp until his head fell back. Pressing her mouth to his throat, she tried to make sense of this but then he lifted his head again, his eyes glowing with heat and need and an infinite, selfless patience she was afraid she'd never understand.

"Breanne," he said—just that, just her name through the falling water. With a strength that seemed effortless, he turned them, pressing her back to the wall, opening her thighs even further. "Hold on," he murmured hoarsely in her ear. "Hold onto me. Yeah, like that." And he began a series of bone-melting strokes—slow, lengthy withdrawals and returns that she wanted to last forever and ever. But she had her limits, and Cooper was one of them. Within a few moments she began to fall apart at the seams.

He thrust a little higher, a little harder, his hands keeping her right where he wanted her. Pinned, she could do nothing but hold on for dear life, panting, blinking away the water, the steam. Nothing about any of this with him made any sense, not the depth of her wanting of him, or how it was that she hadn't gotten enough of him.

That maybe she never would.

But she didn't want it to stop.

"Christ, I can feel you," he groaned, able to talk while she could only pant. "It's like you're milking me. You're going to come."

And with a surprised cry, she did.

While she was still shuddering, she somehow managed to keep her eyes open on his, and saw his face darken, his jaw go tight enough to tic, watched his eyes go blind, even as he struggled to keep them open on hers.

He was showing her everything, every single emotion as it hit him, as he came with a gravelly groan torn from deep in his throat. This is trust, she realized as he trembled. *Naked trust.* Just the thought triggered another orgasm within her, and through the kaleidoscope of sensations, she thought maybe he murmured her name, but she was drowning in the pleasure and couldn't be sure.

Slowly she came back to herself, blinking away the water, realizing that he'd slapped a hand on the wall behind them, quivering as he struggled to keep them upright. Still clinging to him, she suddenly felt oddly close to tears. Not wanting him to see, she tried to pull free.

With what seemed like great reluctance, he let her legs slide down his body. "You okay?"

Chest tight, she only nodded. She was so far beyond okay.

He smiled, but looked a little shaky himself. "That was . . ." Words seemed to fail him.

She turned away to get a grip on her reckless emotions. "Yeah. Good shower sex." She grimaced at her own coarse choice of words. Grabbing a towel, she tossed it to him, hitting him in the face.

He pulled it down. "So . . . do you get a lot of shower sex?"

"No," she admitted. "You?"

"Yeah, but usually I'm alone."

She laughed. Damn, he was something, always able to pull her out of a funk. "You expect me to believe that a guy who looks like you, and has a sexy job like you do, has to have sex alone in the shower?"

"I'm not exactly a chick magnet. And as for that so-called 'sexy job'? You know I nearly let it suck the soul right out of me. I think with some distance I've got it figured out, but the truth is, my love life's a barren wasteland. Or was, until I met you."

She shook her head. "I'm just trying to picture a healthy, red-blooded, innately sensual guy like yourself going for a long time without sex."

"Yeah, well. I'm hoping the dry spell is behind me."

That clammed her up because she wasn't sure how to respond. The thought of jumping into another relationship made her stomach clench. She wasn't going to let herself fall for this man, but having to remind herself felt a bit like putting the lock on the chicken hatch after the chickens had escaped.

Fact was, she'd leapt feet first into many relationships, and none of them, not a single one, had made her feel like she felt with Cooper—like she was on a roller-coaster ride going too fast, like she was going to throw up, like . . . like she was alive—really, truly, vibrantly, thrillingly alive.

Oh boy.

He hadn't done anything with the towel she'd tossed him. Completely comfortable in his own skin, he stood there naked. Actually, he wasn't just standing there, he was coming toward her, then stroking a long, wet strand of hair behind her ear. "You're looking pretty relaxed."

"Funny how an orgasm does that."

"Yeah." He didn't look nearly as relaxed. "Funny."

Don't ask, she told herself. Don't. But this was Cooper, and for some reason, she couldn't turn away. "What's the matter?"

"That rejuvenated you, having wild shower sex."

"It would have rejuvenated anyone."

"Really? So why do I feel more frustrated now than before?"

Not wanting to face the answer to that, she shrugged and began to dry off.

But he waited her out, standing in the doorway when she would have breezed on out. "Why did you cry at the end?"

Her gaze whipped up to his. "I didn't."

"You did."

Embarrassed, she looked away. "I don't know."

"Is it because you're not used to feeling as much as you did?"

Hammer on the nail. "It's just that . . ." Oh, the hell with it. "I really liked it," she admitted in a whisper.

"I know." This was accompanied by a grin. "I was there."

She stared at his chest, trying to find the right words. "I want to say something that's going to sound weird." Lifting her head, she met his gaze. "You're nice to me."

"You're easy to be nice to."

He always knew what to say

"I came here to clear my head." Lifting a shoulder, he shot her a crooked smile. "I thought maybe I'd meet a few snow bunnies, have a great time."

"I can put on a ski hat if that would please you."

"Only if that's all you put on."

She snorted at that, and got a fleeting smile from him.

"I thought being here," he said, "that I'd feel better about walking away from my work. My life."

Her flippancy vanished in the face of his quiet pain. "Oh, Cooper."

"I thought I'd go home with the answers in my head of what I want to do with myself."

"Do you have them?" she asked. "The answers?"

"Not a one that you'd want to hear."

Her heart skipped a beat, and she went very still. "What does that mean?"

He sighed, ran his hands through his wet hair. The muscles and tendons stood out in bold relief with his arms lifted, and her belly quivered. When she was around him, everything within her quivered.

She wanted him. Still. *Again.*

"Remember when we talked about love?" he asked. "You said you didn't believe in it."

"I remember," she said tightly.

"Well, I do. I believe in it, Breanne. I want it."

Oh, God.

"All the time I thought it was my job screwing with my head. And in some ways, it was." He came close again. "But I can move out of vice and not have to go under for months at a time. I can work regular shifts patrolling, or even going the detective route, and still have a life. I want a life, Breanne. And in that life, I want—"

"Don't," she said, setting her fingers to his lips. "Don't say it."

"You."

"Oh, my God."

He just looked at her.

Her throat tightened, her eyes burned. And her heart, God, her heart. It took one big tumble. "It's only been a day."

Reaching up, he pulled her fingers from his mouth, keeping her hand in his. "It's been three, and those were pretty accelerated, intense days."

"But it takes years to get to know someone," she said, sounding desperate.

"I'm game."

She stared at him. *He was game.* "I wrote 'no more men' in my journal. You saw it. It's in stone."

"There's always *Delete.*"

If only she could really erase some of her mistakes. "It's my path."

"Rewrite the path." He smiled. "That's the beauty of electronics."

She swallowed hard. "You sure seem to have a lot of answers."

"You do, too."

She rubbed her temples and wished that were true. "I'm hungry. *Starving.*"

"No, you're scared and you have to think," he said. But then he stepped back and finally began to dry off that mouthwatering body. "It's okay. You go eat. You go do what you have to do."

Yeah, she would. Like a chicken, she took her out and moved to the door. There she glanced back. "Probably in the real world we'd have nothing in common."

"Date me and find out."

"Date?" After what they'd done, dating seemed so . . . tame. "Men say they want to be with me," she said softly. "But they lie."

"I don't. You know that by now."

She shook her head. "Cooper. I don't know what to do with you."

A small smile touched his lips. "Yeah, you do. You just haven't faced it yet."

Keep him. That's what her heart wanted to do. Take this thing where it might go.

But her brain was saying—*are you kidding? Run like hell.*

Since she'd decided never to trust her heart again, she went with her brain, and ran like hell.

Twenty-six

If a man is talking in the woods, and there is no woman there to hear him, is he still wrong?
—Breanne Mooreland's Journal Entry

Breanne stepped out of the suite, then turned back and stared at the door. She let out a slow breath. Cooper turned her upside down and inside out, and when she was with him she didn't know whether she was coming or going.

Mostly coming, she admitted.

Her legs wobbled at the thought. They'd had some damn amazing sex. She'd never been with anyone who could take her right out of herself and then put her back, making her feel like a new woman, a *better* one. When she was with him, she didn't have self-doubts. She didn't wonder what he thought of her. She didn't do anything but be herself.

And he seemed to like that woman. A heady experience.

At the bottom of the stairs, Dante appeared right out of the woodwork, and still dizzy with thoughts of Cooper, she nearly fell over. "How do you do that?" she demanded.

A ghost of a smile touched his lips. "I'd tell you, but then I'd have to kill you."

He was just kidding. Probably.

"Bad joke," he said.

"Really bad." She put a hand to her chest, wondering if the butler had a side career going—murdering obnoxious managers and equally obnoxious guests.

Shelly came up behind Dante and smiled. "Hey. You okay?"

Breanne nodded at her new friend. And Shelly *had* become a friend. She wouldn't fall for a man who could—who would— No. No, she wouldn't.

But how to explain the bloody gloves beneath Dante's bed? Or the bloody towel in Shelly's kitchen? "I just thought I'd try to get something to eat."

"No problem," Shelly said. "I'll bring you something to the great room? Or maybe the library? Where will you be?"

Breanne didn't feel comfortable going anywhere alone— she was afraid of what else she'd find. Before she could work up a good panic over that thought, Cooper came down the stairs and stood at her side, settling a big, warm hand on the small of her spine.

Such a small gesture, really, and yet . . . yet it meant so much.

"What's the snow situation?" Cooper asked Dante.

"We're about halfway. We could be out in a few more hours."

"Just in time for nightfall," Cooper said, sounding resigned.

Dante nodded.

"Could you find your way to town in the dark?" Cooper asked him.

"It'd be a suicide run. Frigid temps, bears . . ."

"Bears?" Breanne didn't like the sound of this. "I don't want anyone to be out there with the bears."

"And believe me, no one wants to be," Dante told her, the big, tough guy letting out a shiver.

"If we kept moving—" Cooper started.

"I'd rather walk the streets of my gang-infested childhood than snowmobile through the woods tonight."

Cooper sighed. "So we all stay another night."

"Another night," Dante agreed.

Shelly bit her lower lip, and Dante set his hand on her shoulder. "It's going to be okay," he said.

Cooper nodded.

Breanne only hoped they were right.

Everyone met in the great room and snacked on whatever Shelly was able to drum up. Stranded as they were, the lines between staff and guest and wrongly booked guest had blurred.

Or maybe that was because of the unintentional bonding that had occurred when they'd all found themselves staring at a dead body.

Breanne didn't know, but she liked having everyone in the same place, where she knew that no one was off getting . . . well, offed.

Despite the relaxation of duties, in some ways, their positions here in the house still very much defined them. Shelly rushed to serve everyone. Dante handled the fire. Lariana kept straightening things up in the already perfectly straightened room. Patrick didn't do much, but he kept his tool belt on and creaked when he walked.

"We really need a new generator," he said to no one in particular.

"Maybe it's operator error," Dante suggested.

"Bugger off."

Dante laughed. "Come on. We all know you hate being the fix-it guy. The wicked witch is dead, dude. Do something else now."

"Like . . . ?"

"Like what really gets you going," Dante said, as if this was the easiest thing in the world to decide. "How about your painting stuff?"

Patrick looked over at Lariana, who smiled. "Told ya," she said softly. "Do it, Patrick. Go for your dreams. Show your paintings."

"It was you," Cooper said to Patrick. "You painted that saw blade. The one that went up the day we found Edward."

"I hung it," Lariana said. "Patrick didn't want me to, but I think the guests that come here would love to see what he can do. Sunshine doesn't have any galleries because it's not a touristy type of place, but just a little bit south of here, closer to Lake Tahoe, there are tons of shops all around the lake where he could show his work. *Should* show it."

Patrick lifted a shoulder. "Maybe."

"You're good, Patrick," Shelly told him. "And your idea of painting on antique tools is unique. You really should go for it."

Patrick clinked his way to the fire, hunkering before it to jam the poker into the red-hot coals, stirring up the fire with a bit more strength than necessary.

"He's dead, Patrick," Lariana said to his ramrod-straight spine. "No more worrying."

"Worrying about what?" Cooper asked.

No one answered.

"Come on." Cooper looked at them. "You're going to hold back now?"

Shelly and Lariana gave each other a long look.

Patrick stabbed at the fire again, making sparks leap and jump.

Dante remained broodingly silent.

Cooper shook his head in disgust.

"You know what?" Shelly surged to her feet. "It's late. And I'm really tired." She didn't look at any of them as she moved to the door. " 'Night."

Lariana shot Dante a worried look, then started to follow, but Dante stopped her. "I'll go," he murmured.

Lariana nodded, then pulled him in for a hug. When he was gone, she said, "It *is* late, and we're all overtired. Patrick?"

Seeming surprised to be so publicly summoned, he jerked

to his feet and moved to the door with her, looking for all the world like an eager puppy.

"Call if you need anything," Lariana said to Breanne and Cooper.

When it was just the two of them, Cooper looked at the empty doorway. "That was fun." He stood up and held out a hand to Breanne. "Come on. There's even more fun to be had."

Her heart stopped. Parts tingled. "What kind of fun?"

"Everyone's going to sleep. Everyone but us."

The thought of "us" made her stomach sort of tremble, but not in a bad way. Oh God, she was getting used to the word *us*.

When had *that* happened?

Everything had been so simple a week ago. Sure, she'd been in an engagement that had been just a joke, but she'd had no major losses. No big disappointment—Well, maybe a few.

But she could have lived with them, because she'd never seen a dead body, she'd never lived in a haunted house, she'd never feared for her very life.

Now she knew what all those things felt like, as well as true, gut-wrenching fear for another person she truly cared about. Maybe staying one more night wasn't the end of the world. She could use it to show him how much she cared.

"We're going searching for the BB gun," Cooper said.

"We are?"

His gaze swiveled to hers. "You sound disappointed. What did you think we were going to do?"

"Nothing."

He ran a finger over the groove in her forehead. "You are such a liar. You were thinking about getting naked and losing some brain cells."

"Losing brain cells?"

He reached for her hand, the gesture sweet and tender.

"Every time I get you naked, I lose brain cells. Hell, you don't even have to be naked for that to happen." He pulled her in for a tight hug. "I want more of this, Bree. When we're out of here, I want more of you."

Now her heart, all warm and cushy—*and locked up tight*—quivered. "Cooper—"

"Don't panic." He stroked a hand down her back, then pulled free.

Thank God.

"Let's go exploring."

In the dark. Damn it, she didn't know which was worse, facing her feelings for Cooper, or exploring this dark, haunted house.

He pulled out a flashlight. "I noticed Patrick did some extra digging," he said as they entered the garage through the foyer door. The large, cavernous room was icy and eerily silent. "I want to know why." With that, he let go of her hand and moved away.

Breanne bit back her pathetic whimper, gasping when Cooper lifted the garage door manually, rolling it up a few feet. "What are you doing?"

"With no power, it's the only way to open it. Come here."

Into the dark night. Into the snow. "My boots are finally dry—"

He vanished beneath the door.

"Damn it," she muttered, and hurried to the door. Taking a deep breath, she ducked beneath it.

The darkness felt different outside; colder, deeper, all-consuming, with no walls as boundaries. Nothing but trees and mountains she couldn't even see. And bears. Let's not forget the bears.

Cooper had trudged past a buried vehicle—"Mine," he tossed back—and through the snow to another parked about fifteen feet away. A truck, she saw, when his light flickered over it.

He was peeking in the windows with the flashlight. "Bingo."

She eyed the still-falling snow and sighed, then stepped out from beneath the protective edges of the eaves. They'd shoveled here, so she didn't sink much more than a few inches into the new stuff. Buoyed by that, she grinned at him as she came up to the car. "Made it."

He didn't smile back.

"What?" she asked, hers fading.

"Hold this." He handed her the flashlight. Then he pulled the sleeve over his hand before opening the door of the truck. "No fingerprints," he whispered. "Light the backseat for me."

She lifted the light and stepped closer, her boot heel catching on an icy patch. The next thing she knew, her feet slid out from beneath her and she was down, the flashlight bouncing twice before going out.

In the dark above her, Cooper sighed at the loss. "You okay? Anything broken?"

"Just my butt, and possibly my pride."

In the pitch darkness, a hand slipped beneath her elbow and lifted her up. Another hand slid over the butt in question. "Feels good to me. Your pride'll heal, too."

"But the flashlight won't."

"No." The disconcerting darkness reigned, and that eerie, utter silence of the woods all around them.

Except for the very distant call of a coyote.

Breanne shifted closer to Cooper, hating the weakness, but hating even more the thought of facing a wild animal out here.

"Did you see?" he asked quietly. "Before you slipped?"

"I saw," she said, and hugged herself. "I saw the BB gun in the backseat. Oh, my God, Cooper. This is insane. Bloody towels, bloody gloves. Edward's shoe . . . *What does it all mean?*"

"I don't know."

Blind as a bat and disoriented with it, she shivered. Cooper pulled her closer. "Come on," he said, and nudged her around toward the house. "Back inside."

"It's just as cold in there."

"I'll warm you up."

"It's also just as dark in there."

"I'll be your light."

She managed to find a laugh. "That was hopelessly corny."

"Yeah," he said in disgust. "I'm not that great at romance."

Breanne set her head on his capable, sturdy shoulder as he led her inside. "I think you're better at this than you think you are."

Breanne woke at the crack of dawn and opened one eye. She was sprawled facedown over most of the bed with all of the covers.

There was a big, warm hand on her butt.

Lifting her head, she turned and found Cooper on his side, head propped on his hand, watching her.

"Hey," she said.

"Hey, back." Leaning in, he kissed her. "Time to rise and shine, Princess. Today is the day we get the hell out of Dodge."

Sounded good.

And yet . . . She looked into his see-all blue eyes and pictured her life back home. Searching for a new job. A new place to live. Seeing her friends and family.

Would Cooper really be interested in that life? He'd said so.

Could she trust him enough to believe it?

"I can see the wheels spinning," he said. "Want to share?"

She looked at him, trying to find the words to express her fears, her worry, but none came. "It's nothing."

If he was disappointed, he didn't let it show. He just kissed her, then rolled out of bed and took his fantastic body into the bathroom.

Breanne stretched, rolling to her back, eyeing her Palm

Pilot, which was on the nightstand. She reached for it, figuring she had a new entry to make, something along the lines of enjoying the moment because that moment was about to be over.

Only there was already an entry for today. It read: **Keep Cooper.**

Keep Cooper? "What does that mean?" she murmured out loud.

"Just that," Cooper said from the bathroom doorway, one hand propping up the jamb. "Or better yet . . ." He pushed away and came closer. Naked. "Take a chance on me."

"Cooper." Her heart lodged in her throat.

"Come on, Bree. I'm falling hard here. Fall with me."

Lodged in her throat and swelled. "It's not that simple."

"Why not?"

"Because I'm bad at it." She let out a low laugh, inviting him to laugh with her, but he didn't. He wasn't kidding. "You know my track record," she said. "I fail at these things, with a regularity you could take to a bookie and make millions."

"If you never try, you've failed before you've begun."

"I *have* tried."

"No, you went through the motions, but you've never really put yourself out there. Not like you did with me."

"Cooper." Words failed. She shook her head. "You scare me, you know that? All the way to the bone."

"You either want to see me outside of here, or you don't."

"This is about more than that, and you know it," she said. "We already know we're sexually compatible. Now you're asking me if it can be more."

"Why can't it?" he asked. "I like you. You like me. Let's take it where it goes."

"But how will we know if it's right? How will we ever know?"

With a shrug, he pulled on his jeans as if they were discussing the weather. "You just do."

"You're telling me *you* know?"

"Yeah. I do."

For some reason, that made her mad. She shoved back the covers and got out of bed. Stalked toward him. Poked a finger in his chest. "Well, maybe it's not that easy for me."

"Why not?"

His eyes were clear and full of things that took her breath. She knew he had a slow and easy smile, somehow both so sweet and sexy that she always felt like smiling back when he flashed it at her. She knew how he made her feel with just a look, which was so damn special she always felt as if she could take on the world.

"Why not?" he asked again, softly, giving her one of those looks now.

"When you look at me like that," she whispered, "I lose my place."

"So start at the beginning," he whispered back. "And tell me again why this can't work."

"Besides the fact that we're so different?"

"Yeah, besides that."

"Besides the fact that neither of us is currently employed?"

"Sounds to me like a great time for a change."

"Damn."

"Is that 'Damn, you're right'?" he asked. "Or 'Damn, he's lost his mind'?"

She just shook her head, frozen to the spot.

His smile congealed a bit but he slowly nodded. "I'll tell you what. I'm going to go start digging."

"What am I supposed to do?"

"I don't know. You could sit here and keep letting life pass you by."

"Hey, I don't let life pass me by! In fact, that's the problem. I jump at things without thinking them through."

No longer quite so calm, he shoved his arms into a T-shirt

and pulled it on. Inside out. Swearing, he ripped it off and righted it. "You get a jump on ignoring this thing between us, Breanne." He grabbed a fleece sweatshirt. "Because I can't convince you that this would be a good decision, or that you're just afraid because deep down you know it's different, that what we have would be better than anything else you've ever done. That this is real and deep and yeah, scary as hell, but worth it. You go ahead and pretend you don't know any of that." His hair was sticking straight up as he jammed on his shoes. "And I'll get us out of here so you can rush back to that life you want so badly, where you can pretend you never met me, where you can pretend you didn't fall as hard and as fast as I did—"

"Cooper—"

"Don't." Whipping around, he pointed at her. "Don't even try to tell me I'm wrong."

She couldn't, she didn't have the breath, and when he'd left, quietly shutting the door behind him, she turned to the bed, looking at the rumpled sheets, remembering how much she'd shared with him right there in that spot. It'd only been a few nights, and yet she'd shared more with him than she had with any other man.

How had that happened?

And what did it mean?

Afraid she knew, she reached for her clothes. She'd just laced up her boots when she heard pounding feet. Going to the door, she opened it. Shelly was running toward the stairs. "Shelly?"

Shelly stopped. Turned back. Wearing a long, flowing, flowery skirt and a blue hoodie sweatshirt with the hood up, she smiled tentatively.

"What, you're taking fashion lessons from Dante now?" Breanne asked.

Shelly's smile went from anxious to nervous as she pulled

the hood off her head. Her hair wasn't neatly pulled in its usual ponytail, but wild and uncombed. Probably from another Dante romp.

"So where's the fire?" Breanne asked her.

"Fire?" Shelly's eyes went wide. "Oh, my gosh, there's a fire? *Fire!*" she screamed, and then went running.

"No, I was just—Shelly, come back! It was just an expression, there's no—Damn it." Breanne took off after her, moving down the stairs.

Daylight streamed in all the windows. It was the first time since she'd been here that she'd seen the place in full light, and she was blown away by the difference. Everything seemed warm and cozy, gorgeously simple, not gloom and doom. Above, the sky was a squinting azure blue, so big and bright as it shined through the skylights it almost hurt to look. At the bottom of the stairs, she could see through the foyer windows. Everyone was outside. Patrick and Cooper were bent over one snowmobile, its hood up. Dante was over the other one. Beside him was Lariana and . . . Shelly. She wore dark jeans and her fluffy white sweater that went to her knees, her hair up in a perfect ponytail.

No skirt. No sweatshirt. No wild hair.

Breanne turned and stared down the hallway past the kitchen, where she could still hear footsteps running away from her. "Shelly?" Feeling almost disembodied from reality, Breanne took one more look outside, then turned and headed down the hall. "Hello?"

"No one's here!"

That was Shelly's voice. Breanne would have sworn it, but Shelly was outside, she'd just seen her there. With goose bumps raised over every inch of her body, Breanne came to the kitchen.

Empty. "Hello?" she called out, half afraid to get an answer.

"I told you, no one's here! Don't you listen?"

The voice hadn't come from the kitchen. Breanne moved

out of there, past the dining room, which was also empty. "Where are you?"

"Go away!"

The voice came from the back, the hallway with the servants' rooms. It was darker here, but not as dark as it had been on previous visits. Uneasily, Breanne stared at the door to the cellar straight ahead, beyond which lay Edward's body. Then she turned and eyed the other four doors, all closed.

She could feel someone behind one of them. "Who are you?"

"I'm not telling," came the soft whisper. "I'm not supposed to tell."

Twenty-seven

Everybody wants to go to heaven, but nobody wants to die.
— Breanne Mooreland's Journal Entry

Breanne stood there in the middle of the servants' quarters, both confused and terrified. "Shelly?"

"You like Shelly. You're her friend."

The voice came from the left. Breanne took a step toward the two doors there. "Yes, I'm Shelly's friend. Who are you?"

"You're nice. You'll understand."

Door closest to the cellar door. The one that had been locked all this time. "Understand what?"

"What happened."

Breanne froze with her hand outstretched for the handle. "With Edward?"

Silence.

"Who are you?" Breanne asked.

More silence.

"Can't you tell me who you are?"

"I'm not supposed to."

Heart pounding, Breanne wrapped her fingers around the handle. "Why not?"

"Because I'm a secret," she whispered, sounding just like Shelly.

But it wasn't, Breanne knew that now. "A secret?" Damn, the door was still locked.

"I'm supposed to stay quiet and out of trouble while Shelly does her job."

Breanne stared at the wood. "You're Shelly's sister."

"Yes." A delighted giggle followed this, and then a click, and the door opened.

Shelly's face, and yet not. The eyes were slightly different, slightly slanted down. The mouth was fuller, softer. "I'm her twin." She grinned. "I'm special."

"I bet you are," Breanne said softly, her throat inexplicably tight. "What's your name?"

"Stacy."

"Stacy." Breanne smiled gently. "Shelly told me she had a sister. She said you are close. She loves you very much."

Stacy beamed. "I love her, too. That's why I'm real quiet. I was real quiet, wasn't I? You didn't even know it was me your first night here!"

The face she'd seen hovering over her, of course. "Yes, you were real quiet."

"I can't let Edward see me. He says I'm retarded, but I'm not. I'm not!"

Breanne's heart twisted. "That wasn't nice of him."

"He's not nice. He's mean. I used to help Shelly, until I broke a plate. He—" She frowned, then hugged herself, turning away.

A surge of hatred for the unknown Edward welled up. "Did he hurt you, Stacy?"

"I'm not supposed to talk about him." She hunched tighter into herself. "He doesn't like it. He told Shelly I couldn't come here with her anymore."

"So you hid."

Stacy didn't answer. Instead she began to hum very softly beneath her breath.

"Edward's gone now," Breanne said softly. "He can't yell at you. He can't hurt you."

"He's not gone!" Shelly tossed a fearful look over her

shoulder at the closed cellar door. "He's right in there. I've seen him!"

"Stacy, he's dead."

She blinked huge, hurt eyes at Breanne. "Are you sure?" she whispered.

At this moment, Breanne was sure of exactly nothing, except she had a fierce surge of protectiveness for this beautiful, sweet woman.

"See, you're not sure, either." Stacy covered her face. "That's why I did it. So he couldn't hit Shelly—"

Breanne went cold with fear, but not for herself. "Stacy, did you have something to do with Edward's death?"

But Stacy was no longer talking. Just humming and very slightly rocking back and forth.

"Stacy?" Breanne stroked Stacy's wild hair. "Can you tell me what you did? Something to protect your sister?"

Stacy kept humming, and rocked faster.

"Oh, Stacy."

"He always yelled," she said unhappily. "He scared me. I'm glad he's dead." She covered her face again. "Bad Stacy."

"*Stacy!*" This shocked cry came from Shelly, standing at the end of the hallway. She looked both horrified and terrified. "Oh, honey."

Behind her was Dante.

And then Cooper. "What's going on?" he asked, locking gazes with Breanne.

"Hi," Stacy said uneasily, shifting from foot to foot, swiping her hand across her mouth. "Hi."

Shelly rushed past Breanne to pull her sister in for a hug.

"I was quiet, like you said," Stacy told her, gripping Shelly tight. "I was."

"It's okay." Shelly looked tortured as she rocked her sister. "It's going to be okay."

Lariana crowded in, took a look. "What now—" When she saw Stacy out in the open, she sighed. "*Dios mio.*"

"I was telling on myself," Stacy told her.

"Oh, sweetie." Lariana pressed close and wrapped an arm around both Shelly and Stacy.

"Am I in trouble?" Stacy asked.

Shelly just hugged her tighter and closed her eyes, resting her cheek on Stacy's head. "You didn't do anything wrong." Still holding her sister, she looked into Breanne's eyes, silently begging her to believe it. "You didn't."

Cooper moved to Breanne's side. "You okay?" he murmured.

"Yeah, this is Stacy. Shelly's twin. She—"

"—Didn't do anything," Dante said, moving to join the fray, putting a hand on each twin, making a united front as he turned to face Cooper and Breanne. "I know what you're thinking, but it's not true."

"I'm not thinking anything," Cooper said.

"Like hell. You're a cop. Your mind is always spinning. But you're wrong."

"My mind might always be spinning but that doesn't make me a coldhearted bastard," Cooper said calmly. "And I'd have figured you knew that by now."

Lariana was stroking Stacy's hair, Shelly was still holding onto her, and Dante was guarding over the whole pack of them like the alpha wolf. The thought of them clinging to each other like a tight little unit, so brave and uncertain, broke Breanne's heart. "We're going to get out of here," she said. "And the proper authorities will—"

"Bullshit." Dante looked at Shelly, who was openly crying. Then he looked at Cooper. "*I* did it." He cleared his voice and said it louder. "I killed Edward."

Shelly gasped. "No. *Dante*—"

"Well, fuck me," Patrick said, joining the group. "First we play the nobody did it game, and now you're taking credit for the deed? Christ Jesus, why, when we all know it was me who done the bastard in?"

Lariana spun around and leveled furious eyes at him. "You'll not be taking the blame for this one."

"Oh, yes, I will."

"No." Lariana whirled back to Cooper. "*I* did it."

"Darling—"

"Don't *darling* me, you skinny Scottish ass!" she snapped at Patrick. "I killed Edward with my bare hands and I can prove it."

"Stop," Shelly whispered.

But Patrick looked ready to explode. "Don't do this," he said to Lariana. "Don't even think it."

Dante stepped forward. "Both of you shut up. I already said I killed him—"

"Stop," Shelly said again, louder now, but Patrick and Dante were toe-to-toe, looking ready to battle.

"Bugger off," Patrick told Dante.

"*STOP!*" Shelly yelled before Dante could respond. She was still wrapped around Stacy, who was staring at everyone, wide-eyed. She seemed confused at Shelly's tears, but solemnly lifted a finger and stroked one off her sister's cheek. "I love you, sissy."

"Oh, Stacy, honey, I love you, too. Remember that, okay? Promise me you'll remember that if I have to go away."

Dante whipped around and looked at Cooper with impotent rage and emotion shimmering brilliantly in his dark, dark eyes. "You want to prove yourself to us, cop? Fix this."

Cooper shoved a hand through his hair, leaving it standing straight up. "First up, everyone to the great room." He put a hand on Stacy, who was shivering. "By the fire. It's colder today than it's been—"

"That's because it's clear outside," Stacy said, and smiled.

When no one smiled back, hers faltered. "It gets colder when there's no clouds to keep the warm air low." She looked at everyone's face. "It does."

"Yes." Dante ruffled her hair. "You're right."

Her smile wobbled. "Am I in trouble?"

"No," Dante said, looking at Cooper. "You're not in trouble."

"Goody." She danced down the hallway. "I can go anywhere now, right? No more hiding?"

"Right," Patrick said. "You go on, we'll be right there."

"Don't stoke the fire by yourself," Shelly called. "Remember what happened last time."

"Yeah." Stacy bit her lip. "But the fire trucks came really fast."

Shelly let out a half-hysterical laugh, then covered her mouth, her eyes shiny. "Yes. They came fast."

"You go with her," Lariana said to Shelly. "Go ahead."

"You go, too," Patrick insisted, pushing Lariana after Shelly.

Lariana dug in her heels. "Look, you tall, skinny beanpole, I don't need anyone watching out after me."

"Sure, you don't. But maybe I be liking to watch after you."

Lariana opened her mouth, but he set a finger to her lips. "I love you, you bossy, infuriating, huffy woman. I love you, and I plan on loving you for the rest of me life, which will not be spent watching you waste away in a jail cell. Now, for once in your life, listen to me. Go. *Please.*"

For a moment Lariana just stared at him, her eyes brilliant with emotion. Then she slipped an arm around Shelly and led her after Stacy. Halfway down the hall, she paused and looked back at Patrick. *I love you, too,* she mouthed, and left.

Dante and Patrick stood united, facing Cooper, Patrick's eyes suspiciously bright.

"Does either of you want to tell me what the hell is going on?" Cooper asked.

Dante's expression went cool and distant.

Patrick's matched.

"Fuck." Cooper shoved his fingers into his hair. "Fine. It's obvious anyway."

"If it's obvious, then you don't be needing us to say it," Patrick said.

Cooper looked at Breanne in disbelief.

Breanne's heart went out to all of them, to the staff trying to protect the sweet, naive Stacy, and to the beautiful, tortured, sexy cop she'd begun to fall for. "I think Cooper means it's obvious you're covering for *someone*," she told them. "And for whom."

"Shelly didn't do anything," Dante said. "And when the police get here, she'll be gone. She was never here. She can't have been here."

"Dante, Christ." Cooper stalked the small hallway and whirled back. "Her prints are everywhere. The evidence can't lie. The truth has to come out."

"You have the truth."

"What I have," Cooper said unhappily, "is four worthless admissions of a murder and not a single truth." He stared at the two men, neither of whom backed down. Swearing again, he reached for Breanne's hand. "Okay, your choice. Don't let me help you." He looked at Breanne. "The snowmobiles are out and running. There's still no cell reception. Our goal is to at least get to a place where we can call out for help. If not, we go all the way into town."

Dante looked at his watch and raised a brow. "You plan on doing that before dark, you'd better get moving. And don't get lost."

Breanne gulped.

"Patrick is riding on one," Cooper told Breanne. "We're on the other. We'll be fine."

Dante lifted a shoulder as if to say *hope so*.

Cooper began to pull Breanne out of the hallway, then turned back to Dante. "Don't do anything stupid while we're gone. At least, nothing more stupid than admitting to a murder you didn't commit."

Dante's face was granite.

"I mean it," Cooper said. "No one goes into the cellar. *No one.* Got it?"

"I think I know the definition of *stupid*."

"Make sure that you do."

Twenty-eight

Among the great lines of all time:
1. This won't hurt a bit.
2. The check's in the mail.
3. I swear I won't come in your mouth.
And . . . the granddaddy of them all (in my humble opinion):
4. I love you (this is the most troublesome).
— Breanne Mooreland's Journal Entry

Cooper had ridden motorcycles all his life, so he figured riding a snowmobile would just come to him. Luckily, it did. It was an awesome feeling, gliding along the thick, powdery snow, beneath towering pines instead of crowded freeways. So was the sensation of Breanne snugged to the back of him, her chest pressed into his spine, her legs straddled around his.

That he could get used to. But it was cold, at somewhere around zero, far colder than he was used to. Being out here for longer than they had to be was a bad idea.

They followed Patrick, and Cooper was grateful the snow had stopped, because he had no idea where they were or which direction to go in. There were two colors; azure blue sky, and stark white landscape. The snow had thoroughly and completely wiped out any of the landmarks he might have remembered on the drive here—like roads. He figured if something happened and they were separated from Patrick, he could at least follow the tracks back to the house. Or so he hoped, because he really did not want to be a "lost in the Sierras" statistic.

Patrick led them straight for a few hundred yards, and then they veered right through a clearing, heading up over a hill. "We're still on the road," Patrick yelled back through his helmet. "Things are good so far."

"How do you know?" Cooper yelled back.

"Truthfully?" He craned his neck and lifted a shoulder. "I'm just guessing."

Great. Terrific. Perfect.

"The snow has never risen above the street poles before," Patrick yelled. "I'm estimating where they are by the slight indentations every ten yards or so. See?"

Cooper saw the indentations, and since they were at regular intervals, he could only assume Patrick was right.

Ahead, Patrick slowed, pointing to a steep incline that definitely was *not* the road.

"Should be able to get phone reception up there," he yelled, and with that, revved his snowmobile, let out a loud "Woo-hoo," and took off at a high speed, bouncing over unknown dips and curves.

Cooper's stomach sank. "Patrick—" Damn it. "He's going to get stuck—"

As soon as the words were out of Cooper's mouth, Patrick's machine took a nosedive between two dips and bogged. The engine died.

Patrick straightened, shot them an *oops* look, and tried to restart.

"He's going to have to dig out first," Cooper said with a sigh.

Sure enough, the motor wouldn't start, and as the snowmobile's entire front end was buried, there was no getting to the engine compartment without digging.

Patrick got off the snowmobile and sank up to his chest in the fresh powder. "Shit."

They dug for a few minutes and got nowhere. They were losing precious daylight.

"You go ahead," Patrick finally said. "Get to the top where you can use the cell. I'll keep digging."

Cooper didn't like the idea of separating, but it was going to take a good, long time to get Patrick's snowmobile running again. He'd feel better about spending that time if they could just get the police notified and on their way here.

He took it slower and smarter than Patrick, or so he hoped. They made it through the trees and ended up along a ridge, looking down onto a breathtaking landscape of crystal-clear lakes, pristine forests, and abundant wildlife.

"Wow," Breanne breathed in his ear when a wild rabbit dashed right across their trail.

Cooper turned off the snowmobile and pulled out his cell phone, pausing first to enjoy the feel of her up against him, her arms around his waist, her cheek resting on his shoulder.

"What's the matter?" she asked. "No reception?"

"There's reception." He closed his eyes and tried to soak up the moment so he'd remember, so he'd *always* remember this.

Breanne ran a gloved hand up his chest, settling it right over his heart. "I was wrong before, Cooper."

He twisted around to see her. "Wrong about what?"

"To let you think I wanted this to be over when we get out of here." She pulled off her helmet, waiting while he did the same. Then she pressed her mouth to his neck, his ear, and when he turned his body, she kissed him, long and sweet. "I was scared," she said when they pulled apart. "Still am," she admitted softly. "I know it sounds silly, but thinking about what I could grow to feel for you churns me up more than finding Edward. More than being in the dark for the past two days. More than—"

"I get it," he said dryly, stroking a finger over her temple along her hairline as a gust of wind hit, sprinkling a dusting of sparkling snow over them. "I scare you."

"Yes." She looked deeply into his eyes. "But you also make me feel. I mean *really* feel, and it's just so good, it might be worth the pain."

"I'm not going to hurt you," he said through an aching throat. "No pain, Breanne."

"You say that now, but you don't really know all my faults."

"They can't be that bad."

She laughed, then pressed her forehead to his. "I can't even tell you."

"I could tell you mine first, if that would help."

"You could?"

He shifted more fully around, facing her now, putting his hands on her thighs. "I let work fuck with my head."

"I know." Everything within Breanne softened as he let her see the things he usually kept hidden: frustration, anger, even shame, and if she'd managed to hold back her heart at all, it tumbled hard in that moment. "Anyone would have after what you went through." She rubbed her cheek to his, feeling her soul follow suit and tangle with his. "That you do what you do, day in and day out—"

"I walked away, remember?"

"But you're going back."

He looked down into her face. Slowly shook his head in amazement. "You seem so sure."

"I believe in you, Cooper."

"Even when I don't." He seemed unbearably touched at that. "You should know, being a cop in a relationship hasn't worked out for me in the past."

"Then maybe I'm not the only one who's made poor choices."

He laughed softly. "Yeah." He took a deep breath. "I guess I am going back. Is that going to affect your seeing me in the real world?"

"Why would it, if being a cop is who you are?"

His eyes were misty, his voice a little hoarse. "I have other faults, too," he warned.

"Please don't say that you like to hum Elvis tunes."

"I don't hum Elvis tunes."

"Thank God. Give me your worst, then. I know you put the seat down, and you don't snore."

"No." He was smiling. "But I don't fold my clothes. Hell, I don't even own an iron."

"But you like me in sweats. You get bonus points for that." She kissed him then, gliding her tongue to his until she lost her train of thought. "I bet you never have problems deciding what to wear. Maybe you'll rub off on me."

"Tell you what." He stroked his thumbs along her jaw. "I'll rub you and you can rub me. Any time."

She laughed. "Stop it. You don't know how bad my faults are yet."

"Name one."

"My Visa is always hovering at the maxed-out limit, even though my closet is overflowing with more shoes than all of San Francisco could wear."

"I don't care what your closet looks like, but I'm rather fond of those lace-up boots. You have any more like those?"

"Stop it. I'm being sincere here. I'm a bed hog—"

"Now *that* I already know," he said, wiping snowflakes from her cheek. "And I'm here to tell you, you can hog my bed any day of the week."

"I also like to get my way," she warned.

"Well, Princess, so do I. Maybe we could take turns."

She stared at him, her throat burning. "You're not taking me seriously."

"Baby, I'm serious as a heart attack. I don't give a shit if you steal all the blankets and can't afford anything but macaroni and cheese. Just so happens I have a closet full of blankets, and a savings account. Not a big one, but it could probably handle anything that comes up, Nordstrom sales notwithstanding."

"The good stuff rarely goes on sale."

"Give me a *real* reason we can't see each other."

She swallowed hard, and a single tear slipped down her cheek. "Because I like you."

He looked as if maybe he didn't see the problem.

"I *really* like you," she said. "And that has never worked out for me before."

"Does this feel like any of those other times?"

She blinked, and thought about that. "No. No, it doesn't. Actually . . . this feels much different."

"How *does* it feel?"

"Real," she admitted.

He let out a rough sound of pleasure and hauled her across him, cradling her over his lap, pulling her close for a long, deep, and decidedly not sweet kiss. "You know," he murmured when they came up for air, "I really thought life sucked. But then I saw you in that dark foyer, lighting the night with that pink vibrator." He grinned when she smacked his chest, but then he took her hand and held it over his heart, his smile fading. "I'm falling for you, too, Breanne, and to walk away now, before we give it a shot, just doesn't seem fair."

"So what do you suggest?" she asked shakily.

"That we get the police here. Do what we can for the others—"

"Oh, Cooper. You do care about them as much as I do." Her eyes filled, and so did her heart. "Do you have any idea how lucky you're going to get?" She kissed his throat, his jaw. "How very, very lucky?"

He slid his hands down to her butt and snugged her closer. "Keep talking."

Leaning in, she bit his ear. "I'm thinking this seat is pretty cushy . . ."

On his lap as she was, she felt his very satisfying reaction as he cleared his throat and pounded out 9-1-1 with shaking hands.

She laughed. "And here I thought maybe you'd want to . . . you know. Right here."

"Princess, I love you, but I'm not risking frostbite to my favorite part of my anatomy. I have plans for that part, and plans for you—Hello," he said when he got a dispatcher.

Breanne just stared at him, stunned at what he'd just said to her, only half hearing as he gave the information, listened to the response, then disconnected.

"They're prioritizing their emergencies," he said when he was done. "They're overwhelmed, but thanks to Edward, we're moving to the top of the list. I guess we can go help Patrick dig out and then get back to the house and prepare everyone. It's not going to be easy straightening this whole mess out."

Breanne was still speechless by his declaration, her gaze locked on his face, her throat burning with emotions too big to hide. "You . . . love me?"

"I do." He put her helmet back on, smoothed back her hair and smiled into her face. "Hold on tight, 'kay?" He nudged her behind him again and pulled her arms around him. "Ready?"

When she still didn't—couldn't—answer, he craned his neck and looked into her eyes. "Breanne?"

"Yeah," she said in a steady voice but with a very wobbly smile. "I guess the truth is, when it comes to you, I really am ready."

And God help her, but she was.

By the time they dug Patrick out and got back to the house, two hours had passed.

Everyone crowded into the foyer to greet them, looking anxious. *Had they made the call?*

Patrick nodded the answer.

"It's done, then," Lariana said quietly, as everyone seemed to deflate. "Someone's going to jail."

Dante looked stoic about that, but then Shelly burst into tears into her apron and his cool façade crumpled as he pulled her close. "It's going to be okay," he murmured into her hair.

"No." She pulled free. "No, it's not." Turning away, she moved out of the foyer.

Breanne went after her, and everyone else followed them to the great room.

Stacy was in front of the fire, staring into the flames, holding her hands out. "So pretty."

"Don't touch," Shelly reminded her, trying to sound normal.

Stacy giggled and pulled back. "I know, silly. It's *hot*."

"Hot," Shelly agreed, and ruffled her sister's hair, her expression crumbling when Stacy's face turned away. Breanne hugged Shelly, wishing she could do more.

Cooper moved to the fire, squeezing Shelly's shoulder before crouching beside Stacy. "The police are coming," he told her. "Do you understand what that means?"

"They're coming for Edward."

"Yes," he said gently, and Breanne fell for him all over again. "And they're going to want to know what happened to him."

Stacy's smile dissolved.

"We told you what happened," Dante said, face stoic. "It's done."

"Yeah, you told me," Cooper said dryly. "You told me you killed him." He turned to Patrick. "And you told me you killed him." He glanced at Lariana. "You said *you* did it." He lifted a brow at Shelly. "You, too. Do I have it straight? You all killed him, then?"

Everyone looked away. Cooper shot Breanne a helpless look and shook his head.

"We're trying to help," Breanne told them. "Please help us help you. Just tell us what really happened."

Shelly looked at Dante. "It's time—"

"Shelly—"

"It started with me," Shelly said to Cooper. "It did," she said when he looked doubtful. "I swear it."

Dante stepped forward, but she put a hand on his chest, and with a pleading expression, held him back. "I'm going to tell them."

"Shelly, Christ. No."

"You know I'm all Stacy has," Shelly said to Cooper and Breanne. "It's just the two of us. We used to live in a small apartment in town over the hardware store. I was commuting out here every day and Stacy was in a day care class at the rec center. A special program so she wouldn't be by herself."

"We painted," Stacy said with a dreamy smile. "Finger painted."

Shelly smiled at her. "That was your favorite, I know."

"Edward didn't like my finger painting," Stacy said, and rubbed the top of her hand as if it'd been hit.

Dante stalked the length of the room, his expression nowhere near calm.

"Edward wasn't much fun, I take it," Cooper said lightly to Stacy, though his eyes were anything but.

She shook her head.

"A month ago the state's funds changed," Shelly said. "And the money for Stacy's rec center program dried up. I brought her here, but she got into Patrick's paints and redid the hallway. Edward blew a gasket, to say the least."

Stacy lowered her head. "I was sorry."

Shelly hugged her. "I know. He had no right to smack your hand, no right at all." Shelly looked at Cooper. "Then the rent on my apartment skyrocketed and I couldn't afford it. But the owner of this place liked my work and told Edward to let me live in one of the downstairs servants' rooms until I found another place. He said it'd be no problem."

"But it *was* a problem," Lariana said. "For Edward."

"He lived here, too," Patrick told Cooper. "And it turns out, he doesn't like to share."

Dante paced some more, muttering something in his native tongue.

Cooper raised a questioning brow.

"I said he was an asshole," Dante said. "He made the girls feel bad all the time. He said shitty things to Lariana—"

"I didn't care what he said to me," Lariana said defiantly, tossing her hair back. "I could handle him."

"*I* cared," Shelly said softly. "But there was no other job where I could have Stacy with me."

Stacy stared at her fingers, twining them together, humming softly to herself as she began to rock.

"I tried to keep her busy during the day in our room, something she could do quietly so she wouldn't bother him," Shelly said. "Like reading and coloring, but sometimes she'd get bored."

"She just wanted to help," Lariana said. "But Edward wanted her gone. He even stole money out of my purse so I'd think it was Stacy. It wasn't," she said bitterly. "But in spite of him, I'd let her help me with stuff. She's a great sweeper."

Stacy lifted her head and beamed. "I like to sweep."

"It was nice for her to be busy," Dante said. "And it made her feel good."

"I'm guessing Edward didn't agree?" Cooper asked.

Dante let out a harsh laugh. "The day before you two arrived, Stacy was helping Lariana dust."

Lariana winced. "Probably not my best idea."

Stacy went back to humming.

"She broke a few things in the dining room," Dante said. "No big deal."

"Edward went mad," Patrick remembered. "Yelling and screaming. He threw stuff, too."

"He scared her," Shelly said as Stacy hummed louder, rocking, too.

Dante's face was granite. "I wanted to kill him."

"We all did," Lariana said. "But that was just anger and frustration. None of us really would have."

"He raised a hand to Stacy," Shelly said, "and I thought, this is it. He's going to hurt her again. And I . . . I caught his hand. I told him if he hit her, I'd kill him." She covered her face. "I told him if he did *anything* to her, even yelled at her again, I'd kill him, and I meant it. *I meant it.*"

A long silence filled the room. Breanne squeezed Shelly's hand.

"I heard him yelling from the garage," Patrick said. "But as the sight of me usually made him more mad, I didn't rush in."

"I knew I was fired," Shelly said. "And I think I was numb. I went to our room to pack, but then I heard him yelling again, at Stacy. When I ran into the dining room, Stacy was standing over Edward, who was on the floor. He was . . ." A sob choked out of her. "*Dead.* He had a gash over his forehead and there were shards of a large glass vase all around him."

"That was the sliver of glass I found that first night," Breanne remembered.

Stacy rocked so fast she became a blur.

"I panicked," Shelly admitted. "Stacy was just staring at me like I was her whole world—" She swiped at her tears. "God. I'd threatened him. Everyone had heard me. And here he was, dead. But I couldn't go to jail—what would happen to Stacy?"

Stacy stopped humming and dropped her head to her knees.

"I knew I had to make it look like an accident," Shelly said. "I tried to drag him to the cellar stairs. They're steep, and it seemed like a good idea to make it look like he'd fallen. So . . ."

"You pushed him," Cooper guessed.

"I intended to, but I had a problem. He was heavy—he got stuck around that tight corner of the dining room. He got blood on the wall. He'd lost a shoe."

"So you got help," Cooper said.

"She didn't ask," Dante told him firmly. "But yeah, she got help. I carried him to the stairs on my own. *I* pushed him."

"I cleaned up the blood," Lariana said.

"And then shoved the towel you used beneath the sink." Cooper looked at Dante. "You left the gloves you wore beneath Shelly's bed."

"We were going to dispose of both when the roads cleared," Lariana told him. "But the roads never cleared."

"How did Edward get the hole in his chest?" Cooper asked.

"That would be me," Patrick looked grim. "When I saw how terrified Stacy was—" His voice cracked. "She couldn't even talk, man."

Stacy's fingers were white as she clenched and unclenched her hands. She'd begun to shake. Breanne stroked her back, feeling utterly helpless.

"I lost it," Patrick admitted. "I just happened to be holding the gun—I'd been scaring away a few squirrels. I looked down at the son of a bitch lying there, knowing he'd ruined all of us, and I shot him."

"You know that wouldn't have killed him," Cooper said.

"Aye, I know. But he'd said those things to Lariana, he'd terrified this poor little thing—" He gestured to Stacy. "The fucker deserved to die, mate."

Cooper sighed, scrubbed his hands over his face.

"You don't think so?" Dante demanded.

"It doesn't matter what I think."

"Since when?" Dante asked.

Cooper looked at him for a long moment. "Look, the guy was an asshole, the worst kind. We all know it. But him dying wasn't for any of you to decide." Cooper dropped his hands and looked at all of them. "Why the hell didn't someone turn him in for harassment? Employee abuse? Hell, *anything*. It didn't have to get to this."

"Please don't tell the police what Stacy did," Shelly whispered. "*Please*."

Cooper let out a long breath, filled with tension and unhappiness, while everyone waited.

Breanne ached for him, and the decision she knew he faced. For Stacy, and her sweet, helplessly contagious smile.

When the doorbell rang, it was like a collective shot in the room; every single person jumped.

Dante and Patrick stood.

Cooper did as well, and stared at both of them. "Let me do this."

Neither man budged.

"Sit down," Cooper said in his cop voice. "*Please*," he added softly when they didn't move. "Trust me."

"You're a cop," Dante said as if *trust* and *cop* couldn't go together in the same sentence.

"Yeah, to the bone, I'm discovering," Cooper said dryly. "But at the moment, I'm not anything but a guy on vacation, Dante." He waited until the tough butler looked at him. "Trust me," he said again.

Dante stood for another long moment, then slowly sank back in his chair, arms crossed, the picture of arrogant punk.

Scared arrogant punk.

"Here's the thing," Cooper said to all of them. "The evidence never lies. You have the bloody towel, the gloves. Where's the vase that Stacy hit him with?"

Stacy turned her head. "I didn't hit him with the vase."

Everyone went still.

The doorbell rang again.

Cooper walked to Stacy and hunkered down beside her. "You didn't hit Edward with the vase?"

She shook her head, her wild hair flying about her face. "I

don't hit." She leaned in with a conspirator's whisper. "I'm not allowed."

Cooper gave her a lopsided smile that Breanne felt to her toes. "Good girl. How did Edward end up on the floor?"

"He did this." Stacy stood up, clutched her chest, bugged out her eyes and stuck out her tongue, then fell sideways to the floor, gasping for breath. After three seconds of writhing, she sat up with a smile. "Like that."

Shelly clapped a hand over her mouth. "Oh, my God."

Cooper reached out and put a hand on Shelly's shoulder to keep her quiet, never taking his eyes off Stacy. "And the vase?" he asked her.

"He grabbed it on his fall. It made a pretty noise. Tinkle, tinkle, tinkle, tinkle, tinkle . . ." she sang.

The doorbell rang again. Cooper leaned in and hugged Stacy. "Thank you," he whispered. "You've been a huge help."

Stacy beamed.

Breanne raced after Cooper as he walked to the door, her heart so full she could hardly stand it. "Cooper."

"I have to get—oomph," he said when she flung herself at him. Fisting his hair in her hands, she pulled his head down for a quick kiss. "I'm not just falling for you," she whispered. "I'm falling *hard*."

Looking stunned, he stared at her.

"You." She put a finger to his chest. "Extremely lucky tonight."

That tugged a staggered-looking grin out of him. "Hold that thought."

Three hours later, the police were gone, and thankfully, finally, so was Edward's body.

Once again, everyone gathered in the great room. Cooper looked around and realized what was different—the tension was gone. He looked at Breanne and got a brilliant smile.

"Heart attack," Dante said, looking just as flummoxed as Cooper felt. "Who'd have thunk it?"

"The coroner will have to say for sure," Cooper warned. "We're only assuming heart attack, but it makes sense."

"The police thought so, too," Breanne said. "They figured Edward was yelling at Stacy, got chest pains, gripped the vase hard. She thought he meant to throw it at her and screamed. Patrick ran in, assumed the worst, and shot in self-defense." She looked at Cooper. "Sounds like that's what's going to stick."

"It's unbelievable," Dante said. "No one's going to jail." He looked at Cooper. "You're not so bad. For a cop."

Cooper smiled at the backhanded compliment. "Thanks."

"So what now?" Lariana asked. "You two have half a week left. The weather is going to be gorgeous, and the skiing amazing. You staying?"

Breanne looked at Cooper. And with one smile, stole his heart.

"I could use a vacation," she said. "How about you?"

"A vacation sounds like just what the doctor ordered," he answered. "Starting right now." Getting to his feet, he swept her off hers and into his arms. Turning back to the staff, who were all grinning from ear to ear, he said, "I hear there's a hell of a honeymoon suite. With amenities. We'll be enjoying those tonight. Now that the road's cleared, you guys can all go home and take the rest of the week off. We'll be fine."

They whooped and hollered while Cooper kissed Breanne, then carried her out of the room and up the stairs.

She slid her arms around his neck. "Don't hurt yourself," she warned, her mouth on his ear. "I have plans for you."

"And I for you." He shouldered open the door to the honeymoon suite.

"My plans first—" she started, her words ending in a gasp as he tossed her to the bed.

With a grin, he followed her down, stripping off his shirt as he did. "Sorry. But I'm bigger—"

She rolled him. He couldn't believe it but she rolled him, held him down, and smiled wickedly before going to work ripping off his pants.

"Okay," he said, happily caving. "You first—"

This ended in a groan when she took her mouth on a happy cruise down his chest, his flat belly, to the prize between his legs.

"Wait," he gasped.

She lifted her head.

"Earlier, when you said you were falling for me—"

"I meant it."

"So this is—"

"Yes."

"Say it."

"I love you, Cooper Scott." Her eyes stung with it, but she smiled because nothing had ever felt so right. "Now, pretty please may I ravish you?"

"For as long as you want, Princess. For as long as you want."

Get more Jill Shalvis fun in

AUSSIE RULES!

Please read on for an excerpt.

One

If you asked Melanie Anderson, nothing was sexier than fly-ing. Not an eighty-five-mile-per-hour ride in a Ferrari, not any chick flick out there, nothing, not even men. Not that she had anything against the penis-carrying gender, but flying was where it was at for Mel, and had been since the tender age of four, when she'd constructed wings out of cardboard and jumped out of a tree on a dare. Unfortunately, that first time the ground got in her way, breaking her fall.

And her ankle.

Her second try had come at age eight, when she'd leapt off her granny's second-story deck into a pile of fallen leaves. No broken ankle this time, but she did receive a nice contusion to the back of the head.

By age twelve, a time when most girls discovered boys and their toys, Mel had discovered airplanes, and had taken a job sweeping for tips at a local airport just to be near them. Maybe because her own home never seemed happy, maybe because she didn't have much else to look forward to, but the magic of flying was all she ever dreamed about.

She wanted to be a pilot. And not just any pilot, but a kick-ass pilot who could fly anywhere, anytime, and look cool while doing it.

Now she was twenty-six and she'd pulled it all off. She ran her own charter service: Anderson Air. That Anderson Air consisted of a single Cessna 172 and a not-exactly-air-worthy Hawker was another matter altogether. Having fueled her dreams from cardboard wings to titanium steel made her proud as hell of herself. Now, if only she could pay her bills, things would be just about perfect, but money, like man-made orgasms, remained in short supply.

"Mel! Mel, sweetie, the oven is kaput again!"

Mel sighed as she walked through the lobby of North Beach Airport, a small, privately owned, fixed-base operation. The cozy, sparsely decorated place was dotted with worn leather couches and low, beat-up coffee tables and potted palm trees—low maintenance to the extreme. A couple of the walls were glass, looking out onto the tarmac and the two large hangars, one of which housed the maintenance department and the other the overnight tie-down department. Beyond that lay a string of fourteen smaller hangars, all rentals. And beyond that, Santa Barbara and the Pacific Ocean, where Mel could routinely find her line guys and aircraft mechanic riding the waves on their surfboards instead of doing their job.

The far wall held a huge map of the world, dotted with different colored pushpins designating the places where she and everyone else had flown to on various chartered flights. Red pins dominated. Mel was red, of course, and just looking at the map made her smile with pride.

Just past the map, the wall jutted out, opening up into the Sunshine Café, an ambitious name for five round tables and a small bar/nook, behind which was a stove, oven, microwave, and refrigerator, all crammed into six hundred square feet and painted a bright sunshine yellow. On the walls hung photos, all of planes, and all gorgeously shot from the ground's viewpoint.

Charlene Stone stood in the middle of the kitchen nook, bottle-dyed maroon hair piled on top of her head, her black lip gloss a perfect match to her black fingernails. She'd turned forty this year and wore a T-shirt that read TWENTY WAS GOOD BUT FORTY IS BETTER, and a pair of short-shorts that rivaled Daisy Dukes. As the eighties had been Char's favorite decade to date, she had Poison blaring from a boom box on the counter while staring into the oven. "I can't get my muffins going," she said in her Alabama drawl.

"I thought *I* was your muffin, baby."

This from Charlene's husband, Al, the photographer who'd taken the pictures on the walls, who despite being forty himself had never outgrown his horny twenties. Medium height, built like the boxer he'd once been, he waggled a brow and grinned.

They'd been married forever, had in fact raised two kids while they'd still been kids themselves, but they had empty-nest syndrome now, and were currently revisiting their honeymoon days—meaning they talked about sex often, had sex often, and talked about it some more.

"People come here for my muffins," Charlene said, and smacked Al's chest.

"I love your muffins."

"You're just kissing up now."

This brought out a big, hopeful grin. "No, but I'd like to." He shifted close, put his hands on Char's hips. "Kiss up, and then down . . ."

Char shot Mel a long look. "Men are dogs."

Mel tended to agree with that assessment but she knew enough to keep her tongue. "I'll get the oven fixed."

"Oh, honey, that'd be great. I know you're swamped and this is the last thing you need."

Yep, on the list of things Mel didn't need, the oven going on the blink fell right behind a hole in her head. "We need the oven. I'll get it fixed ASAP."

"Good, because if I keep disappointing the customers, we aren't going to be able to pay our rent this month. Sally will freak."

Ah, yes, the elusive Sally.

Sally was the owner of North Beach Airport, and everyone's boss, from fueling to maintenance to hangaring. Mel herself rented space from Sally for Anderson Air and in return for a lower fee managed the whole airport for Sally. Since Sunshine Café happened to be one of the few profitable segments of North Beach, the broken oven fell into Mel's already-overflowing pot of responsibilities. She pulled the radio off the clip on her belt to call their fix-it guy, who sometimes fixed things, and sometimes didn't. Mostly didn't. "I'll get Ernest."

Charlene sighed.

"Yeah, yeah." Mel brought the radio up to her mouth. "Ernest, come to the café, please."

No answer, which was not a big surprise. No one was sure exactly how old Ernest was but he'd been at North Beach as long as Mel could remember. According to other sources, he'd been around since the dawn of time. Only thing was, he was grumpy as an old goat and was rarely anywhere he should be when Mel needed him.

Like now.

"He's probably rescuing a spider." To Al's credit, he said this with a straight face.

Ernest loved spiders. He actually carried around a special species book in his back pocket so that he could characterize each and every spider he came across, and here just off the Santa Barbara coast, in the shadows of the Santa Ynez Mountains, he came across a lot. The only thing he loved more than spiders was computers. The man, strange as it seemed, was a computer god. He probably could have gotten a job anywhere for more money, but undoubtedly he couldn't nap on the job anywhere else so he stayed at North Beach.

"Ernest," Mel said again into the radio. "Come in, please. Ernest, come in."

"No need to shout, missy."

Mel nearly jumped out of her skin at the low, craggily,

grumpy voice behind her. Ernest stood there, all five feet of him packed with attitude, from his steel-toed boots to his greasy trousers and long-sleeved, button-down plaid, to his bad comb-over, which was rumpled now, telling her he'd been sleeping in the storage closet again. The crease on his cheek that resembled the side of a can of oil was a dead giveaway. "The oven's down," she told him.

"Eh?" He cupped a hand to his bad ear. "Speak up!"

Mel would have fired his curmudgeonly ass a long time ago except she couldn't afford anyone else. "Oven! Broken!"

"You never talk loud enough," he grumbled. "Sally's the only one who talks loud enough."

Ernest hadn't actually spoken directly to Sally in years, but arguing with the man was like betting against the house.

Never going to win.

"Can you fix the oven?" she yelled in his good ear.

"I'll fix the damn oven soon as I fix the damn fuel pump!"

Mel's stomach dropped. "What's wrong with the gas pump?" Muffins they could live without. Getting fuel into their customers' aircrafts, some of which landed here daily for the fuel alone, they could not.

"Nothing I can't handle." Ernest was already walking away, his pants slipping down because he had no hips to hold them on. He stopped, hitched them up, then kept moving.

The radio squawked with the announcement of an unscheduled plane arriving in twenty minutes. Mel waited for one of the linemen, Ritchie or Kellan, to respond to the news, but neither did. Once again she lifted the radio to her lips and called for her employees.

No response.

"Gotta love those brain-dead college students," Char said.

Mel resisted the urge to smack her own forehead with the radio. "If those two are in the back hangar getting high again, I'm going to kill them."

"We're falling apart at the seams." Charlene hugged Mel.

"Look, honey, you've got your hands full. I'll go see what I can wrangle up without the oven, 'kay?"

"I'll get on it," Mel promised her just as the Poison CD ended.

For one blessed moment silence reigned before a new CD clicked on. Journey. "I just wish we could give this place the makeover it needs," Char yelled over the music.

Mel wished that, too. They were making ends meet, and they all had jobs, two really good things, but no one was getting rich, that was for sure.

Not that she wanted to be rich, but comfortable would be nice . . .

Al followed his wife into the kitchen, his hand sliding down her back to squeeze her ass.

"Albert Edward Stone!" Charlene said in her most Southern-genteel voice. "If you think that instead of cooking muffins, I'm going to 'cook' with you—"

"Come on, just a quickie—"

"That's what you got just last night!"

"Hey, that wasn't a quickie, that was some of my best work!"

Mel covered her ears and walked away. She didn't need the reminder that everyone was getting quickies and she was not. So it'd been a long time for her, so what? People could live without sex.

Or so the rumor went.

"Mel? Mel, are you around here somewhere?"

At Dimi's voice drifting through the lobby from the front receptionist desk, Mel changed direction and headed that way, wondering, what now?

Dimi Wilmington sat perched on the edge of her desk, head tilted as she studied the view out the window of sweeping coastlines bisected by the magnificent Santa Ynez Mountains and a typical low-lying morning fog. Willowy, with legs long past the legal limit, Dimi had a body and face that could launch a thousand ships, make the fat lady sing, and put grown men on their knees to worship at her altar.

She used them to her full advantage, too, rarely coming across a man she didn't like—which probably explained the new whisker burn along her jaw.

Terrific. Everyone was getting lucky except Mel.

It was said she and Dimi were night and day, a modern-day odd couple. Mel being the anal one. The one who gathered worries and stress like moss on a tree. She also tended to gather the heartaches and responsibilities of others much like a fraught mother hen, bitching after all her little chicks, pecking at them until they did as she wanted them to.

Dimi was more a live-and-let-live type of soul. She cared, deeply, she'd just rather light incense and meditate than actually solve a problem. She was both a thorn in Mel's side and her closest confidant.

She wore a multicolored, filmy, gauzy miniskirt and a snug, white cap-sleeved tee with a pink heart in the center that brought the eyes to immediate attention of her brand-spanking-new breasts. But the thing that never failed to amaze Mel about Dimi was that she could go all day and that bright, clean white tee would stay bright, clean white.

Mel didn't even bother to look down at her coveralls, already filthy from just a quick maintenance check on the Cessna. "What's the problem?"

Over the steam of her herbal tea and the faint smoke from the incense she'd lit, Dimi shot Mel a wry smile.

Right. What *wasn't* a problem was a more likely question.

The two of them went back a long ways. As teens, Mel had swept and assisted in the maintenance department, and Dimi had answered phones. Each had been far more at home here than either of their decidedly not *Leave It to Beaver* homes.

Sally Wells, a woman with more dream than cash, had taken them under her wing—Sally, who'd lived as she wanted, wild and free with men and fun aplenty. As their first real role model, Mel and Dimi had both worshipped the ground Sally walked on; Mel appreciating Sally's directness, the way she ran her own show and the world be damned, but for Dimi the worship had gone deeper. She'd wanted to *be* Sally.

Unfortunately, Sally had been unavailable to them for a long time now, and without her around, there was no one for Mel to share the stress of holding all this up with. No one except Dimi. "Tell me," she said to Dimi now. "Believe me, the day can't get worse."

Dimi put her hand over Mel's. "You look tired. You're not drinking that tea I gave you."

"I hate tea. And it's just stress."

"You only hate tea because I tell you it has healing abilities and you think that's a crock of shit." She sighed. "Money's tight again."

"You mean *still*. Money's tight still."

"That's all right." Dimi stood and, primping a little, played with the hem of her skirt, adjusted her top. "We have a couple of hot ones coming in today."

"Hot ones" being Dimi-code for cute, *rich* customers.

"What we have is an unscheduled," Mel said. "I've gotta get out there and do tie-down because God knows where Ritchie or Kellan is."

Dimi pulled out a compact and checked her gloss, ran her tongue over her teeth. "I'll do it."

"Uh-huh." Mel eyed the short, short skirt, which at every move flirted with revealing Dimi's crotch. "You're going to go get your hands dirty, risk that manicure, and tie down a plane? In *that?*"

Dimi smiled. "Should get me a big tip, don't you think?"

"That's not even funny."

"Hey, I'm going to hit on them anyway, might as well get something for it."

"Stop it." Mel knew Dimi was only kidding. Or half-kidding

anyway. Dimi enjoyed men the way some women enjoy breathing. "I have enough to worry about."

Dimi sighed and stroked a long, wayward strand of hair from Mel's face. "We'll be fine, hon. You'll come up with something, you always do."

Right. She'd just wave her magic wand and figure it all out. And while she was at it, she'd conjure up a happily ever after for all of them as well. "The oven's down, the gas pump is acting up, and morale's getting low."

"They need a phone call from Sally."

Their gazes met for a long beat.

"You do it this time," Dimi whispered.

"Actually, I was hoping you could, from—" Mel broke off when Ernest appeared out of nowhere, shuffling past the desk, pulling his noisy cart stacked haphazardly with tools and the ever-present jar for liberating spiders.

Mel didn't know how many times she'd asked him not to walk through the lobby like that, to instead go around the outside of the hangar, where customers wouldn't have to see him, but he never listened. At least not to the stuff she wanted him to. "Ernest?"

He'd stopped to stand in front of the vending machine next to the wall map, scratching his head as he contemplated rows of candy bars. "Yeah?"

"Did you by any chance ever clean out that maintenance hangar, the one Danny wants to stock new parts in?"

"Not yet. Busy, you know."

Right. He looked really busy. She and Dimi waited until he'd made his selection, shoved the candy bar into his pocket next to his spider book, and left.

"I hate the secrets," Dimi whispered.

Yeah, and Mel just loved them. *Not.* She looked at the time. "I gotta go meet that flight. Then I have a flight myself, to LA."

"You're changing your clothes first, right?"

"Yes," Mel said with irritation. "Of course."

"You say that like you don't regularly forget to change from mechanic to pilot. Daily."

Mel rolled her eyes. "I'll be back by two."

Dimi nodded, looked wistfully out the window. "You're so lucky."

"Lucky?" Mel laughed in disbelief. "How exactly?"

"You get to get out of here."

"But you hate to fly," Mel reminded her. "You throw up every time."

"I know, I didn't mean . . ." Dimi searched for words. "Look, don't you ever . . . just want to get in the plane and, I don't know, fly off into the sunset?"

Mel just stared at her incredulously. "Never to return?"

"Well . . . yeah."

North Beach was Mel's home, her *life*, and no, she'd never ever thought about going away and never coming back, and she'd always figured Dimi felt just the same. "Okay, what's wrong?"

Dimi lifted a stack of mail. "Just the usual. Here's your incoming pile. Bills and more bills, if you're wondering, though what's the point of opening them, we still can't pay last month's."

"Officially no one can even bug us until . . ." She glanced at the desk calendar. July ninth. "Tomorrow, the tenth." Oh, God.

"Also we need fuel for the pump, and they won't deliver it without their bill being paid." Dimi leaned over and lit the three candles lining the front of her reception desk. The crystals on her wrists jangled, as did the ones dangling from her ears. The scent of vanilla began to fill the air, joining the incense she'd already lit on the credenza behind her.

"You're going to make people hungry," Mel said. "And the oven's down."

"I'm going to make people feel warm and cozy and at home," Dimi corrected, and smoothed her skirt. "Helps our karma."

Mel wanted to say that she didn't believe in karma or fate, that they each made their own, but the sound of a plane coming in ended the conversation. "They're early." She understood early, she herself was always compulsively early, but it meant she had to run through the lobby, grabbing an extra orange vest off a hook as she went, slipping into the lineman's gear as she moved quickly across the tarmac to greet the plane.

The Gulfstream was a beauty, and her pilot's heart gave one vivacious kick of envy as the plane swept in for a honey of a landing, perfectly controlled by a pilot who was clearly a master of his craft.

When the engine shut off, Mel moved in, squinting against the early chill and wind, using the tie-down blocks to hold the plane steady, her mind wandering as she worked. The oven had gone out twice this month. She needed to look into the cost of a new one. The linemen clearly needed another ass chewing regarding responsibilities, specifically theirs. And then there was the little matter of fuel. She'd have to find a way to pay that bill pronto.

God, her brain hurt.

Finished with the tie-down, she straightened, patted the sleek side of the airplane just for the pleasure of touching it, and blew a stray strand of hair out of her face, wishing she had put on an extra layer of insulation beneath her coveralls because despite it being summer, the early-morning wind off the Pacific cut right through her.

From the other side of the aircraft, the door opened. A set of stairs released. A moment later, two long legs emerged, clad in dark blue trousers, clean work boots, and topped by a most excellent ass. Not averse to enjoying a good view, Mel stayed in place, watching as the rest of the man was revealed. White button-down shirt, sleeves shoved up above his elbows, tawny hair past his collar, blowing in the wind.

Yep, there were a few perks to this job, one of them catering right to Mel's soft spot.

Pilots. This one looked more like a movie star pretending to be a pilot, but you wouldn't hear her complaining. And just like that, from the inside out, she began to warm up nicely.

The man held a clipboard, which he was looking at as he turned, ducking beneath the nose of the plane to come toe to toe with her, a lock of tawny hair falling carelessly over his forehead, his eyes shaded behind aviator sunglasses.

And right then and there, every single lust-filled thought drained out of Mel's head to make room for one hollow, horror-filled one.

No.

It couldn't be. After all this time, he wouldn't *dare* show his face.

His only concession to the surprise was a raised brow as he lifted his sunglasses, his sea green gaze taking its sweet time, touching over her own battered work boots, the dirty coveralls, the fiery, uncontrollable red hair she'd piled on top of her head without thought to her appearance. "Look at you," he murmured. "All grown up. G'day, Mel."

And look for Jill's delightful Christmas romance collection *Merry and Bright* this holiday season!

"Shalvis makes me laugh, makes me cry,
makes me sigh with pure pleasure."
—Susan Andersen

Finding Mr. Right

Brilliant chemist Maggie Bell has a knack for choosing Mr. Wrong, and with yet another lonely Christmas looming, she decides it's time to alter the equation—and seek out someone who seems totally wrong for her. Eureka! The heart is a genius. . . .

Bah Handsome!

Behind on her bills, B&B owner Hope receives an unlikely guest: stranded solicitor Danny, who's been threatening to put her out of business. Funny how the holidays can bring people together no matter how much they resist. . . .

Ms. Humbug

Born rebel or overgrown man-child, Matt is the kind of man no woman can tame—until an unexpected encounter with his nemesis, Cami, at the office holiday party proves there's an exception to every rule. . . .

Connect with Us

Visit us online at
KensingtonBooks.com
to read more from your favorite authors, see books
by series, view reading group guides, and more.

for sneak peeks, chances to win books and prize packs,
and to share your thoughts with other readers.

facebook.com/kensingtonpublishing
twitter.com/kensingtonbooks

Tell us what you think!

To share your thoughts, submit a review,
or sign up for our eNewsletters, please visit:
KensingtonBooks.com/TellUs.